Without Trace

Without Trace

Héctor Münster

First edition, 2023

*Dedicated to my mother,
because she suffers the abandonment
of her family, her country, and her people...
But the eternal thanks to my father
who rescue her. Gave her back a country,
and identity, and a new live.*

*PostMoster, to my father, who teach me
and form what I am.*

*Specially to mi wife, for her unconditional support in
this life project.*

To my daughters for perpetuating my legacy.

PREFACE

The re-creation of this work, that is a fiction base in real facts, is dedicates to all those persons that went by the life without hardly neither glory, coming from faraway places, leaving behind families, remembers, and lives to get to these lands and that no one knew of their existence until now. This is a compendium of facts that according the tradition could be a legend, maybe fiction, maybe fantasy o just a chance that unchain some social consequences of which we are victims today.

Nothing is casual; all that happen to us has a real effect in the lives of others, everything happens for a reason that somehow allow other things to happen or not.

Live is a complex web of events connected and how they are communicated our thoughts, attitude, actions, and descriptions that each person sees in each situation that is presented, being the consequences of our actions. The direct results and collateral, represent a dose of reactions in this intricated social web of changes; our relations, contacts, and influences. They provoke, where the "how" and the "when" appear and with "whom." All the components good and bad, have their consequences.

For this reason, I can say that an event in the past can alter, as a direct consequence the present. There is no existence of isolated facts, there is no chance existence, all has a moment, everything is connected and the future of any person, family, social group, town, or nation is in the same reference plan, perfectly trace back from a global perspective, generation to generation.

No one leaves an emptiness in this life; everyone always leaves something: a trace, an identity, a tread, a mark... Nothing is in vain. No one goes unknown for simple the existence is of a being, even if they are poor, simple, sick, hide from society or is rich, powerful, all have the same effect in this complicated mechanism. Free will activate a microproject of unique power and superiority that is totally divine and comes from a perfect plan for being the supreme delirium of a greater love for our humanity and for all creation. That same love, more than material, is totally from another world, from an eternal Kingdom where the human being and all creatures belong, as a part of a body formed by millions and millions of lives form all generations of humanity that are part of the same time, but different moments, conforming the active part of the project that is building a web day by day and generation by generation. Inside this web, the ones who went through, are moving to another energetic web and spiritualty is found in the eternal kingdom of celestial love, going by from one web to another to get to the total highest love.

Do not get surprise that the misfortune of some, can be the happiness of others, because the consequences that life dictated; a sense and a logic that take humanity to their perfection in all senses. That's why no one can despise the life of any person, good or bad, important for some or insignificant for others, because their profession, activity, or the role it play in society; from the humblest to the most important, are needed, we all are important.

Even the encounters between persons in a bus, in a bank, in a store, in a trip or anywhere are causalities, no matter the distances, the ways, the letters, telephones, or contacts. The words, thoughts, ideas, everything is linked together and influence fall on the moments of each person, from a sermon, a talk, a song, a musical tone, or a book and why not? Even a phrase, a bad word, any element of the verbal communication or not verbal, sensitive, audiological, or seen, at the end this thought, idea, inspiration, dream or ideal, was created for one person that can convert into a specific action. To take a decision, to make a selection motivates, for that impulsive connection, generates a shot and the execution of thousands of activators in the society.

That is why, when someone move things, shares them, allows it, or avoid it, forms an infinite chain of reactions that have a direct or indirect to effect on us since we are connected, all without exceptions.

Lots of leaders and groups pretend to break with the social order and dictate their own destinies; but destiny is already determined and no one can change it since it is divine, is of our God and not earthly, the negotiator, creator, and generator of his mission. This is the reason why the facts and our earthly bodies and souls for this world, only possess free will, that at the end dictates the necessary change to achieve to take this work to destiny. All we do or not base on the established order, provokes effect at the end the destiny of each of us. It forms part of the intricate web, complex and totally ordered and perfect; most of the time doesn't make sense in human understanding, in a such a way that a piece of paper won't move, a grant of sand, a drop of water, a rock or an insignificant muscle of our body won't move, but the purpose to generate the process before all times, being only an instant of personal decision. All puts the human being in the part of the web where they belong, so at the end, for good or bad, all of us form part of the same universal web.

INTRODUCTION
THE TRACE OF THE PAST

In a European country, Germany to be specific, is the place where this story begins, and where the facts originate, pouring out their consequences from the lives of several individuals that are part of this story. Within this novel, we will find some historic moments that took place in real life and point out important events of this country which gives us the beginning of this story.

Germany at the end of century XVlll was in a state of peace, but because of the consequences of its past, did not have good relations with many countries. France, for example, had resentment because of past wars and invasions. Germany and the Reich had a thirst for conquest and that's why their people fought for nationalism to protect their land and to expand their territory and influences in Europe.

The story originates in the lives of several families that joined together. During that time, there was a family settled in Lucerne, Switzerland, a city divided by the Reus river, under the solid alps mountains and founded in the century Vll, around a monastery (once the property of the Hapsburg family). Lucerne was part of the Helvetic confederation which fought for their independence from Germany since 1332. During the last decade of the XVlll century, the French revolution expanded into this zone, serving as support to the French people in 1798. Germany was controlled and threatened by the military presence established by

Napoleon himself, which at that time, made people in the business world look for new commercial business elsewhere. But these political and military events did not stop regular business from the Rhine area throughout San Gottardo; that was the traditional way since the XIll century for business and products of these zones and their surroundings. This was the case of the Whent family that travelled in these areas on a regular basis to offer their products.

The Whent family were producers of dairy products and wood carving supplies to several Switzerland cities and where their products became famous.

On the other hand, in this story there is another family of influential and rich origins since their ancestral formation was known as the nobility of the Earl Friedrich lll von Münster. He was a well-known diplomat, highly educated on social arts, business, and politics. He was also the beneficiary of great inheritance from his ancestors from several generations back, who had survived several wars and invasions at that time. It was because of this tradition that the community named him as a member of the group of powers and a representative of the Hanseatic league.

For these reasons, the family of Friedrich lll von Münster was established in Koblenz. This city was part of the French dominion; it was the main city in the districts of the Rhine and Mosel area where the family had its political influence and had big land holdings in the Rhine area. They also had wineries and properties (some inherited and as payment of spoils of war because of awards or donations given by the families of nobles that died in combat). These were passed on from generation to generation and preserved and managed carefully by Earl Friedrich lll von Münster.

The roots of Friedrich lll von Münster come from the city of Wuppertal, his father's hometown, where during the mid XVlll century the train system was controlled (needed for commercial exchange with the north and with England). This influenced their movement of residency to the city of Koblenz (the original city of the Ehrnbreitsta fortress destroyed in 1799 and rebuilt because of the strong desire and work of the nobles in 1816).

Earl Friedrich lll von Münster's father was a land owner of the nobility and his mother belonged to the upper middle class. His character was due to having lived in a conservative province and having great intellectual talent. He studied law and started to work for the state in 1850. He resigned a year later to oversee the management of the family business of goods, which were not very productive at the time. He built them up and made them available for rent. He met his future wife in 1855 and married her in 1857 in the Lutheran church, as tradition of the aristocracy.

During this prosperous time, attendance at the wedding was very important to people of royalty of the second empire of Germany because the new wife, the young duchess Margarette, was part of the heritage of the Carolingian court. She was not a direct line, instead, was a niece of Charles l of Romania. This relationship between families was distant because of political fights and family problems. This beautiful young lady was known as the little duchess of Sigmaringen; she was active and modern for her time, she was an intellectual, and best of all, very kind with others, which gave her that name in her native city of Koblenz. By being part of the high society, one of her qualities most known was her philanthropy for the neediest people, leading her to be the founder of the House of the Vineyard, a place where the workers and poor families received consistent help with food and work for their needs.

That house was so famous in the region that besides being a shelter, it became one of the first cooperatives (not well seen by the aristocracy and neither by the land owners) but was accepted because of the need for manual work and the social relations pressures of the laborer reforms in Europe during those days. (It was a prosperous place and harmonious time).

At the beginning of 1815, Prussia was claiming this zone, but it was after a strong resistance in 1822, that it became the capital of the new Prussian province of Reinabia. It was then that the Von Münster's inherited the properties, and later under the new reign, Earl kept it as the main commercial place for exchange. This beautiful property view was by the peninsula between the Rhine and Mosel rivers. In this zone, the market was located during the months of August, where the Occidental European commerce attended to do their most important commercial business. It was also the place for the Fire Festival, where per legend, Germany was born because of the conquest of the Teutones and the order of Knights that found the basis of such a nation about 1216.

In this spectacular scene, the upper-class men attended to this festivity, being one of the special occasions when the land owners, also known as the Junkers (land owners of Prussia and owners of big extensions of land and with a great influence in the conservator party of Germany) mingled with the towns people. The Junkers were so influential which is why they were the ones who nominated the powerful Otto von Bismarck to the head of German military, being that he was from the second German empire.

Around 1878 the business men and producers from Lucerne, Italy, France, and all Europe, met to show their products at one of the first biggest European displays, and of course the traditional dairy products of the Whent family couldn't be absent. Herr Arthur Whent attended with her daughter Heidi Marie, after a long trip through the beautiful Switzerland Alps and with the goal to come back with good business connections and to enjoy the popular celebration of the Market.

In Koblenz, walking around the main plaza, was Earl von Münster and his three children: Heinrich, the first born; Mark and little Otto, the presumptive heirs of the legacy of the knights. The family was enjoying their walk around the new monument to the German unity built in honor of Kaiser Willheim l. The music being played was well known by the nobles. The musicians at the plaza were playing the most recent hits of Johan Strauss like "Die Fledermause" (The Bat), which invited all the audience to dance, as well with the "Wiener Bult" (Viennese Spirit) by the same author, and other popular music of the time. Meanwhile, Friedrich, while wandering around listening to the music, was admiring the view, and thinking of the love he had for his land. This encouraged him to come up to his sons and ask them to never lose the unity of the family, and to maintain and defend the beautiful inheritance of the legacy of their family land. With his eyes lost in the view of the sunset and feeling the wind on his face, he said, "What a beautiful view!"

The two rivers joined in one, "It's the way this land is, a real beauty..."

He repeated it over and over in silence to himself, within his heart and his Prussian soul, "What a beautiful view...!"

Heinrich, his first-born son, was tired of listening to his father's inflexible thoughts and ideologies that were boring him and exhausted his patience because all these crazy and stubborn ideas were no value for him at the time. He was an unusually simple young man that was not following his father's ideals; he was a rebellious young man with a thirst to fight for equality and justice for the unfortunate people who wanted change and justice.

At his young age, Heinrich was feeling pride regarding what he wanted to live for, but in the meantime the young man was looking for something to put his attention to divert himself from his boring life and the agony of listening to his father's speech; prying for a way out of his boring and strict life. He was looking for something beyond the society rules that were affecting him and in which he did not agree, "Those rules, but what can he do about it?" He was born there, and the rules were part of his genes and he cannot change that. Also, it was part of his father's traditions, which his dad followed to the "T". He did not have any choice but to obey and respect them, but only due to the love and loyalty he had for his dad.

While he was keeping his mind busy trying to find some answers, his sight was looking to the people without faces. His sight was lost, just like his dad's sight was; but for Heinrich, suddenly like a meteor or a star in the sky, shiny, beautiful, and captivating, in front on his eyes walked Heidi Marie. The shiny blue eyes caught his sight, and she blushed when they looked at each other without taking their eyes off each other. It was there, where love at first sight began; it was such a clear scene that Heinrich's Dad got his attention and said, "Heinrich, listen to me! I'm talking to you! Turn around and listen to what I'm telling you."

Friedrich, insisted on getting the attention of his son, "Are you listening to what I said?"

And his son answers him, "Yes father... I have seen it..."

He was talking about the beauty of Heidi Marie.

The music continued playing and the festivity invited everyone to dance. Heinrich started moving slowly over to get right in front of Heidi Marie. He looked at her and without taking her out of his sight, he took her by her hand and walk to the middle of the dance floor, dancing, and dancing. They danced a famous waltz of Lerhner of that time and other Tyrolese beats. It was a memorable time for both being that close together.

The evening was long, especially since it was getting late. All the people were watching the young couple dancing. At that moment, Friedrich turned his sight and saw how his son was dancing, and asked one of his companions, "Look, is that Heinrich! Or not?"

The companion answers him, "Yes, my lord, it is him."

He continued asking him, "Who is he dancing with? Who is the young lady he is dancing with?"

"Look at him... Smiling!"

The Earl was thinking and believing that the young lady was from the nobility, because her beauty was notable. He pulled out his watch and with his finger indicated to his first-born child that it was time to go home, but the young man ignored the signs, and turned away from his father and got lost on the dance floor, leading the couple to the other side of the dance floor where Heidi Marie's father looked at them. She saw him and just from looks enough knew what he was saying to her in a way where no words are necessary. The instruction, "Let's go and right now!" But his order was ignored.

When Heidi Marie separated from the young Heinrich, she couldn't resist the challenge of looking at his dad, and she ended up leaving the young Heinrich as soon as they turned, ending with a mutual bow as part of the dance. Heidi Marie used this to leave him and got off the dance floor as quickly as possible. She left Heinrich in the middle of the bow position and when he returned up, she was gone.

Like a dream, like waking himself up, she vanished. But he knew her way of walking among the people. He tried to catch up with her, but he stopped suddenly when he saw how she was leaving with an older man whose identity was unknown. He saw the unknown man putting his cape on and walking away; he tried to catch up, and shouted, "Hey! Wait! What's your name?"

He followed her, but he couldn't catch up with her, watching her go away and not knowing who she was.

He did not wait one more day. The next morning, he went to look for her at the Market Platz downtown, and he was not going to stop until he found the beautiful Heidi Marie. Heinrich got nervous as he got closer because of her origin, and he knew she was not what his father wanted for him and even worse, she was not German... But all this did not stop him from looking for her. Call it curiosity or cupid hitting him in the middle of his heart. Consciously or unconsciously, he looked for her. He saw her selling in the market and bought three pieces of cheese from her, he tried them and with no words, they kept looking at each other; she got the coins. Then he broke the ice, and said, "What's your name?"

With a simple and courteous response, "I'm Heidi Marie Whent."

After a brief pause, but with a deep look between them, they stayed together like they were out in space by themselves, looking at each other and opening their hearts in silence. After a few moments of looking at each other, they started a conversation, which ended in giggling. Heinrich was there for a long time helping her sell her products.

Several hours after, Heidi Marie's father, Herr Whent found out about the encounter, and immediately separated her daughter from the place, but there was nothing to stop Heinrich during those eight days when the Whent family stayed there. He continued to meet her and remain as close as possible to her. No one could stop the destiny of this young couple; they were starting a long trip to the deepest of the human heart, "The endless love."

Heinrich asked the Whent family to stay longer, because he wanted to ask his father if they could spend the day with his family, but Herr Whent felt intimidated by the young one, like he was a snob. Herr Whent did not believe him and did not listen to him so they left town that night as scheduled. No one could change their plan. Heinrich couldn't find his loved one, and discouraged and sad he went with his father and begged him to let him go after her.

"I wish to go and look for Heidi Marie to ask her hand in matrimony."

With such a petition, Earl reacted and was upset, and answered him, "What's wrong with you Heinrich? Are you crazy? What is guiding you to such an impetus?"

He stopped questioning and tried to reason with him, "If you want to meet a girl, we have lots of them here and they come from good families."

And his father asked, "Is that what you want? Right? The father continues "You are still young, you have a lot to learn about the family business, and you can't drop your studies for someone that you do not even know where she is coming from. No Heinrich! Wait, have patience," the father contained himself from screaming at him. "Try to understand what is best for you."

"And love father? Where do you leave it?" Heinrich answered.

He answered, "Love... Is something heavenly, can't be defined, you can only feel it. Lots of times love can be confused with a corporal need or missed affection. Are you needing something?" The father asked Heinrich, but his son answered, "No father, nothing."

Then, the father proceeded, "Why are you so obsessive and persistent in wanting to be with that young girl? What is her name?"

He answered right after the question, "Heidi Marie."

"Oh... Yes, that Lucerne girl?"

Heinrich blushed and said, "Please father, don't call her that."

"Ok," with a mocking pause, the father continued, "Whatever, she is young, so you need to wait some time and you will see that as time goes by you will forget all this nonsense."

As the father calmed down, he started thinking very seriously of acting on his plan of sending his son to the law school in Berlin, so he could prepare better. Without wasting more time, he prepared the procedures thru his old friend Klaus Hartan from the university, which he attended in 1855 and where Klaus was a professor.

Young Heinrich couldn't do anything; due to obedience and respect for his father, he did not have any choice but to go to Berlin to the Königliche Friedrich-Wilhelms-Universität (Real Fredrick William University) in honor of Fredrick William lll, king of Prussia. The same place where his father studied law and Fredrick hoped that the young Heinrich would have the same opportunity as him and finish a political degree in the conservative party that he belonged to.

In September 1878, the young man left. He was sad and full of anger, and did not answer his father; he put his face down and walked away fast, trying to get lost in his father's house.

Several weeks went by and no one talked about this subject. Heinrich waited until Heidi Marie arrived in the beautiful city of Lucerne to let her know his homesickness for her and how the distance separated them, but did not separate the closeness of his heart. Furthermore, he addressed her with a beautiful love letter in which he explained to her why he was going to Berlin. When the opportunity came along for Heinrich to leave, it was not too long after she received the letter, and it was not good news for her since she was still living the unforgettable sudden love that happened in 1878.

Time and distance did not interfere with their feelings for each other; on the contrary, the love letters came and went between them; they were intense and were the only way to keep developing their love. It was a motivation for Heinrich in his loneliness and study, and for Heidi Marie in her work and homesickness.

The love between them was a secret deep in their hearts, since the parents of both did not know about their existence. That was enough for them, and they had hoped to someday be together forever.

Heinrich, because of studies and other problems didn't write often to his parents. Something even worse; War was again in the area. France was claiming their lands, and the towns people were claiming their part of the land from owners and to the aristocrats; it was a difficult time. The economy was down every day, the business was not good, and the social press was putting pressure on the upper class. All this brought misfortune, starting in 1898. Earl Friedrich had a heart condition illness at the same time when the region was having constant rebellion and devastation. Duchess Margarette, now with no help from her husband, became the head of the business dealings. Earl was sick and asked his friends to help advise his wife on the business and prevent losing them, but the rebellion was present.

The bank money was lost, the friends were gone. The duchess took the lead of the family business even though, the women in that time were not allowed to do any administrative business (it was considered only acceptable for men) but, she was different; she liked to fight for ideals contrary to the aristocracy; she was in favor of justice and always looked out for the well-being of the people.

This situation brought her to be involved in the foundation that she once created and still was working in an altruist way. She created a pact with the foundation and it was converted it into a cooperative, passing all her wealth to the cooperative and become the head so she did not lose it all.

The Schmitt brothers (Johan and Kart) signed a pact and agreed that the cooperative would manage the goods of the family for some years. It was then when all the Von Münster family move to Koblenz.

Earl Friedrich was suffering from angina pectoris and was worn out and having problems breathing. His sons were not happy with the move, but it was the only option even though the area was suffering from a typhoid fever epidemic. The lands were abandoned, and the workers left to go somewhere else until this illness passed, giving the thieves the opportunity to rob the places. No less, the invasion by the enemy was very strong in that area. Earl Friedrich died in 1884 in the company of all his sons except Heinrich.

"My son Heinrich," said Earl. The illness devastated him; he could not sustain himself standing. When he was on his death bed, he asked his sons to look for their brother.

"He is the only one that can help us," he continued talking. "He should be well related now... My good Heinrich. He said in a low breath."

In his delirious state, he kept calling him on and on, "Heinrich...!"

And after a deep breath, they answered him, "He is not here yet."

But the father insisted, "When he gets here, tell him that I'm resting for a while and that I love him."

At that moment, Earl closed his eyes, and stop breathing. He was gone.

There were horrible moments in the minds of the sons, and they were also suffering the typhoid infection. They tried to get to Berlin, but the local health department did not let them in, instead they were admitted to the general hospital of Koblenz.

Their mother, the duchess, was on the brink of hysterics since she needed to take care of burying her husband and her two sons were in the final stages of the illness. Only a brave and heroic woman could handle such pain, and like a soldier with no expressions, she kept herself in front of the coffin with the accompaniment of some friends during the burial. Heinrich did not know about his father's passing, because the situation and the danger on the roads. It was almost impossible to communicate long distance, like in this case.

Heinrich's brothers couldn't fight the illness and died almost simultaneously in 1885. The frightful illness took them to a tragic end and after a long suffering their mother, Margarette, got ill with the same illness that took her sons lives, but this time it was different, she was treated with an injection called Penicillin. This medicine still was in an experimental stage, and she was one of the first humans to be tested with it. The results of the reaction to the new medicine were satisfactory and she survived the illness. She recovered in Koblenz with the care of the foundation.

Little by little the illness dissipated as well as the violence and the war. By that time, the duchess tried all types of resources to communicate with her son. To her surprise, he had been out of school for a year and was not there anymore. He enlisted in the imperial military to fight on the front line. When she tried to look for him in the military, it took her more than six months to find him. She wrote to him and told him the horrible story of the death of his father and what happened to his two brothers.

When he received the letter from his mother in 1885, his face became full of sadness, surprise, and remorse as well as he cried because of what happened in Koblenz. Soon he asked permission from the military to assist his mother and take care of his father's house. The worst part was the remorse he had for not contacting his father because of all the resentment he had towards him for sending him to Berlin against his well and not understanding him. This blinded his will to write when his father was doing it for his own good, and he understand this too late.

He started a new life after being in the war, nothing was the same but, Heinrich came back to Koblenz and help her mother. He looked for the Schmitt brothers, so he could get back control of his properties, but when he finally found them, he got a surprise. They denied everything and told him they did not have any signed documents of the pact; the greediness of the brothers caused them to create a plot to keep everything but the father's house, which was abandoned, and thieves got all they could since no one was living there. Luckily, because of the size of the property and thru the intervention of the town hall, it was not taken away from the owners.

Tired of the fights and constant threats from the Schmitt brothers, Heinrich gave up on trying to get his family heritage back. His mother and he started getting some of their possessions that were not in the pact, and both tried to start a new life.

Heidi Marie's communication was less often, but their love continued live; Heinrich decided to leave his mother for a while and try his luck in Switzerland and continue looking for his Heidi Marie's love, since she moved to another house, but his letters were still being delivered to the old house. As time went by and Heidi Marie could not find the new address of Heinrich, which was the reason they lost contact for a while. Meanwhile during the time, that they were trying to keep communicating by mail, Heinrich's mother started recuperating and continued with her life, Heinrich left to Lucerne, but never lost contact with his mother.

Another reason that made him leave was the fact that he could not provide for his mother nor for himself, so leaving for Lucerne was a good option. He resigned from the military and went out to look for a job in that city. Thanks to his firmness and preparation in law subjects, and his business knowledge, after trying several jobs, he quickly found a job in the Switzerland government as a tax collector for Lucerne, place where he continued looking for Heidi Marie.

Heinrich worked hard for several years, and all his income was sent to his mother, he only kept the minimum needed to live in a boarding house and have a comfortably life because now the salary allowed him to do so. He was doing this because he wanted to rescue what they lost.

Heinrich started to put into practice all that he had learned from his father since that was one of the things, he missed the most. Also, the fact that nothing had changed his love for his love one and to give up everything for her; made him live with guilty feelings but at the same time he had a strong conviction of looking for his love one and finding her; for him this hope would never die. In his mind the power of love that he had for Heidi Marie was his motivation to keep looking for her.

After several years, Heinrich was feeling no hope, and he was thinking of going back with his mother, who was financially recuperated, thanks to being a hard-working woman. That made him feel ease in his mind to continue working in Lucerne. During that time, Heinrich had the habit of going out to all the markets in the area thinking of the possibility of locate his love easier. He knew the vendors of all the city markets by memory, and wishes to find her again. Every day and on his days off he visited all the stores in Lucerne. It was causing him despair that he could not find her and soon he started looking outside of Lucerne.

In those days, it was a popular attraction to visit the Lucerne Lion. One that day there was the precious moment, when he was walking towards the wooden bridge that crossed the Reus river, not knowing it would take him to his love one. It was a cold evening; he was walking slowly with his head down and at that same time looked up trying to find her. He said, "Heidi do not leave me, let me find you."

Without thinking he stopped in the middle of the bridge, while the river flowing with a strong noise letting him think about fragile human life; it was at that moment when Heinrich stopped and leaned on the bridge and start crying.

The feelings he was having were because the memories of his father which made him think and say to himself, "Father, I left you for my love one, and did not find her. Now, we are alone, but I won't let my mother down, this time I will be with her always, I will take care of her, do not worry, my mother... And my beautiful Heidi... I do not know where she is, I'm lost... I will quit looking for her and get back with my mother."

He was questioning himself and said, "This will be the las time I will be looking for her in this city."

As he continued crying, the river kept flowing like it did not care. He turned up his face crying and in silence for a few minutes as if he was out of this world, and breathed deeply for a while. He calmed down and listened to the noise of the people on the other side of the bridge. He pulled himself up slowly and put his hat on and started walking towards the people. When he was getting closer, he heard the music, laughs, and saw the festive environment. At that moment it came to his mind the memory of that evening in Germany when he saw Heidi for the first time. The Reus river noise was behind him as he heard a small market where they were celebrating a local festival. He was getting closer, walking slowly and the night lights were illuminating the houses, and Heinrich turned his sight to the left and he couldn't believe what he saw, it was Mr. Whent.

"Is it him...?" He asked himself while his heart was jumping. His heart palpitations were increasing and he was breathing with a lot of emotion. He couldn't believe it, as he approached him very quickly and stopped in front of him.

"Mr. Whent..." He paused, but couldn't say anything else. The silence and his look paralyze him.

Mr. Whent saw him and said, "What can I help you with?"

He couldn't talk, at first and then with a little doubt in his mind, he asked, "Herr Whent?"

Mr. Whent looked at him very confused and said, "How do you know my name?"

Heinrich kept in silent.

A shiver following with suffocating emotion and a strong body shake, but Heinrich kept looking at him and Mr. Whent repeated, "What can I help you with? I do not know you; Why are you not responding to me?"

At that moment, a person asked him for some products, and interrupted their talking, so Mr. Whent started attending to his customers, "Yes, how can I help?"

Heinrich just stood watching him without interrupting his sale, but when this ended, Heinrich spoke up, "Are you Heide Marie's father?"

"Yes, why? How do you know her?" He responded.

Heinrich continued, "Don't you recognize me? Don't you remember me Mr. Whent? I'm Heinrich!"

"Heinrich?" Answered Mr. Whent:

"Yes, I'm Heinrich von Münster. Do you remember me?"

And Mr. Whent responded surprise, "Don't tell me that you are the young man from years ago."

"Yes, yes, the same one," Heinrich answered emotionally and at the same time, with lots of questions and glad to know that was Mr. Whent who answered him in an indifferent tone of voice.

"What are you doing here young man, so far from your home? Or are you coming with your family?"

At that moment, Heinrich was sure of his discovery, and answered him in a firm voice, "No sir, it has been a long time since I left my family..."

But Mr. Whent in a cutting way interrupted him and questioned again, "So, what are you doing here?"

While he was attending to other customers, he kept watching him standing there. Mr. Whent was getting upset and desperate, not for who he was but because he was not moving and was like stunned and mute in front of the stand; so finally, Mr. Whent turned toward him and looked at straight in Heinrich's eyes, "Ok, I know who you are; very good! Nice to see you, GOOD BYE!"

He turned to continue working, but Heinrich was still there, so Mr. Whent couldn't stand it anymore and took his apron off, pulled his shirt sleeves up and pushed him to the side. He went straight to Heinrich, took him by his arm and tried to pull him out from the stand because he was not happy with Heinrich's attitude, and told him again with a strong tone of voice,

"What do you want?!" And again, with a stronger tone of voice. "What a hell are you doing there, standing like an idiot?" He tells Heinrich very serious. "Are you going to buy anything or not?"

Heinrich was paralyzed cold. Mr. Whent touched Heinrich chest three times with his finger, following with the same questioning, but this time with a strong tone of voice and upset, "I'm asking you, what do you want?"

Heinrich finally responded, "Mr. Whent, with all my respect, I need to talk to you."

He responded, "Not now young man. Don't you see how busy I am? Wait or come back later, but do not waste my time, you already have me in a bad mood, stupid boy! Do not bother me anymore."

But Heinrich insisted, "Please Mr. Whent, I need to talk to you."

Between interruptions with the clients and Heinrich just standing there watching, Mr. Whent was upset and call out to his son Helmut, "Come here Helmut! Son! Help me because I need to take care of something."

After this Mr. Whent told Heinrich, "Come over her boy."

He took him by his arm and with anger and no discretion in front of the clients he said, "Tell me right now what is that you want."

With his adrenalin flowing around his body, his pall skin, he turned red that made the color of his eyes highlight like blue lights, when Heinrich saw this, instead of being scared or fear, he remembered the color of the eyes of his loved one and that made him feel brave to talk to him, but Mr. Whent said, "Ok answer me... Are you talking or not?"

They moved out from the stand, and after a silence, Heinrich used all his strength and all his bravery to explain to Mr. Whent his story...

After several minutes of this conversation, Mr. Whent couldn't believe what he had just heard. The silence was dominating and the only noise was from the people and the water of the river. Mr. Whent was quiet until he finally said, "But, how could you have left your parents?"

Heinrich responded, "For me there was no greater motivation than to look for Heidi Marie."

Mr. Whent continued, "Young man, look at all you have done... And your mother? Does she know you are here?"

Heinrich answer him, "Of course, part of being here is because of her... And the other part is to look for your daughter."

In a lower tone of voice with a sad look and pleading he continued, "Now my mother depends on me, but I always thought of Heidi Marie... In my job... In everything. Well, you understand me Herr Whent. We have been able to come out thanks to the strength and work of my mother. Now I'm working very hard, and I know that we will recover from all our problems, Herr Whent, but you know what..." Heinrich continued very emphatically. "I had hoped to someday to find you... I mean find her."

After silent moment with a supplicant look, Heinrich asked, "Did you hear me? Do you understand me? Herr Whent!"

After looking at him at his eyes and then turning down his sight to the floor while reflecting, Herr Whent touched his chin, crossed his hands, and continued with an extended arm to mark his distance and at the same time touch Heinrich's shoulder with his right hand, "Look boy, the only thing I can do for you, is to talk to my daughter, and if she agrees and remembers you... We will see. In the meantime."

He said in a strong tone and with an authority he had over her daughter, "Do not bother her! I won't tell you where we live."

At that moment, Heinrich interrupted, "But, Herr Whent, can you see how I am and all I did to find her?"

He responded, "NO! I will let you know."

He got up, but Heinrich stopped him and touched his shoulder questioning. He tried to stop his walk, "But, When...?"

Without turning his face. Mr. Whent answer him shortly, "I will let you know at the right time. I have a lot to think about, and a lot to talk about."

Heinrich couldn't wait any more, he was desperate and asked Herr Whent, "Herr Whent, please understand me!"

Whent push him away and said, "Calm down boy."

He looked up to the sky over his shoulder thinking of the suffering boy.

"Look Heinrich, come back tomorrow, in the afternoon and we will talk, I will see what I can do, but I cannot guarantee you anything... Ok..." And while he was telling this to the boy, he was thinking to himself "This bourgeois! Is he on an adventure or what? Or it is real love?" he sighed and ended up saying to Heinrich."

"She is the most precious I have, my daughter, she is the one who should see if she remembers you or not..." Heinrich answered him.

"Herr Whent, thank you very much, you don't know how much you are doing for me, and I will thank you forever. Thank you, thank you! And I will be here early tomorrow morning."

But Herr Whent said, "No, not until the afternoon!"

And Heinrich answer him excitingly, "Yes, I will be there."

That afternoon was the coldest of October... But become the warmest and full of happiness, for Heinrich since love was in all its splendor.

"My God, you had heard me," He was thinking to himself, and a big smile came to his face. Heinrich left screaming of happiness to wait for the next day. He continued walking and screaming in the street, "I found her!" Even louder. "I FOUND HER!"

It was the longest night and longest morning of his life, but next day, just like Herr Whent told him, anxious and punctual he waited. Several hours went by, suddenly he saw Herr Whent walking and to his surprise he was accompanied by the beautiful Heidi Marie. It was such a happiness of Heinrich that he couldn't wait to get there, he run to find them and the same happened to Heidi Marie, she took off from her father's arm to meet her love. At that moment, Herr Whent understood what was happening and did not have any other choice but to see how those two-in-love hugged. With a breath and walking faster Herr Whent, got next to them, and said, Heidi Marie, "Do you know him?"

She responded, "Father, I had never stop thinking of him, and I had hoped that he was looking for me, just like he promised me... And he did it, father!"

Heidi Marie couldn't be happier, "He is the man that I have given all my love to in silence, during all these years."

The father starts crying and hugged them.

"Look, how is this happening?" The young Heinrich answered him with a strong tone but tearing voice.

"Herr Whent, do you understand now that we are both in love that started long time ago and it was worth it to leave everything for her?"

Mr. Whent nodded his head, "Yes, I do understand."

The couple in love spend all afternoon talking and Mr. Whent left them with the understanding that his daughter was happy.

Time was the witness of their love and little by little, Heinrich kept very close to her, a year went by of waiting, time that Mr. Whent set us a minimum time for them to get engaged. In the meantime, Heinrich respect that agreement and he was the best of the boyfriend, the most cordial, discreet and help with the beautiful Heidi Marie.

In the meantime, his mother knowing and depending on him, she arrived at Lucene to visit since their economic situation had change for good, and with the time family relations will endure. After three years of engagement, friendship, and real love, they finally got married and started a new life together in beautiful Lucerne.

The happy couple couldn't wait and got married in 1881 under the catholic church for her part and in the Lutheran for his part and with the blessing of duchess Margarette.

It was an emotional ceremony that had two celebrations. One in Heidi Marie's house for all the businesses of Lucerne; friends and family attended with music and served beer and wine and where Herr Whent celebrated the happiness of his daughter with a magnificent party full of joy. The other celebration was in Heinrich's house where they had the same magnificent party, with an emotional gathering and the acceptance of love that the couple were waiting for.

By this time, the Heinrich's family had, achieved through hard work of the mother, recuperated most of their goods and settled a suit by the duchess to the Schmitt brothers which they couldn't prove in trial. The legality of the properties and the judge after years of dedication and constant legalities, pronounce his verdict in favor to the defendant and give her the sole administrator of cooperative to the duchess Margarete.

Two years went by after the celebration of their marriage, when Heinrich and Heidi Marie, now von Münster, well known and residing in Lucerne, were recommended by several people and by Heidi Marie's father Herr Arthur Whent to administrated his business.

While this was happening to Heinrich, another story was developing at his father's house.

"You can't get back in time, you can't see ahead what is going to happen, only the opportunity that life gives us at that moment," Those were Heinrich reflections and meditations. Each word coming out of his mouth, each thought he analyzed carefully, since he learned that his thoughts became plans that took him to action both consciously or unconsciously. He understood at that moment the importance of his thoughts and emotions had on his life and that he must control them because they could change the life of a person. Like when lies recited oven and over become reality, not only of the fact of the lie itself but also the power the mind has over the free will of people. When someone wants to hear a truth, is not acceptable if it is not what we want to hear. For Heinrich, his truth was over everything, his truth was the passion for his wife, his truth was to follow her and find her without analyzing its consequences at that moment. Heinrich thought of his actual life, all he was going and knew he couldn't come back anymore. All his thoughts could happen in the future and what he was doing today was reality.

The Duchess, Heinrich's mother asked him to come to visit her, since she was feeling tired. He went immediately as in past occasions; he left to Koblenz with Heidi Marie to assist whit his mother's health. Even though his mother's physical and moral straighten, it was visible of the wounds of life and from the illness that almost took her. When the couple arrived at Koblenz and started taking care of the business, they found out that everything was in excellent condition and in order; the business economically was in good shape and the old cooperative was now property of his mother and working the winery productions that kept the name of "earl of Von Münster."

Heinrich understood what happened and admire what his mother did, with her spirit of hard work bringing out the lineage of her ancestors; that was the miracle of Koblenz that allowed the business to continue and the Von Münster to recuperate most of their wealth. Besides, Heinrich decided to join the business of his father-in-law with the ones he had in Germany, that way the goods of both families increased. Even though the Von Münster did not have some of their past lands, they kept two of their castles in Koblenz and the mother's house in Wunppertal. Those were valuable at that time, but was difficult to manage the business, so the family left to a small town close to Hamburg, Elson. Where the country and rivers were ideal to start a new business: livestock and milk processing, as well as cold cut processing.

This was a place far away from the noise of the big cities of Germany, where they lived and procreate decedents in a cordial, friendly atmosphere beginning the origin of lots of destine and initiating the story of happiness and abundance for several years to come for the families in this story.

The atmosphere at the end of century was a problematic Germany, with their threating states and the threat of war that finally ended with the union of Germany in 1871 and being proclaimed independence by the emperor of Germany William I, and Bismarck being named the first chancellor or the Republic of Germany.

Economic progress could be seen in the region, with the milk industry and the wine-making. The Von Münster family resurged in a new Germany, and became vigorous and progressive at the end of XIX century.

CHAPTER ONE
THE FORMATION

By this time, the inheritor of the Von Münster dynasty already had a well-known place in the German society; he was a friend and collaborator of conservative movement of the country. His friends included a banker and a jeweler Jude: Abraham Hoffman, a commercial strategist political conservative that assessed and helped in finances; also, political conservative and liberal Hans Jägger (representative of the region for the conservative group of the German monarchy). Also, a special hunting friend, captain Mark Henkel, who was also his security assessor and in charge of the safety of his properties.

Mark took this position because of his good-fellowship with Heinrich from when both were part of the imperial military, together lived through innumerable intense fights on the front, as well as several special missions where they were together and more than one time saw their lives in danger. But thanks to a strong friendship and their military cleverness they came out alive from all their adventures. Even though Heinrich left the military, his friendship whit Mark continued and their lives joined at several times.

Mark was very close to the family, he had the rank of Capitan from his participation in heroic combats, in addition to being outstanding as a solder of the union of Germany and giving himself and combat. The reunion of Mark with Heinrich, was in a day for Franco

Mark, where he was traveling in the region and wanted to visit his mother's house. When Heinrich Knew that, he tried to look for him in the train station at Elmsohrn. It was there where they had an emotional welcoming and after a long talk, the day ended in one of the longest most pleasant evening parties for both, where they recalled the stories and adventures they had together.

The reunion was so pleasant that Heinrich asked Mark to stay and offer him a good position, that consisted of guard the security over his family and other activities like the supervision of all the employees, so Heinrich could be closer to his old mother. He was the ideal person for the job, because his military formation, his close friendship, and was 100% trusted. Mark immediately accepted, with the only exception that if he was required for military service, he would leave his job and go with no regrets to his call. But before leaving he would leave someone of trust in such an honorable position, because of the dear Heinrich family. At that moment, a new friendship stage began and learning from each other, they created an environment of arms, security, and order that had an influence on the Earl von Heinrich family.

The Keiser William I family; specially Frederic Von Hohenzollern "valued friend" of the family, during their summer vacation times used to take walks around the beautiful fields and mountains that look like they were engraved in scenery, unique fields and the calmness of the Rhin and surrounding areas where you could go to contemplate nature and admire the mountains where the air from the north travel without frontiers and whispering songs of work, pace, and harmony between men and nature. That was the place where the nobles felt present and felt part of their own nation and spirit of courage where their arise and their spirit fight to increased and kept them dominant in.

The Von Hohenzollerns had a tradition to stop at the Heinrich house on his way to Hamburg or Kiel. He was known as an excellent host beside being a good politician; since life taught him that it was better to be good to the nobles as well as with the town people. This kind of mentality allowed him to maintain a privileged position in the area, giving him the advantage of growing economically and stronger even though there was not the dominance like during the past dynasty but for this was more than a middle-class could possibly wish form.

On one of Hohenzollern family trips, a hunting trip with their son Victor Albert, grandson of the Prussia king, and belonging to the lineage of Victoria Queen of England, a onetime event in this area, he arrived was like a big party. Attentions was on the nobles, and obviously, this connected the two families, the Hohenzollern and Von Münster.

The atmosphere was favorable for generating great changes in Germany. Years of formation, where the nobles dedicated their time more to the military due to the war verses Russia and France, there were times where tension was high between the people. The thirst of revenge and conquest by the German nobles was clear. William II, the young noble and sport hunter was the new emperor and Kaiser of Germany, but it was obvious that he vehemently desires to be the Teuton conquest.

More than hunting, there were social events where the politician art and relations were the daily practice. For Heinrich, it was normal to relate with this kind of people but thankfully this kind of events were not frequently since it was a fortune to serve them.

By 1890, Earl Heinrich had an inheritor, Otto son of a traditional Switzerland heritage and from the German noble, was named by his father in memory of his brother who tragically die in the disgrace with his other brother and the pain of losing his father. This caused Heinrich a guilty feeling that was consuming him inside, but in 1895 his first-born son could justify the long absence of his loved family. The little one was presented to the Lutheran religious community where the family was part of. To this event there were invited aristocrats to include little Otto in an early age to the society where Earl von Münster was part of.

Now, Heinrich said proudly about his offspring: "I will educate and take care of my children like my father did, but I will never place in front of them my desire over them, I will give them the biggest gift a father can give... I will give them their freedom, but they will always have my guidance and support, they will always be Von Münster. The suffering I had for the intolerance, rigidity, and arrogance of my father, won't happen to my son Otto"; after saying that, the child was taking to his room with Heidi Marie, his mother who was waiting for him to give him the best she could give: her love.

After two years of this important event arrived Arthur, named by his father in honor of his father-in-law, by 1898 was celebrating his presentation in the same manner that happened with Otto years past. This event felt proud to both families and during the happy celebration, family and friends invited gave the same good wishes as they did with Otto without distention between Arthur and the first-born.

Five years later in 1902 arrived the most beautiful of the surprises, the most beautiful of the creatures to the eyes of the family; it was Ana Marie, the little one who seduce the heart of Heinrich forever.

The time went by. It was imaginable the type of education that the inheritors of the Von Münster destiny were getting. Mark function as surrogate and tutor of the boys Otto, Arthur, and Ana Marie with the help of the young Heike (instructress and nanny of the little ones) together with his mother Heidi Marie was taking care of them day and night, starting a new meaning of life for the family, preparing, and formatting them for whatever the destiny had for them.

CHAPTER TWO
THE LEARNING

Heinrich wanted their sons to have the best education at that time, which besides the tutor, he wanted them to be educated at the custom of his family, in which was accustom like all the aristocracy of the moment, the Bach, Wagner music (the favorite ones of Heinrich) in addition of much more like Lieberman, Lehner, Zor, Düren. In between the music, the work, and the family education and more, the children were growing up and learning most of the greatest legacy of the German culture. The time was passing and in between the readings of Götze, Luterek, Nietzsche, and first one Humboldt, since it was the most profitable in the family. Recognizing the influence of the mother education giving a special personal touch, it was a special distinguish with the combination of the greatest values of the German culture of the boys, the traditions and Switzerland customs were present in the behavior of the children that was accepted by Heinrich in conjunction with his love Heidi Marie worked and lived in harmony taking the best of both cultures and mixing it in the refine of a new family, leaving behind old traditions of the Von Münster family.

All this was giving a different touch to the German traditions, they were different, the were not the typical aristocrats stuck-up, arrogant, superb, impulsive, and martial like the Prussians use to be, they never felt superior to others, they never looked down to people in a lower class than theirs, thanks to the roots of Switzerland origin. Their mother, came from a working family of a middle class, she dedicates oneself with painstaking those qualities, knowing that their sons couldn't be like the aristocrats, she cultivates in them an affable character, friendly, accessible, generous and worker; mainly worker, a characteristic that distinguish them mainly and allowed them that the people in the town and employees recognized and respected them.

The German cohabitation in between the social classes it was impossible. Between the traditional German aristocracy and the town people, the interaction was ridicule most of the time. The most common case was the Hohenzollen family who ignored or pretended not to see Heinrich during their visits, it was during this time when they got closer with the people. The only reason of these visits was taking place, was well seen by the empire. Remember that Heinrich was a good politician and maintain in harmony his family interest and social with the German empire as well as to get along with the liberal line of that time, obviously without deposition openly as that.

However, the hunting even thought was not inculcated to his sons, ended absorbed as an own tradition being Otto the best targeted shooter giving him to become fond of weapons, hunting, and furtive formation in the annual hunting camps organized in between the families of that time, where the Münster family was aware.

CHAPTER THREE
THE PRESAGE

The time for school and knowledge formation did not wait; it was how by the influence of his father and mainly Mark, the boys define to take a liking for mechanical; the engineer, hunting, and their maximum fascination: airplanes. It was such a captivation that Otto and Arthur spend entire days imagine furrowing the sky hopping someday to conquer the skies. There was not a day when the two boys spend time laying in the grass looking up in the sky and imagine thousands of flights in that marvelous sky that cover the country of their home.

The economic and social position of the Von Münster family allowed the two boys to have the possibility to choose where and what they wish to study, always in between the most important educative institutions of the country.

As a Germans aristocrat, born in the side walls of the Rhin and on the side or the Krükau river, had a better chance among the other applicants for higher education, since they had to meet with several requirements, one of them having the intellectual capacity to pass the admission evaluation and none less being fond of the fine arts. It was how their father Heinrich, send them to Stuttgart city at the Heidelberg University.

The Heideiberg University, a German institution of high teaching located right in Heidelberg which its official name is Ruprecht-Karls-Universität, was the oldest university that exist in this country; being an autonomy center subject to the authority of ministry of science and investigation which headquarters was in Stuttgart and finance by the state of Baden-Württemberg.

Was founded in 1386, in Heidelberg (at that time belonging to the Palatinate) by Rupert I elector of the Palatinate. The first superior of the university, the religion academic Marsillus von Inghen established it as a catholic institution. In XVI century, during the reform, Heidelberg became prosper university; reorganization that had a fundamental role, the protestant scholar Philip Melanchthon being later reorganize in 1652 after the thirty-year war as a lay institution. During the next 150 years, the activity of the university continues in difficult conditions, due to, mainly the France wars. The stability did not return to the university until 1803, year in which the Palatinate hand over the city of Heidelberg to the Gran Dukedom of Baden.

For XIX century it became a prestigious study center that attracted a lot of foreign students. Available with several faculties like biology, chemistry, classic studies, and oriental, social, and economic sciences, law, mathematics, modern philosophy, physic, astronomy, theology, and theory medicine and clinical. Included also more than 80 institutions, clinics, and seminaries associated with the different faculties. The courses were normally four years to obtain the Diploma or the title of Doctor.

Here is where after four years (from 1911 to 1914), the young ones were already impregnated of the philosophy and studies from authors like Nietzsche, Kant, Goethe, Heine, and Shiller, not leaving behind the inspiration of Luther and the philosophy influence of the theological flowing of Sebastian Münster, Calvino, Engels Marx and Humbolt, basing his searching of new worlds and feed their hunger with adventures and discoveries.

The music played an important role in their formation; between pentagrams, masterly pattern, that were generators of great dreams day and night for the young students, they developed an admiration dependency and love for music: plays like Brahms, Beethoven, Wagner, Lieberman, Zorn or Duere couldn't stop to marc those thick strokes.

The university of Heidelberg was recognized for the great formation of a new type of sciences in Germany, true born creators with a bigger vision of possess an intellectual power insuperable in the world of that time, they were considering in several sense invisibles productions of science like Bosch, Rötingen, Hertz Bauer, Leibniz, Einstein, Blümmer to name some, that only the experts and the world knew what they could achieve.

To be able to understand what happen in that time, is important to refer what was happening in Europe: Germany it was already an economic power to the extent that all the products were prefer in Europe better than the French or England products. The Europe power number one by excellence were a great export of coal, steel, and much more products for the pharmacy industry as well as machinery of high performance and precision; the German products conquest not only Europe but the whole world. It was a strong economy growing and supported, the per capita income was the highest in the world and its influence was already in United States, where the consume of the German products were more than other countries. This incite that their economy outlines to be the stronger powerful economy in the world, situation that started to disturb the neighbors from the south, mainly England, since several events started happening that were not favorable for the French and neither to the English, seeing clear that Germany was taking the rule of the economy and it was that little by little things were getting complicated.

The first world war: a military conflict incited by the European power, French, and England, when they saw the German supremacy, situation that they must stop somehow. There was an intent to stop this great economic trade in Europe, but not until a war that found the only way to stop this giant. This started the 28 of July 1914 as a curbing between the Astro-Hungary empire and Serbia that became in a curbing armed to the continental scale when the war declaration Astro-Hungary extend to Russia the 1 of August 1914 and end finally to be a war world with the participation of 32 nations, ending in 1918. Twenty-eight of the nations, denominated "ally" or "associate power" where Great Britain, France, Russia, Italy, and United States fight against the coalition of the call central empires form by Germany, Austria-Hungry, the Ottoman empire and Bulgaria. The main cause of the beginning of the hostility between Austria-Hungry and Serbia was the assassination of the archduke Francis Fernando of Habsburg inheriting of the throne Austro-Hungary assignment in Sarajevo (Bosnia being part of the empire Austro-Hungry now Bosnia-Herzegovina) the 28 of June 1914 by the Serbia nationalist Gavrilo Princip, hire by the French to initiate a local war and weaken the German power. Nevertheless, the deepest causes of the conflict refer to the European history of the XIX century, concretely to the economic and political tendency that rule since 1871, year that were founded and surface as a grant power of the II German empire.

Another of the most important factors that unchain the war world I were the ardent nationalist spirit that expanded in Europe along the XIX and beginning of XX century, the economic and political rivalry in between different nations, as well as the military process and the rapid armament course that distinctive the international society during the last third of the XIX century, since the creation of two systems of alliances confronted.

The French revolution and the Napoleonic wars divulge in most of the Europe continent the concept of democracy, extending the idea of the towns that share an ethnic origin, language and some same political ideals had the right to form independents states. However, the beginning of the national self-determination was totally ignored by the dynastical and reactionary power that decide the destine of the European matter in the Vienna congress (1815). Lots of the towns that wished their autonomy would stay subdue to local dynasty or to other nations. For example, the German states, integrated in the Germanic confederation were divided in several dukedoms, princedom, and kingdoms in according with the Vienna Congress terms; Italy was also distributed in several politic units, which some of them were under the foreign control; the Flemish Belgian and French from the low countries Austrian remaining subordinate to the Dutch dominion by decision of the congress. The revolutions and the strong nationalism movement of the XIX century attain annul most part of the impose reactionary agree in Vienna. Belgian obtain the independents from the low countries in 1830; the unification of Italy was ended in 1861, and the Germany in 1871. However, the nationalists conflict continues without getting solve in other areas of Europe at the beginning of the XX century, that provoke tensions in the involve regions and other European nations. One of the most important nationalist courses, the Pan-Slavism fulfillment a main role in the events that proceeds to the war.

The nationalist spirit also makes evident the economic way. The industrial revolution started in Great Britain at the end of XVIII century, in France at the beginning of the XIX and in Germany in 1870, inciting a great increment of manufactured products, being these countries compelled to look new markets in the external. The area where there was developed mainly the European political of economic expansion was Africa were the respective colonial interest start in conflict with frequency. The economic rivalry for the dominion of the African territory between France, Germany, and Great Britain was from 1898 till 1914 to provoke a war in Europe in several occasions.

As consequences of these tensions, the European nations adopt ways for the interior and exterior politician between 1871 and 1914 that increase the conflict danger; maintaining several permanent militaries that constantly increased by recruiting in times of pace and creating bigger war ships. Great Britain with the influence of the German military that start 1900 and by the curse of the war Russian-Japan, modernize their fleet under the direction of the admiral sir John Fisher, because the martial conflict between Russia and Japan demonstrates the efficiency of the naval weapons of long reach. The advance in other areas of technology and military organizations encourage the constitution the bigger states capable to manufacture plans of mobilization and attack very precise, integrating often in programs that couldn't cancel them ones they were started.

The leadings of all the countries took conscience of the increase expenses of weapons unload with time in national bankruptcy or war, that's why the intention to support the world disarm on several occasions, especially in the conferences of La Haya in 1899 and 1907.

However, the international rivalry got to the point to be impossible reach any effective agreement to decide the international disarm.

In a parallel way to the armaments prosses, the European states establish alliances with other power for not being isolated in case of war. This attitude generates a phenomenon that in itself greatly increases the possibilities of a generalized conflict: the alignment of the great European power in two hostile military alignments: The triple alliance, form by Germany, Austria-Hungary, and Italy and the triple entente, form by Great Britain, France, and Russia. The own changes that were produce in the center of these associations contribute to create a crisis atmosphere present because the period was denominate "the arm peace"

The Von Münster family was not alien to this event, but even there were times of prosperity, their products, and their finance resources were in a perfect time, they sold all the properties form Koblenz and reinvestment their profits in Switzerland and Germany in processing equipment, agriculture machinery as well as several heads of cattle.

The imports were not coming in to the country and with the Dölling family initiated an alliance of business for the production in series of sausage, cheese, and milk products of the highest quality.

CHAPTER FOUR
THE DECISION

Europe had a chaotic situation, the shadow of the war was imminent, the conditions in the country were complicated, the Kaiser William II had a thirst of conquest and an evident pride for trying to defend himself. This combining to the envy and greed of the French and England, who were supported by the Russians; who were also living times of changes in their monarchy as well as the excessive paranoiac of a Kaiser that couldn't control anymore the power and that day by day were getting out of his hands inciting the unavoidable. The streets of the main cities of Germany were evident the presence on more military everywhere, the in and out of buses full of soldiers and the medals of Kaiser to the heroes of war with the iron cross of first class for the participation in the great work of the now obsessionist German leader. This made the young ones involved in a zone favorable to go to war and leave everything for their country.

Heinrich, was worried for their children and knowing what was being in war he tries to persuade them. He had a conclusive talk In Stuttgart, with Otto and Arthur; same conversation started and repeated when they were small kids, and even when Arthur and Anne Marie were not borne yet.

"You decided the best for yourselves and what your real wishes are but consider that the decision taken will determine and can mark OUR lives forever."

Otto was the one to continue what his father Heinrich did not conclude when he was in military stage for dedicating to his family; while Arthur will have had a destiny inside the commerce boundary and the administration, like his father. Everything was just suppositions at that moment. Heinrich return to Elmsohrn ready to prepare himself for the new war that was everywhere. The news did not have any other subject beside victories of Kaiser, without mentioning all the thousands of soldiers dying each day in the seas, land, and air, horrible deaths and the hurt of families because of the loss of their loved ones.

That made Heinrich meditate even more, when he arrived home, did not tell anything to his wife, like he was caring a heavy load on his shoulders, he must confront a new reality with a loud shout.

"Holy cow!"

In silence, in a whisper Heinrich said, "My God! What kind of men are these, that destroy everything they touch?"

He strongly bangs on the table and walks to the closes chair and let himself fall in the chair with his two arms covering his head.

In silence and with tears in his eyes, when they heard noise in the dining room, Heidi Marie and her daughter, Anne Marie run to see what was happening, with respect and at the same time scared for what they heard from Heinrich, so his wife said to him, "What happens Heinrich?"

In absolute silence, couldn't avoid a new question made, "Heinrich, Are you ok?"

At that moment, he put himself up and looked at his wife and daughter and hugged them like he had not seen them in years, and ended telling them conclusively and with a great assurance, "Our lives are going to change totally, we must prepare ourselves, I had to talk with Otto and Arthur, and probably we won't see each other again."

The three of them start crying.

"I'm very scared, hug me."

Anne Marie whisper and suddenly her mother answered such a petition, while his father asked them to keep hugging strongly. They started listening to the in military marches passing in front of their house that was going to fight in the French border.

"Come here?!, that's what I mean, our lives won't be the same. Prepare your things and let's go to Lucerne now that we can, at least we will be better than here," Heidi Marie Ordered.

Heinrich hurried up and took care of all his pending, however he took the necessary time to order his business in Germany and to have a meeting with his friends, one of them was his assessor and almost administrator Abraham Hoffman.

"What's going on? Why is this happening now?" Asked Anne Marie.

While looking at her eyes and in silence put her hand over her shoulder, Heidi Marie strongly said, "My love, come on, cheer up, we have always gotten ahead, not this time and never will we be defeated, we are great, my love."

"Let's go then, we still have time to get everything ready," said Heinrich, talking about the proposal of his wife, but she took him by his hands and told him, "There are things in life that we can't change, but we must accept and get ahead."

Heinrich looked at her and said, "My love, you are right, there is nothing to do here anymore, let's go."

The next days, they were gathering all their belongings, and by the end of fifteen days they were on the train to Berna then Lucerne. It was a dangerous crossroad; they must avoid the French borders since the conflict was prominent. Thanks to the relations of Heinrich and the Switzerland safe-conduct, they could leave Germany, since Switzerland was neutral in the conflict. He granted the safe-conduct, because his father in-law request as a Swiss his granddaughter and his son in-law an answer that was obtain in short time.

Looks like a never-ending trip; more than 10 inspections stop by the military. It was the same story when they asked for documentation... Where are you going? What's the matter? etc. The distress was constant and the sensation of the urgent to escape from hell.

When they arrive at the border, before crossing to Switzerland, the German authorities requested them.

"Herr Heinrich von Münster, came to the immigration office."

There was the General in charge of the last point of inspection, they took him to the office and start a long interrogation.

"Herr Heinrich, German... Why are you leaving Germany? What are you going to Switzerland for?"

He responded to the official, "I have business to attend, my wife is swiss, my daughter..."

With a firm and strong voice, the official of immigration answers him, "They should get out, but not you."

Mein Herr! The doubt was invading so the anxiety, so he nervously asked him, "But why?"

His look turns pale, and he try to ask the official to be reasonable, the situation in a state of war is difficult and each day is becoming more complicated, especially in places like this, where violent events happened here before.

The officials were inspecting everything, and they were also nervous like the persons having the inspections in that moment, the tension was such that everyone was a suspect.

Heinrich took out his documentation and try to explain the official, who retrieve the documentation and took then to another place, meanwhile he was taken to another room where he was uncommunicated for couple of hours, but after a while, he starts to scream of desperation saying, "Wait a minute, you can't detain me! Please official... Come back!"

Two officials arrive to the room and one of them told him, "Please Herr. Control yourself, you don't want to upset the General and make it more difficult, ending here without your family."

Heinrich became quiet and obeyed. Finally, after an hour of a long waiting, the General came back to the room and said, "Herr Heinrich, an apology, here are your documents. You can leave from Germany."

Heinrich, did not say a word, took his papers, and got out of the immigration office. Promptly looked for his wife and daughter, he found them siting on the bench of the train station; they missed the train of that day and the last train going out to Switzerland was until early morning... They stayed there in the cold temperature of minus two degrees with a shake wind like predicting a war...

It was two in the morning and far away the seeing of vapor getting closer and the noise of the train tracks. The train the most beautiful noise that he ever heard in a long time, almost screaming of happiness was waiting the arrival of the train, in less than twenty minutes they were on board, despair to get out to their last shelter: Lucerne, there was the point where the family converse the separation of a marc destiny forever.

No more than three days went by of their arrival to Lucerne when the French started mobilization of their power to the border between Germany and Switzerland closing them.

Otto and Arthur did not have anything to say, their passion for airplanes gave them the golden opportunity. The enthusiasm and the adventure thirst as well as their gran nationalism, and the presence of the French on the German border, gave them a chance to enter the Luftwaffe (German air force), Otto entered the group of air engineers and his brother Arthur the group of tactic operations. It was little by little; the war starts to separate the two Münster brothers that were distancing day by day since each of them has a different destiny.

The German troops crossed the border of Luxemburg on August 2nd and Germany declared war to France the next day. A day before, the German government informed the Belgium government of their intention of marching over France crossing Belgium to finish off the route to attack Germany by the French, however the Belgium authorities denied allowing the pass by their territory to the German troops and appeal to the signing countries of the treaty of 1839 (where there was guarantee the neutral of Belgium in case of a conflict in where Great Britain, France and Germany were implicated) so they can carry out what they establish in such agreement. Great Britain, one of the countries signing of the treaty of 1839 send an ultimatum to Germany on August 4 where demand to respect the neutrality of Belgium; Germany repel the petition and the British government declare war that same day. Italy kept neutral until May 23, 1915, when it broke its pact with the triple alliance to satisfice their territorial aspirations and declare war to Austria-Hungry. The unity of the ally got stronger in September 1914 thru the pact of London, signed by France, Grant Britain, and Russia. While the battle keeps going more countries were adding to the conflict like Ottoman empire, Japan, United States, and other nations of the American continent. Japan, which signed an alliance with Great Britain in 1902, declares war to Germany on August 23, 1914, and United States did it on April 6, 1917.

It was inevitable, Europe was in war, while Heinrich sheltered in Switzerland, he was hoping to hear something from Otto and Arthur but was pointless the war parts were confusing every day and Heinrich did not have choice but to wait.

The European military operations start developing in three fronts: the occidental or frank-Belgium, the oriental or Russian, and the meridional or Serbia. Otto trained in aeronautical was integrated to the elite group of the Earl Alfred Von Schlieffen, old friend of the family Von Münster, reason why the course of the young Otto was driven by his important incursion in missions and programs of training very special and strategist for Germany, meanwhile Arthur kept one's distance in Berlin in the tactics operations team and administrative control of the imperial military, because being also grandchild of Frederick von Münster had the opportunity to manage a full logistic operation in the oriental front. With these both brothers lost contact for several years, their ways were separated in a year, all because of the war.

The initial plan of the German strategy was to defeat France in the west in a short time, while a little part of the German military and all the power Austro-Hungry were controlling the Russian invasion expecting it from the east. They were reliable on conquering France fast, thanks to the "lightning war" strategy controlled in Schlieffen plan; elaborated by the Earl Alfred von. The anticipate project was the following: The German troops should conquest Belgium, surrounding the French with quick movements, then change the front and defeat fast and contusive. When they applied this plan in the fall of 1914 to be a success. The fast incursion of Germany at the beginning of August to exterminate the Belgium military that forsaken the fortified town of

Lieja and Namur and refuge in the fortress of Amberes. The German troops push forward quickly defeating the French in Charleroi and the British retail force in Mons, that provoke the withdrawal of Belgium in all the ally line. At the same time, the German throw out the French from Lorena that were invaded but obligated to remove from the border of Luxembourg.

At the end of 1914 both factions were entrenched on trails lines that extended long by 800 kilometers, from Switzerland until the North Sea. Changes just start happening in this front for three years. Since the end of 1914 until almost the end of the battle, this becomes a war of trench or "wear and tear."

The world war incentive greatly affected the manufacture of airship with military purposes and development of the air war; project in which Ott von Münster participated very closely, since the German aristocrats had the opportunity of having strategist positions and even Otto since was supported by Schlieffen, because Heinrich von Munster had very good family relations with him since several years ago, Otto enter to this team of work where manufacture blimps, aerostat balloon and airplanes. These last ones were used mainly for two types of missions: the observation and the bombard.

Otto kept in the elite engineer group of developments of a new model of air hunter that threat to be a destructive weapon never seen before while the prepare for their surprise act, the Luftwaffe bombard for the first-time Paris from the air on August 30, 1914, and Dover (Great Britain) on December 21, 1914. During 1915 and 1916 the German blimps knowing as zeppelin, assault the east of England and London in seventy occasions. The first assault with airplanes was on November 28, 1916, and this occasion were frequently repeated the rest of the war.

The appearance in 1915 of Fokker German E-2 initiate the time of air battle. The Fokker has a synchronized machine gun with the helix, so the shots go through cross. Advance obtained because of years of investigation by the German elite group.

The fight for the air space control over the trenches develop quick technical advances. The private factories start build airplanes. Names like Nieuport, Sopwith and Fokker become famous, and the relative qualities of their different models were tested in several combats. The technologist leadership jumped from one faction to another with the building of airplanes furnish of better weapons or capable to fly higher and faster. In 1918, the skies were furrowed for enormous combat airplanes like Fokker D.VII, German; the Spad 13, French and the British S.E.5 and Sopwith Camel, capable of fly 200 kilometers per hour in 6.100 metros of high.

The pilots who fly these airplanes become the most famous pilots of the battle. The chief of the German squadron, Manfred von Richthofen, had a lot of losses and there were not enough train pilots available; it was how Otto from the engineer area put his name in a waiting list with the illusion to be trained to fly in the battle like the famous of the time and with the only vision of furrowed the skies and to fight for his country.

CHAPTER FIVE
FLYING IN THE SKY

It was morning and the dawn of the spring on Tuesday April 12, 1914, with a freezing wind that penetrate the bones was challenging, it was a morning like never seen before, at the sound of the military alarm, Otto woke up with the only hope miss for a long time: it was his first fly. The young brave and venture were a helper of airplane mechanic and pilot apprentice couldn't do anything else but wait that sublime experience for someone who have in his blood the adventure, the challenge, and the passion to be the same as the angels over the world. That morning like a tradition in that place, the persons who were waiting to start their daring challenge they were waiting to risk everything for all, took a morning shower with cold water that woke the bones to live; in the case of Otto von Münster that sensation was obtain for his enormous emotion of his Albatros D.II than for the water.

All for his illusion to "Fly" in those machines where for a long time he maintained and repaired.

He quickly dressed up with his pilot uniform, very respected by their own people and feared by the enemies. At his arrival, Otto never imagines being part of the elite the most selective of Luftstreitkräfte of that time. Manfred Albrecht Freiherr von Richthofen himself known as the Red Baron was present; an extraordinary situation since normally the one in charge of the air field was the one who did the selection of pilots, which in this occasion the reason of his presence. Knowing the Red Baron and his eccentricity, like a rich aristocrat he was practically the owner of the air field and had maids at his orders in the field, he also had servants, and tents who were taking care of their family, the baron was very careful on the selection of his pilots since that depended of the wining or losing the battle; he did not like to wait and in the necessity of assure the victory sometimes he had the custom of selecting his own pilots.

This is how he surprisingly ended up assisting in this occasion. He was walking to his airplane the distinctive triplane Fokker Dr1, when enfilade himself instead to go up to the airplane, he left the plane running and directed himself to the commander of selections that was Ernest Udet. After his traditional salute, Ernest remembered that he did not enter after many try outs, when the Red Baron himself selected him even though his height was shorter than 1.60 and didn't meet the profile for a pilot.

The commander Udet in that moment was his major priority of that place, however before the presence of the red baron, immediately gave the authority of selection. In silence, he remembered how he used the same technique of selection of years back, to become part of such an elite unit. It was a similar day when the Red Baron selected him, now his friend and associate of lots of victories; while he was looking at all of them to select one by one scanning them without taking down his look.

Again, just the way the commander Udet remembered, the Red Baron watch fixedly each of the candidates and when was turn of the first cadet from Luftstreitkräfte, couldn't resist that permanent and dominant look. Intimidate to anyone, there were few who has the courage of dare him and maintain with decision their wish to battle, one by one of the candidates were deserting, with an authority voice scream in front of each candidate and said, "My live depends of each of the members of my team and the ones I select will put their lives in my hands..."

And continue his speech, "The discipline is mandatory, after that, the obedience, and the country, is the maximum value of our mission."

With his looks, his words resounded in the ears of each cadet in turn.

In the middle of the sepulchral silence, with an infernal cold, was a feeling of a wind with adrenaline flavor.

His tone of voice plotting and demanding during the little seconds of looking, it was impossible supporting, he reflected his spirit in his posture and while looking for answers to the confuse riddle from a mind that rejoicing to any hesitant thought: like he could detect the scent of fear of each cadet.

With the sagaciousness and intuition that distinguish him, dig deeply in to each candidate like investigating to the last part of their conscience of each candidate to find out if they were brave enough to battle until the death. He continues one by one until he got to Otto, he stopped in front of him, hit his boots, put his eyes on his eyes, with a deep look, getting so close grubbing the limit between the privacy and the braking of the identity; the Baron looked at him from top to bottom and stopped his look only to scream at him without visual contact, "And you, why did you come? answer me!"

Immediately, Otto with a firm strong voice and determined gave respond saying, "For my country... With my country."

Watching him like looking the moment where he gets intimidate, become frightened and not look at his eyes, insisting with strong scream, "Is that all you have? I can't hear you; can you scream louder?"

But Otto continues repeating his scream, "For my country... With my country! For my country... With my country! For my country... With my country!"

Three time he repeated the same, Otto did not give up... More was his bravery and courage that he achieves for one minute embody a battle of looks until finally the Baron told him, "Step forward cadet."

After this, he was accepted in the pilot unity.

When Otto did not feel his presence, he looked for him with his sight to confirm that the Baron continue with the next candidate, however the Baron turned with Otto and like his last challenge to him and with low voice told him, "I hope that anger you are showing, have it when you see your enemies... That could be myself."

Otto kept looking to the front like ignoring him, but at the same time challenge the Baron saying to himself, "Will see what happens in the air..."

Did not pass like an hour when they were selected the new 14 cadets of the select unit of the famous Baron of the Jagdsstaffle (or Jasta 2), which also was part the famous airman Oswald Boelcke. The Baron took his plane and left to a descry mission and recognition to prepare the battle...

In the meanwhile, the new cadets left to the scream voice of, "March! go...! Take your positions!"

For Otto in that moment, he was born to a new live full of adventures, intrigue, and drama, but for him the biggest sensation and satisfactory was to dress for the first time the uniform of a pilot of the unit.

It was four minutes to eight, the smell of fuel was notice, the machinery was ready and the breaking or the crank to start the roar of the planes to the unison and same time noisy sound of war.

The noise of battle, beside of screaming orders and discipline was the only registration in the minds of each pilot. It was the time to put on the leather helmet, go up to the pilot cabin and position in front of the most lethal weapon of that time: a German battle airplane. The restore and powerful Fokker III or the Eindecker to be debut in April 12 until July 1914, it was an exhaustive training day and night until the first incursion of recognizing the enemy sky... First with recognizing flights, then with approximation flights, higher objects and little by little getting closer to the enemy territory.

Otto was feeling freedom when in the air and take advantage to feel the cold air that became his friend rather than his detracting, the fright become his ally... Arriving, landing, and enjoying a thick black coffee and hot to maintain him alert...

His adrenaline of everyday to the maximum... The machineries were in a position line to departure at any time when they were call to battle, and that day arrive...

The siren sound in the unit of the air field; Otto always ready listen the siren as a scream of battle and he was there: Otto Von Münster to battle, airplane 4; Jürgen Schmith, airplane 8... One by one run to place themselves in his biplanes, in the same order they made roar their own motors and start without losing the formation, they departure in the presence of the Baron that was happily watching the design and new weapons that Anthony Herman Gerad Fokker himself created and from that date were the terror of the airs because of his secrets operations and lethal weapons.

It was so impressed that the Red Baron, the grates pilot, did not change his airplane until two years later when he got the dreidecker DR1 and the VII D, making both famous; weapons so lethal that at the end of the war were destroy by his own designer when the Versailles treaty was signed.

Meanwhile, everyone was flying testing their weapons; Otto for moments feeling the sensation of the dominion of the air and having the trigger and determine live form death must formulate a strategy for searching and battle to shoot down, attack, and express the power of the German air.

Day by day Otto abilities were improving in the military dispute were practically infallible, the airplane was almost indestructible, the attacks were targeting and surprising to any opponent.

In that moment, Otto was now part of the squadron; same as Max Immelman and Boelke Oswald, who were the ones with most victories and medallions attribute. At the end of 1915 were decorated with the iron cross of first class given with a seal from the letter hand of King Wilheim.

The glorious days and fights versus enemy airplanes were daily, until one day in a battle, the allied develop similar weapons as theirs in the squadron.

In a confront, they were received in the same way: with the lethal canister shot. It was the beginning of the frenetic and desperate evasion action of the members of the squadron, getting out, trying to avoid the enemy fire. The labored breathing made Otto understood that the airplane was not the lethal weapon anymore.

The enemy counterattack without mercy, just the way he did in 23 interventions, this was number 24; 17 days, they were in the month of June 1916. They apply all the offensive technics of Dogfight, but there were surpass, learned by allied and enemies, they were pointless. Otto decided to try something new. Cut through the sky in vertical ascending and in a dead fly descended vehemently verses his opponent; he shoots down, but in his concentration during the persecution, didn't notice that at his left ambush an enemy airplane that was after him and shot him implacably. Each of the bullets trespass his airplane, receiving Otto a hit in his leg side to side. Collapsing the airplane and the pilot.

"Aww!" screaming because the burn and the pain of his wound.

With overturning and maneuver directing to land in a rapid and none stop, Otto made the possible to control the plane, almost destroy from the tail and because of his maneuvers he rapid landed in an enemy territory.

The smoke and the smell of gasoline, oil and blood was the only thing you can breathe in that moment. Between the destroy iron and wood, he managed to drag out, injured in both legs, several ribs, and his left arm totally damage.

As he drags himself like a serpent until he got to some bushes, the only thing he was caring with him was his Luger Parabellum of 9mm, icon of the German officials which also help him to defend himself or to pass over his secrets for ever. Was what he trained to do.

It that moment he remembers the words of the officials during the training, "If you fell and survive, you have your lovely country as a companion, use it with no doubt, a weapon is to fire not to warn. And if you are capture by the enemy: better be dead than lost your honor to reveal and betray your country."

Between laments and pains could get to his hiding place and seconds later an explosion was heard... His airplane. The noise travel throughout the valley like calling the enemies to come for him. With the adrenaline to the maximum, blows in his face and bruise in the right eye that made his visibility difficult; No more than two hours went by when the enemies arrived to inspect their trophy shouting.

"Look around for any surviving!"

Immediately the searching for the pilot start, even if they were not sure to find someone.

Meanwhile Otto knocks down, throw himself in an old trench full of water and mud, between branches, plants, and old trunks, next to the rest of a decay lamb; it was the ideal place to hide, it was not far from some bushes, so he was immersed in that place.

He was submerged in such a mixture in a way that his body was confused with the mud and the animal remainders, while was a small crack cover by vegetation, the only of his face that stand out was his nose plater of mud. He tries to wait, his heartbeat decrease... And maybe because the hypothermia he starts losing conscience. With the Luger in his hand pointing to the entry of the place, he stays there. The search went by, the solders crew continue ahead searching for a possible injured pilot.

"Look for and find that dog! Bring him alive or dead!" It was the scream defying from the Capitan of that regime.

Almost eight hours went by, Otto finally recover partially his conscience. He did not know the gravity of his wounds, but he couldn't believe he was alive. He made it out of that dirty ditch, he couldn't do anything else but dragging himself, he did not have knowledge of time, but apparently, it was daybreak.

For his good luck, in that area of the field it was summer, so the sun and the brightness of the late afternoon were very special. The sun rays were shooting in between the clouds that mark to an orange horizon that every time was turning red and presage Otto destine.

He had the advantage that during the summer, the days were longer, like the destine was denying moving or stop the time. But he couldn't take such advantage since the battles were taking place during the day light to be useful in the sight and in the combats. When the lights were dimer only astonish to his eyes the dark colors, grays outlines, shadows, and the light of the European sunset and nocturnal, was the only thing that can be capture...

It was how he took off from his body the jacket, the boots, everything he was wearing to got almost naked under a three and with his touching he tries to feel his wounds checking his body; found out that he got a clean shot in his leg, the bullet pierce from side to side, but did not touch any artery, he had the wound in and out. However, he had the certainty not having a hemorrhage. He was feeling a pain in his ribs because two of them were fractured, but fortunately did not reach the lungs. His face only had contusions, several on his right side, but in excess on the left side.

Despite all previous, the swelling of his face was down, so notable that his blue eyes like the sky can be reveal again in his face. Even after received such hits, the water, and the mud looks like help to heal, so he discovers that was not mud, it was like clay and immediately he remembers one occasion during training of first aids and surviving, when was told of the curative quality of the clay; that were many, but for his fortune, the remarkable power for refresh, reduce inflammation, relieve of congestion, purifying, cicatrizing, absorbent, and soothing.

He also remembers in that training advising of their use in case of superficial inflammations, like bites, wounds, bumps or burns, since act by the cold and loose his relieve of congestion action while is heating, situation that favor him to cure in a natural way his wounds of his face and even the wound of the bullet, the only unknown was how he stop the loss of blood. When he took off the clay from the wound notice that he had four leeches in the side of the wound. That avoid his loss of blood! When he saw this, and taking his own conclusions immediately thought the warning of not taking off at once these animals, the only adequate way was applying heat, because the own animal was controlling the flow and exiting of the blood. With a mixt of surprising and repress nausea left them there until he could find a place where he can clean the wounds and comely take off these animals that save his live.

At least he still has in his hand the Luger (he did not let it go for nothing). He was in a complete darkness, inside his clothing had switchblade used to peel food like peaches and pears (his favorites).

With that he prepares to look for a shelter or at least a safer place; he left and cut some branches that helped as crutches, with his cloths he applies bandages without taking the mud off and start his searching.

No more than two hours went by when he discovers one of the many bombard ruins by himself; they were abandoning stores that previously were farms. When he was getting closer in silence between shadows, wolf howls and other nocturne animals, he arrives to that place. He notices that was an abandon place and almost destroyed where he finds rest of once being a bran, he got shelter with fright and precaution throw himself on the floor and cover himself with straw. He stays there until the tires and sleepiness overcome. He stays there with the possibility to be discover; "What else can happen to me?" He thought. "To be arrested? And if is? Die for the country!" And in seconds he loses conscience.

It was morning, he opens his eyes, and the first thing he saw in a blurred and vague way: the light of the sun that enter between of once being a sealing; now almost destroyed with pieces of wood hanging. Otto cofed and little by little started to focus. After a deep breath, oxygen his brain so in a little time recover with clarity his total vision.

He says to himself "This is truly a disaster. What do I do now...?"

He meditates and begins to create his plan of scape and return to his country. After creating mentally his plan, he reviews it over and over, and start analyzing the resources he needed, the times and distances, the possible obstacles; everything was being processing in his mind like he was a robot programing himself to achieve his objective with everything and anything. He began to put hands on in his plan.

He reincorporates while reviewing his bone structure, his wounds, and his labels of energy. It has pass more than 24 hours of the accident, the clay did his work, his body react favorably to the possible infection and the leaches also did their work.

"It is time to go over to the first stage of the plan," Otto said.

In that moment, took one of his garments and with a rock did a small bonfire, he put his knife in it and wait until were red hot to begin to touch one by one the leaches. These ones when feeling the heat free their faces and detach without causing bleeding of the wounded area. He repeated the process one by one until finish with all of them. Couldn't be a better operation ever.

After this, with his still humid clothing, began to take off the clay form the wounds and clean them, very carefully and little by little did his body and face until being free from the clay. When he saw, his wounds were in a process of healing he breaths deeply, was incredible!

He incorporates and try to locate something to cover himself, he enters to a farm where there were rest of animals everywhere, the wolfs had a feast and look like the house was destroy. He pokes in the place and found some clothing, maybe from a country person from the zone, shoes and even a coat. Couldn't be better, so he burns quickly his uniform, put his maps away and after that he continues the way to the border.

It was proximally 2 in the afternoon when he fills out some old saddlebags with water to continue his way. Otto knew the danger and the searching squad and him being in an enemy territory. He never let down his defense and continue in the forest hiding and guiding himself thru the sun and the stars during almost three days. Building primitive's traps to hunt some birds that hide them to used later to eat. He was passing from hill to hill avoiding populated zones, but always inside the forest, when taking breaks, he always set traps in the zone where he slept to avoid animals or person finding him and in case happened, he could scape form the place with enough time.

He was like that for almost a month, he was close to the border, which he was bordering. Listening the eco of bombs and attacks from far was every day for Otto. The screams of dead from both flocks gave him horrible nights of audiological terror, some nights can hear the low fly of the air raid from friend and enemies, but he knew that couldn't asked for help to anyone, because in his condition neither his fellow-citizen could recognize him. It was a voyage of a real survival.

Because the time has been passing on, his aspect was very different: The beard covered his face; without shower, his food being birds and wile fruit, his teeth were dirty; clay and mud all over his body, with a pen-etrate odor; unrecognizable... It was almost November and the cold start doing its work, it was probable that Otto could survive the inclement weather, but he has a new hope when he hunts a deer; he did a coat and boots with the skin. Believed or not, he manages to get to the border and start study the zone to cross in the middle of the fire from his friends and enemies, he had to pass to the other side, but how to do it? He must pass in front of the battle or go by the mountains.

The time passed but meanwhile what was hap-pening in the base? Of course, that his absence should have effects in all! When he was shoot down in battle, two more associates lost their lives and the Red Baron himself when saw the attack shoot down the airplane that shoot Otto and almost shoot down another three more (but they escape because the accurate attack) When the Red Baron saw this he came back to the base, out of 9 airplanes only 6 comebacks. In the absences ones was the pilot Otto von Münster, when they call the roll for the war report, three pilots were fallen in battle. The Baron was hothead and gave a hard beat in the airplane frame; anger and frustrated for the loss of his three-excellent means.

"This is not going to remain like this!" The Baron said furiously...

When were declare the part of war, was stand out the courage and determination of the attack of the pilots in the heroic exploit, mainly for Otto?

Was like this how was stated in the acts of part of war...

The days pass in the parallel absences of Helmut, Frederick and now the Capitan Otto, which bodies couldn't be rescued because the circumstances. They were waiting for information of captives or fallen in battle, but in the meantime, they were considering for their heroic postmortem or for being captives or war will be taking to each of them as aces of war.

The days passed and there was no news, until finally they received confirmation of the dead of Helmut and Frederick, situation that made the Baron very sad, and each battle he attacks ferocious and inexorable to avenge the dead of his associates even though something was telling him that Otto was alive, maybe a prisoner, but alive. He has the hope to know from him. He maintains himself like that for several days, but when did not appear as a prisoner after several weeks, it was giving as fallen in battle or lost in the battle.

He deeply laments the loose of Otto while he remembers how he had performed several contributions to the attack technic. They have good disposition, and their strategies were hit upon to such a step that even the Baron himself follow them, knowing them in between the pilots as the trick of front attack.

This consisted on disappear in vertical ascending as much as possible until the gasoline couldn't inject the motor, initiating a free fall and in silence against the enemy; a descend rough and mortal for the enemies, because they did not know where was coming from and always took them by surprise. It was a dangerous operation that required a skillful pilot, because must be precise to dominate the ignition and glide the plane in a dead fly without using, but the gravity and the expertness. Not all can do such acrobatics so effective on the front attacks.

It was so effective that made his own quick command, that consisted on sign with three fingers of his left hand while put his arm up then to close his hand in a fist form taking it down very fast to his body. Indicated the mortal angel (sterblichen Engel). This, like other innovations to the battle that continue to use were establish as a routine of war. Very proud they were of the contribution of Otto to the war squadron and because of that was remember like: the mortal angel.

This situation of assigned nick names of battle to describe the skills or like a scream of war to maintain the unity and presence of the team, it was usual in between the militaries.

All this was happening, while Otto in his inevitable banishment, he sees himself immerse in an adventure to achieve the return to his country; he devotes himself to watch, observe, and study the enemy, He couldn't have such a valued opportunity to know their movements, strategies, and actions in a such a grade that he becomes an expert observant and learns a lot of things in relations to the operations management of attacks.

In his last pass for the mountains, after a dissipated attack, practically by himself in the battlefield, he passes by the trenches and observed a terrifying scene: between fog and corpses everywhere, it was impossible to identify which ones were from one party or other. Horses, dead and destruction everywhere. Thousands and thousands of burned, twisted, and torn bodies with anger and pain in his face still, lots of them with their eyes open, like screaming and begging clemency for his pain and some others like cursing his existence, carrying the hate in their sight since the short time prior to their brutal death.

With the smell of death, between decay and sulfur, gunpowder and coal, the smell was intolerable to Otto, to such a grade of vomit of much horror. Was there that he understood the misery around him and feeling like he was being scraper alive, he discovers the true face of the horror war. He visualizes the evil and the hate at his max expression, conceive the dead and the griminess of battle, the power, the thirst of dominion, the extermination in between members of the same species, the disregard, the grudge, the envy, the anger, all those grudge disguise of patriotism worldly ephemeral and not sense.

After all this, at the end in between the men itself can distinguish who was from one party or other; at the end, all were the same: men who die for fruitless causes and for honors of leading that never remember neither feeling their pain, because their mobiles were the selfishness; the anxiety for keeping the power; the desire of dominion between them, destroy themselves and win land and money that at the end in that battle of field was only dirt, mud, and rottenness.

That what they were fighting for. Paying the price, these poor unwary souls, that were used only by sick of power and excessive ambition people.

These lives have had lost in vain, getting in return a foolishly and sporadic glory and metros underground, next to others; paying in return with the subjection of lives. The souls that look like wander lost in the battle field without sense of purpose. It felt a presence of pain, confusion, and loneliness.

A horror bigger that the defaced bodies and deformed, that was the presence so infernal that Dante himself was short in the description of hell itself.

The wars, Otto comprehended, at the end it was a genocide verses oneself, verses humanity, versus the most sacred: the human been.

It was when he falls, scream, cry and his throat split seen such a terror, that almost get him in a crisis stage; to get out quick like he was been chased by the demons, like it happens after meeting the horror in person at first hand. He runs and runs without stopping towards the forest where he was hiding. He felt weaken and the suffocated fear to be caught for such diabolic presence. That scenery was chasing him and didn't stop running, his eye had seen the dead at his max expression. His life was reduced to a second and the horror chase him along all his way.

He felt the hands of all those bodies were pulling and taking him to the infernal cliff, where the fire and grinding teeth were not stopping. It was like he was listening claiming for his presence, like since he was caught for these impure beings, and their work was to chase him. The screams of those souls and diabolic beings were inside his head and that moment marked his life forever.

Otto continued running like crazy, trying to get away as far as possible thinking of the despicable and vile his life was. Nothing was important for him anymore, neither that he was bareheaded, captured or even losing his life. So, what? Living like these was horrible enough. Get out of there was his only way out, he continues running until he got in the deepest of the forest, in his desperation of running way he fell and stumble with tree branches, he knocked himself out,

He got up and suddenly fell; on the floor even though he incorporates himself exasperatedly. Almost lost one's voice with broken screams for his tiredness, he felt suffocated from the hyperventilation obtain in his escape route... Between screams and tearing moans, only the eco of his shout can be hear in the middle of the forest while he continues running without course. Until he fells in a ditch and lost conscience entering in an indescribable nightmare that looks like he couldn't get out.

While that horrible nightmare was going on in his mind, his body lies immobile in the ditch and without breath looks like he had died alive.

A whole day went by, until between murmurs and whispers of distant voices, an inspection battalion went by the place and found Otto. For his good luck, all that crazy escape; that unruly run took him to his country. He was in a friendly territory, the squadron mistakenly with a civil (maybe a farmer) they were trying to identify if he was alive or dead, if he was a compatriot of an enemy...

In that precisely moment, Otto open his eyes and he couldn't talk, his throat was completely close, shaking, with his swollen and red eyes, and a lot of pain, with tears because of the effort to talk, full of wounds in his mouth, hands, and his body full of blood, mud, clay... The captain asked him in an arbitrator voice as a Prussian authority, "Identify yourself!"

Since he did not have any badges on him, just his weapon hiding in his clothing; couldn't talk and with a lot of difficulty try to put his hands in his pockets, when a soldier gave him a pistol butt (imagining that he was taking a weapon out) Otto got knock out.

The same soldier decides to look what was the now innocent man was trying to get out of his pocket. He starts to pick the pocket, looking for any object that he could carry, and determine which will be his destiny of that men, same that could diversify enormously depending of what they found. Fortunately, he only carries with him his Luger pistol, the map and behind this, all the inscriptions and information as memories of his observations. When the captain saw this, he determined the identity of the unconscious and deducing.

"This is one of our, pick him up and take him to the camp."

He still was unconscious; Otto was taken in a stretcher to the camp that was 30 minutes away where he was found.

Two days passed, it was the month of February of 1917 when Otto recover his conscience and when he awakes he was in a hospital, which he only could see lights and breath the smell of antiseptics, medicine, and alcohol; when he incorporation a little better, he notices that he was connected to a serum, bandage and with a horrible headache...

He opens and closes his eyes, to each time see clearly, he looks around him, his eyes trying to recognize the place, but in his confusion, he couldn't comprehend what was going on. Slowly he recovers his senses in that moment, a nurse that was doing her checks in his pavilion, she opens the curtain to discover that Otto has his eyes open, reacting very fast she went to let Dr. Kuller know, and who quickly appeared before Otto. He starts checking on him...

Otto's cardiac rate start increasing, the fear invades him, and a cold sensation travels his body; the Dr. Kuller notice that and immediately try to calm down and told him "Calm down! Calm down, you are well cared for. You are in your country."

Otto, immediately try to talk to show him his name and his rank, but his attempt only babbling came out of him.

"Oswald Boelcke Jast Do... My unit..."

The effort exhausts him too much and couldn't understand anymore.

The doctor asked him to calm down, he took notes and wrote down in his file the name and rank and division. In that moment, Otto felt he was born for second time.

The news didn't wait to arrive to his barracks. In his unit, the medical report came to Manfred von Richtofen hands, who received the notice that one of his pilots was alive and recovering. He immediately let his battalion know, "Otto is alive and recovering."

The Baron couldn't believe it! immediately went to the hospital where was the pilot recovering. It was a great happiness sensation for all his workmates, who did not wait too long on visiting him.

Meanwhile, Otto could clarify his situation and the Baron informed that his great boss, Oswald Boelcke had died on October 28, 1916.

"We lost a great aviator, but we gained a hero."

The Baron said, who thanks and remembers with admiration his contribution to the team work. Quick, didn't distract his attention and talk for several hours with Otto, who told his observations, same that he took in account which in the future will be good to give value to the new stage that was begin of this event.

Meanwhile, at the end of his interview with such a personality, suddenly was a sad and loosening atmosphere, that farewell looks for both like the last time they met in life. And his effusive exit of the Baron left a sensation like it was a trace of hope... Or a mortal farewell...

Otto was invading of nostalgia, so he asked the nurse to bring him a pen and paper to write a letter to his father. He told him all he had done; he describes in detail all he endured; he points out how much he misses him and thanks all he had have learn thanks to his formation; thanks to that he came out of this situation and saved his life.

That letter did not take long to arrive in his father's hands. Heinrich and Ann Marie were taking breakfast crestfallen and in a total silence, because two months ago, they knew that his son had fallen in battle. They were sad; they didn't have much communication with Arthur, who had met his father when he exited the military requesting his discharge because he couldn't handle the depression and death. His family as well as Arthur, did not know anything from his brother Otto, so meanwhile he starts working in the activities with his father and Abraham Hoffman, this last one in companion with his wife Sahara and her daughter Esther were together with the rest of the Von Münster family.

All of them continue working in the business that Heinrich and Heidi Marie had consolidated in Switzerland. Because the situation in Germany the fear was constant, when they hear a knock at their door, the fear choke each of the members at home until Ana Marie decided to get up, and open the door: it was the mailman...

He gave her a letter, Ana Marie, sense something in that paper, she felt in her hands a fear sensation. Impatiently to know from her brother Otto, and to take away the restlessness of his death and let the anxiety live, she went with her father and without a word, she gave him the letter; both looked at each other's eyes and with the communication of their bodies, the father looks down to the letter, slowly he opens the envelope and with tears on his eyes starts reading, not finishing reading the text, when he said in a whisper, "Otto is alive" "OTTO IS ALIVE!" He strongly exclaims while hugging his daughter. He jumped of happiness and suddenly run to give the news to his wife, as well to Arthur... And everyone in that place. The happiness came back to all.

In his letter, Otto told them that he was going to be transfer to another division, and later will let them know since he had new plans... But the most important thing is that he was alive, and they were comfortable and happy.

"At least my son is alive, and I know that we will be meeting soon," Heinrich was saying to himself.

Soon the good news was diffused; Abraham, in his office, receive the scandal news. And like this all who knew Otto knew of his adventure, because he describes to his father everything that happened, it was a subject that sat for months in the mouth of everyone, they were feeling very proud of him, especially his father.

Heinrich, by letters, asked Otto to come back home to Switzerland and offered him to be integrate on his business; but Otto answers him that he couldn't in that moment, without giving a reason for his refusal, everyone was asking their selves, what could be most important than the proposition of his father. Without knowing that in his answer was the code of a whole new adventure for Otto.

The German army at that time, did not have an efficient system of military intelligence, because since his creation the Abwehr (Amt Ausland Abwehr) not very desirable. Founded in 1866 during the Austria war had a foolish activity until were taking in 1870 by Wilhelm Stieber who carrying out brightly in the Franco Prussians wars, which generate a whole tradition and a series of strategies to obtain information very advanced for their time. Remaining with no use in a great part of the first world war.

CHAPTER SIX
THE COLLISION

It was March of 1917, Otto, by this time had describe precisely how the French were moving and how little by little the Americans, Australians and England were associating to create an army of allied that was prudently forming to the defense of France, a battlefront, that was folding and attacking to the Germans.

Otto gave this information to his division, Jasta 2; but at his return was transfer to the front in the division Jasta 11, known as the fly circus, because of his bright colors that their 14 airplanes shows; like in a circus traveling by train to the place where required.

It was exactly inside this division where the Red Baron gain such a nick name, because his airplane was painted red, so his rivals will recognize him; clever psychological operation, because his enemies were frightening of him and admire his war skills. Instead, Otto had his airplane painted light blue with white tones, that was confusing with the sky and the clouds, that was what he wanted, because of this, he always took advantage since he couldn't be identified by the enemy airplane's meaning that he could get out faster from the battle; it was for the same reason that his camouflaged was mortal. He was always snare and his flights were of high altitude and very low temperatures, this was like that because he modified the motor of his plane so he could go up high and in rapid dead flight descended. His operations like acrobats gave him the pass to participate in 58 missions successfully in which the Baron knock 80 airplanes, something that no one exceed before in any flock during the rest of the war. Adding on April 20 knock downs by himself.

In mid time Otto got 15 planes knock down, his followers insinuated that he was their leader and that he had a suicide behavior. Few months after he was transferred to the JG 1, form by the Jasta 4, 6, 10, and 11. This unit knocked down 644 planes with only 56 lost. In that unit, Otto met Lothar, the Baron's brother, that together brought 40 victories, being 16 of them by Otto. At the end of the war in this units the most recognize were like Kurt Wolff with 33 victories, Karl Allmenroder 30 knock downs and all the integrates of this team received "Cross Pour le Merited" even though they had lost who were recognized, since the original unit the 30% was knock down and decorated for his heroism and fell in battle for the country of their parents.

There were times of changes, and this will bring a lot of important consequences, within the feast and the profit, the shade of the failure was showing and could see the first pressure of a big storm consequence of the end of a conflict with no sense or logic and consequences of an absurd war that first was chasing economic purpose and the demolition of the monarchical German order.

Otto was disgusted of all he had live: the excessive killing and useless of many soldiers, pilots and friends, his life routine was miserable, after the air incursion his demons and nightmares were attacking him every night; he was capture of panic nights. Enough reason for ending to get use to drink too much black coffee, to sleep the least possible and avoiding falling in nightmares. The arrogance and pride of his friends was such that they vain not less that heroes full of power and that was translated in his lost sights, like if they were possess for a maligns spirit at the time of attack; situation that was becoming impossible atmosphere for Otto, making it more complicated to stay there, captured of this feeling of repudiation.

What heat the fun was the night between nightmares, he dreamed that he was back in the battlefield and was seeing himself lay bare in front of his father... A shivering scene, he saw children that in between pain shouts and mockery pulling out his eyes and skin and were asking Otto to stop mockery about them, while he was immobile, he try to run, but he couldn't move; he try to close his eyes and was not getting success, it was a oppress terror scene... he try to scream in his dream, but he couldn't, as much effort he did, inside his unconsciousness between dreams and reality he couldn't omit any sound.

He kept like that until the desperation and mental impact made him react to the body and in a desperate shout, he got to react with a desperate shout made him get out of his body and comeback to himself to finally stand up... In the tent where he sleeps, it was common to hear screams and cries at nights in such a rate that his friends were used to and knew that was Otto.

"Again, is Otto..."

"Enough, go to sleep and let us rest!"

But Otto was very worried in that occasion, he couldn't stand that situation anymore, so early morning took his things and went with Freiherr (earl Red Baron) Von Richtoven, who never left to be an aristocrat, he stayed there, mostly because his passion to fly in that war, that he knew they were lose...

"My commandant..."

With his military salute, he responded, "Parade rest! What happen?"

With determination and steady that characterize Otto, he was direct and precisely, "I'm requesting a voluntary drop out from the empire service."

The Baron answers him, "What? It's surprising me, this is not normal of you. Why do you want to drop out?"

Otto continues, "I'm not good on my faculties and I'm determining that I do not want to expose the squadron to a failure in the air battle; In this moment, I do not feel capable to continue. I'm in a personal conflict..."

The Baron at first petition did not want to allow him to exit and gave him instructions of not getting out, but Otto continued, "I came here for the passion to fly, the same that you thought: we are not murdering, we do not kill people, we knock down airplanes and try to win a war... But is very strong the pressure. You have had to tell us: we are not butchers; and seriously I am not welling to continue doing this, if you could understand me... I would like to get out from the squadron..."

He had a tight relation, in silence the Baron watched him; deep down he also thought the same as Otto, but the great difference between them was that the Baron could not exit the squadron, since he was an image of stimulation for their troops and the Kaiser himself named him general leader of the imperial German air force. He perfectly knew his situation; he was compromise and had clear that resigning was not an option. Otto's determination was such that combine to his consistent vision of the implication of war, The Baron allowed him to analyze his situation before the Wehrmacht (high-ranking) of the Reichswehr or the king army.

Most of the officials and generals were not only part of the aristocracy but were part of the select group of the earls and the Ritter. Otto was not the exception, son of an aristocrat and known inside the family group of the Kaiser, he knew of the situation about to confront and had an ordinary rule regent that regulated the process of disunite from the army force of the empire. Yes, Otto knew and even though he decides to continue, since was his mental health that was at risk.

The Baron to his regret of his closeness and friendship did what he has to do and apply the dictation rule by the Reichswehr, and immediately, Otto was suspended, but since he belongs to the aristocracy couldn't be incarcerate for his action, even in spite that was consider as a deserter. With this military disrespect, Otto was sent to Berlin to remain confine in the central base doing office work, giving maintenance, on whatever were required for the empire force in their moment.

The news arrived to his father, Heinrich Von Münster, who from Switzerland continue operating caused by the war. The most part of his success was keeping well fed the German army; he had the privilege to be the provider of food supplies.

His company was German, but he controls all his operations from Switzerland, however with the time passing, start to be present the lack of payment and from resources for the company and consequently must suspend all the operations in Germany. Between many fell operations and problems rising; Heinrich, worry, for his son decide to go with his old friend Mark Henkel that even he was retiring he kept contacts in the high military influence.

Mark received a letter from Heinrich, asking intervention in his son Otto's case, which they only knew he was in Berlin. Mark receives this petition and immediately try to look for Otto; his search was positive and, in a week, identify the situation why Otto was suspended and as arrested in the general quarters. After this, Mark could contact Otto as a visitor in his isolation.

Otto was called to the visitor room and met Mark; when he saw him, he welcomes him with a hug and initiated conversation... Mark listens attentively all that Otto was telling him, while he analyzes a way he can help. Mark couldn't avoid his surprising of all Otto had live, because he describes to him his exploits, adventures, and problems; Mark based on the narration, sense that he had great potential in experience, but also bring out the grand mental tiredness that afflicted him. It was obvious that he was affected, and had to find an exit for him; he had to help him in some way.

After several meetings and interviews with Otto, Mark suggested to write a document saying all he had contributed to the Reich and stand out that he had been decorated with the iron cross for his several contributions in the great war. This allowed him to establish a strategy to take Otto out of there, he looks for an old friend that was still inside the militia, and it was like this that after several months later, in October 1917, Otto was out of the military without a sentence; but he was resulted to work giving out his knowledge in an institution of independent war report, where he collected information that the ex-militaries were obtain during their service. It was an organization of German intelligence directed by an old friend of Mark: Walther Nocolai.

It was like Otto got out of the military alive and start to share all his experiences and information that he obtains during his participation. A valuable information that allowed him to receive economic bones, and acknowledge of Walther himself and the possibility of continuing to obtain new knowledge; since it was very rare of a pilot to remain alive before the sudden attack and actualize of the ally that day by day race with the German military.

Consequently, He stayed in Berlin for the rest of the war, but now as part of the Abwehr.

At the end of 1918 attempt to continue in this institution was complicated, because the military pressure was confused because the social situation, the military came across fragmented, the small internal wars for the power were growing with the end of destroy the German marquee... The Russians in their behave, with a new ideology communist-popular had manage bear upon the moral of the German population, the military, lots of unions in Hamburg, Kiel, and others production places in Germany; that sooner or later will join the new social order, provocation great waves of revolts.

Before such a situation, Otto got out of the disorder and went to Elmsohrn trying to reestablish what was left of his father's business. One he was there; he sends a letter to his father where he describes that he was out of the military and was trying to get ahead; as a respond from Heinrich obtain the signs that his friends and acquaintances soon will support him. After the respond of his father, Otto received Johan, an old friend of the family, right there to start a new stage in his live, waiting for the end of the war.

Was not too long, when he knew that Werner Voss and most of his friends had been kill in battles; one by one, all his associates... Otto was devastated, he did not get out of his house; he devotes himself to rebuild and fix all the machinery, tractors, and in general all in front of him.

In times of war no one had time to rest, every day was a supplicate and hopping for the worst; Otto was trying to earn one's living as mechanic, but he continues in communication with his new friends from the Abwehr like Erick Fullman and Fritz Meyer, meanwhile because the lack of economic feeling in the country, he did not have other choice, but use his creativity and start to plan a way to rescue the land of pasture, he studies and puts in practice the techniques of water use, since that was the only exit to generate light, irrigation and food.

There were only some waterways, Germany was commercially blocked and couldn't even obtain parts to do repairs. That was how Otto pictured a series of home machinery that allowed them to be implemented on his farm, in the production of cheese and in the sowing pastureland, and in this way feed the fewer heads of cattle left, because each day these ones were reducing for the lack of food.

For the moment, no one had money to buy their products, everything was a chaos, so not long-time pass when Otto wrote to his father, "Father we are in really bad conditions... Here we don't have anything to maintain the farm. We are requiring more resources What do you suggest?"

His father answers him to please go and look for Elias Hoffman, Abraham cousin, his administrator, that was still working in the central bank... To see what can they do in this situation.

Otto travel to Hamburg, but when he arrived, he discovers that the city was a chaos, everyone running, everyone going up and down with no direction, abandon shipyard... What once was a commercial city, now was a ghost city. It was eminent that Germany was defeated and France had taken his part or the war. The Versailles treat forced Germany to pay the high price of the war.

Otto couldn't believe what he was seeing, that great nation was looking reduce in total humiliation; France and Great Britain were collecting the cost of the war. It was a spitfire of strikes everywhere, the town was demanding the exit of monarchy, the Hogenzollen family were giving up; all the nobles and popularity escape to Holland, a country that welcome them and gave them polite shelter, most of their friends and rich families also escape while all their properties were claimed for a new social order. The Russian revolution it was a reality, and the tsars were destroyed; Germany was not a monarchy anymore, but now it was the country with the most debt in the European history and none the less France and Great Britain immediately impose their products, leaving Germany of being the power that 10 years back was threatened to dominate the European market. Finally, France and Great Britain achieve their aim at high price for the Germans.

Otto was impressed; the hungry on the streets was touchable and like always happen in a confusing surroundings, the social behavior and personality of the people change radically, reflecting it in the enormous increasing of robberies, plundering, and confusion, the frighten took the power and the uncertainty attaining domain to all the people in all the nation. Otto did not have other choice but to return to Elmshorn.

Once in the train going back, Otto in his distress and confusion observed how a high outstanding character climb up in to his new destiny. Boarding in the central station of Hamburg arriving in the precisely moment of his live. Like everything in live the events, the people and facts produce an effect with reaction in a change in the lives of individuals.

Who can imagine that all the events of the world and the people are tie by the thin bond of a great net that interweave in the lives of all people, some tangle than others but all tie in between? In an unimaginable form, but some achieve to impact in their lives of the individuals, in the society and even in a nation...

Otto was annoying and very absorbed, plunge in the concern for what was looking a tragic ending for the great losers of the great war: the Germans. At the time of climbing up to the car, his thoughts were distracting when he observes that in the same car was boarding a slim woman: with a fit elegant dress, wearing out for the use; since the hem digest seen the thread, like wanted to leave a trace on her path walk, like losing a little of herself in each step made...

She remains to himself in those days of surviving, she was showing tiredness and loneliness. Otto kept observing her form his anonymity distance.

In those days, the cars were taking and bringing people from one place to another, but the silence was predominating, only the movement of the wooden cars at the rate of the tracks and squeak of the iron wheels of the train were making noise. The vapor smoke and the smell of coal that move that iron beast frame a picture that between the mists, the two unknowns were shooting gazing to each other. She looks down, but in the seconds when they cross eyes they were transmitting messages like they were talking... There expression was whispering "I'm destroy." Her stooping body was trying to hide her face between the veil that was covering her hat decorated with dead flowers, however, it can still see a beautiful and enigmatic face.

During the trip, the looks were more frequent between them, in silence a dialog was participating actively between both. Otto in his behalf was projecting a disappointing look, his oppress distress, and a sadness... It was like a dialog without voices, like each of them want it to tell their story, like two souls wanted to be free of all the conflict and oppress feelings. These were the longest hours for them.

The noise of the whistle machine was announcing the passing of a town; people going up and down, but they kept themselves in their seats even when the sun was hiding. They were almost by themselves in the car. Otto was trying to avoid disturbing his mind trying to find out what was happening to that woman, in guessing who was she... Suddenly came up a soldiers regimen which destiny was to return back home, such a scene looks like a show of Spector's alive with their disconnected faces, with sadness and defeat swinging in their walk; some of them were wounded and others mutilated physical and morally. With not notice and with surprise in all the spectators, the train suddenly stop, most of them fell on the ground, others scream, but Otto and the unknown lady in an almost imperceptible way, they interchange despaired looks, like trying to explain to each other what was going on.

"What happen?" More than one asked, but no one answered.

The train, was usually prisoner of attacks and the suicide in the tracks was very common; in this occasion, a soldier throws himself to the tracks like wanting to scream the defeat that for many nationalisms was unforgettable, wanted with his dead punishing the nation, but for misfortune didn't do much. The brakeman took the body away and the train continue their way.

That moment was the occasion for Otto got closer to the woman that was showing signs of anxiety was asking for help or at least someone to indicate what was going on. Otto notice that and quickly walking throughout human bodies bulks dressing as soldiers, he got where she was and try to calm her down, "Calm down, everything is going to be ok."

Between gestures of anxiety and fear, with an imperceptible voice she asked, "What is happening?"

Otto with a serene voice, try to explain her what happen and gave her a brief outline of the recent event.

During the trip, a dialog continues that aloud a relation that would bring numerous and remarkable consequences. Let's say, all things in life bring consequences, the good or bad decisions change the context and environment of the people to such a degree that if it's ignored gave step to different chapters or different types of lives.

The changes are eminent and where the points of the web are branching in other ways that are building over the same action second by second in the lives of the people and only leave the trace of their existence in the invisible outline of time. But at the end always leave with no trace since it's a web that is mingle in the time and remain only during the time that existence last.

That's why for Otto that moment got recorded in his time, inciting changes in his behavior. Just as it happens in the human behavior, the influence of the combination of feelings and desires, what each wants and look for consciously or unconsciously, eventually find a reaction in their lives and bring specific actions that give extraordinary overturn to their existence.

No one can track a person if is not by their influences and by their decisions in their lives, that always result in and have a beginning and end according to the build of the web that have been build or forming. Why and end? Good or bad, this is part of the link that join to the people one way or another building what it is, according to what they were and will be base of what they build day by day to finish in a second their work.

So, it was those 84 kilometers of journey in a conflictive route, between the great ports of Kiel and Hamburg it was common this type of scene. When arriving to the station, Otto continues accompany the unknown, who ending being Hilda Dölling, one of the daughters of the very important families of Elmshorn. She was very worried and anxious to continue to get out of difficulties their company of product of cold cuts and sausages.

The Münster family was one of the first providers of meat, even for those dates before anything they were in the worst time. The region of Pinneberg belong to Schleswig Holstein; a territory of rural people, where the production of calf, grains, dairy products, and cereals were very important in the economy during the period in what Otto's father accumulate lots of extensions of land for the calf, the head calves were selling to the Dölling family where they process and make famous cram of the region.

Then, Hilda and Otto in the trip and during their pleasant conversation arrived to the Buttermark plaza, (now known as Karl Marz Platz) a choice place as a point of reunion of the town and where after that day several friendly encounters start between them.

Otto farewell from Hilda and went home, which was 20 minutes away by the border route of the Kru-kau river, between the beautiful forest; apple trees and peach trees and much more while fruit trees as well as different vegetation that touch the cultivation fields and prairie of that zone until the outlet on the Elba river and finally, Otto arrive to his house. Tire fell in his bed and did not wake up until the next day.

A new day was to start and a new adventure in his live.

CHAPTER SEVEN
THE PASSION

It was a late night, Otto couldn't stop thinking of Hilda, she was on his mind even in his dreams although his nightmares that still chase him got calm and decline his night's anxieties when put his attention in that woman.

Hilda left him impacted, Otto didn't know the effect that she made on him, but both in their absences start to think in each other. The thoughts are like a magnet; call to many things and sometimes good or bad.

Their situation of loneliness, in a moment of national distress and the frustration in both, start to generate an appropriate atmosphere to cultivate sensual feelings since both start to tingle their human instincts. The next day, Otto got up like never and decided to work, there were problems with water supplies to the waterways, there were no factories neither parts for the tractors, only old pulley, and old motor gears... With those elements he got in his shop and remain there for three days working. After this time, he took his motorcycle and went to the plaza Buttermark; it was Sunday, a day where was custom to made the reunion of the town in this place. Otto was hoping to meet with Hilda and like it was planned, he found her. Form far away they saw each other and look for each other in between the people; now they were two different people a difference of the first time, their spirit was different: Otto very euphoric and her with a new dress on.

Something happen between both that change them totally, looks like, whenever were together, the bad moments was the less to think about while they were talking what each other wanted to talk about, they interrupted to each other, until the laugh took cover.

Once the light of the day ended, they finish their conversation and agree on a new date to meet: their first date... After set, the day and time each of them left to their house. Otto was looking exiting; he was another person. When he arrives to his shop, he finishes his idea of the new machine, which he named it Hilda trag-bare pumpe (portable water pump) incredible he built a back wheel of a tractor with a device that generate the extraction of water thru a host, so the tractor when moving their wheels prior suspend in a hydraulic jack, sacking the water from one water ways to another.

This invention was too good, to the grade, that Johan, as soon as he saw it in action, he asked to build one for his farm and like that one after another start making orders. It got too many orders that Otto must hire several mechanics to build more "Hildas." Also, in his time of cre-ation he builds a system of rejection for gravity irrigation and create the first system of irrigation canals in his land, it was very difficult to buy machinery in that time and the necessity make him to create a lot more inventios to excel, since he has the necessity and the knowledge.

Otto wrote to his father; the situation in the new Republic of Weimar was indefensible: the inflation was something impossible to carry, the Versailles treat put end to Germany and for none the less an internal battle starts for the power with the Bolshevists in one side, and the conservative for the other side; the German coup and the anarchistic rebellious for another side. It had to take a side; the town was taking a desperate solution...

As a respond to that letter, Heinrich, answer him, that he will go to Germany to see what he can recuperate and to please prepare all things to welcome them. Three months went by after that answer for that visit become reality.

While all this was happening, even in the worst scene, Otto was keeping himself out of those outcomes; he was focus on his work and in that stilling his time (and the hart): Hilda.

It was a hot summer evening in 1921, the relation with Hilda was getting stronger, and with the heat of the evening, both decided to go for a walk to the river border... It was a spectacular evening between glasses of wine, cheese, and sausages that Hilda brought in his basket. Otto so attracted to Hilda line never, Hilda so beautiful for Otto... A special moment where it was not necessary even talking, their bodies and looks were interlacing, their gestures and hands were touching like they were talking.

The courting was taking them to get closer increasingly, until their breaths and mouths got lost in to each other; their hands, their sweats, their fluids, their odors... Their chemistry made reaction, their totally combine between them in one act of hands. It was such a passion for each other that their clothing was in their way so all their skin unified, so all the fluids from all parts of their bodies mixed, like wanted to run through each other bodies. It was such a union that did not take too long to generate a rhythmical rate, where both between their encounter breaths and moans create a melody of fluids, breaths, and grub of bodies.

They live the moment full of intensive caress and grubs until they consumed all their sensual wishes, their bodies emptied to the last breath and their souls were full, both went up to heaven... It was a unique moment of youth; the venting, all was consuming in that evening. And in a gentle calm, both bodies were left in the oasis of a melody that the pass of the rover play, the frogs, the crickets, and the birds coming back to their nests; a unique melody and full of peace.

Just like that, both, immobilizes, immutable with their sight lost in each other, like they were still talking internally, superior and sublime only when you give your soul is possible achieve, there is no body that limit their knowledge, there is no passion that limit their ecstasy, is a supreme sensation that take them far, very far, in their mind leaving their bodies arrived to places never seen before by their souls and only to get there after braking the meat bow, when you achieve liking, unmask, to free for seconds from the body slavery that contain the soul to aloud touching and get to the sky.

After this corporal and mental ecstasy, both were feeling free since the frustration of the moment they were having was so strong that the fiery moment of a total contact it was like an oasis in their lives, they couldn't imagine how in that moment will radical changes in their lives, Otto and Hilda were not apart for any seconds, like they did not want to be apart from each other, but the tiredness of the ecstasy made them little by little relax and separating from each other like saying good bye, like leaving one from the other one until in one breath and without letting go the sight to each other came back from their sidereal trip, each of them to their own body, each of them to their reality... Hilda got up, dress up and with an agreeable look, told Otto, "You are wonderful..."

Otto throws himself to his feet and kiss her again, finishing with a kiss in her mouth, when, like a lighting splitting their attention, they hear something...

"Hilda, did you hear that?" Otto said.

Both got silence and they hear at back a noise like a swarm but also seem like a song... So, they dressed up very quick.

They got up, picked up their stuff, Otto run towards the noise that was getting more intense, leaving everything to the side.

They move and hide in some bushes from far, close of some trees beside the river, they wait and for their surprise they look a wild army of men with torches marching by the other side of the river like going to a revolt, manifestation, or an event of violet demonstration... From far they recognize some neighbors and workers from their respectively houses. The people were going towards the city. Otto broke the silence, "Hilda, I had better take you to your home."

Hilda answered him, "Yes, it's better, I do not like this..."

In that moment, he accompanies her until the gate of her home and then he left to his home... Otto was very worried, since that revolt was like a rebellion and was going to town.

They hasten and when closer they notice that in fact it was a reunion of a group of neighbors that were unionize to a socialist party that was taking power in that area. He did not get near, but he was able to identify several of his workers that from far away notice of his presence and with their sights send Otto a message, "The aristocrats going down soon..."

Otto went to his home and immediately wrote a letter to his father, asking him to comeback, that the situation in Germany was getting worst; he asked to comeback urgently.

Next day, he tries to organize the work and notice a great portion of his employees were not presented at work. Immediately went to look for Hilda at her home to asked her how she was doing, he was very worried for her, because the situation. Between the worries, the memories of their caress and what happened that evening, he got reasons to look for her. She as well as him were totally infatuate, however, they knew that things were not good in their outskirts.

While this was happening, the day by day of the Germans was full of news that were showing that the end of war was prominent and the greater looser, Germany, will pay very highly the devastation of these, which did not achieve but compromise the town future of an economic power that now was coming down in a giddy manner; was eminent an economic collapse, the German mark was felling in accordance with the winners initiating the actions of economic freezing, the value of the mark was equivalent to 5,000 per dollar and continue going up. The prices of the products going up, anywhere, when the people wanted to buy something, they notice that the cost of a coffee was 43,000 marks, a piece of bread, 18,000, a piece of cheese, 120,000... The big families had to sell their animals and the value of a cow was more than 10 million marks... The people were feeling very confused.

The live of Otto was in between dates, hard work, and a lot of desperation; he continues to be meeting Hilda and they were unified sharing this crisis of live, but at the same time they feel very identified to each other reason both share beside their feelings, the responsibility to bring up their family business, the support of Elias Hoffman, who lend money and had a community bank. Elias was cousin of Abraham that was also the trustee of Otto's father, and who already went to look for at the Simmons Central Bank days ago, but he couldn't arrive because the situation happening in Hamburg. The situation was very delicate since devaluation was letting feel their consequences, the interests of the loans were contemplating disconcerting rates that jumped in a range between eight percent and twenty percent until forty-five, sixty or even an eighty percent and continuing up. It was a situation that Otto was trying negotiating with the bank, leaving once more to Hamburg and there in Elias office, after some minutes of waiting in the lobby in a cold, heavy, desperate, and distressed atmosphere, surrounding of people with disconnected faces, one by one requesting help since Germany was destroy, and were lots of indebted, Otto was hearing their stories and how some of them were able to pay with their lands, and how each of them had a different case, until Otto's turn was on. When Elias saw him, he got up of the chair and told him, "Otto my good son... I'm glad to know that you are here, I had seen that you had been a great hero; I'm very proud of you... Even though your father should be more, no matter that the crown, couldn't maintain that victory... What a shame!" And continue talking, "Bur Otto, you know that we love you very much and we are very proud of you and your successes."

With his attitude and the use of his hands, dress in an expensive suit and shiny shoes, he continues, "Ok son, sit down."

Between laughs and hugs, Otto sits down and made a comment, "Thank you, Elias," making a pause and looking him to his eyes continue. "As you know, I came back to rescue my father business and we have been working hard; Johan request several loans to your bank, and I can see we are behind even though we start delivering much more to the Dölling..."

Elias interrupted him, "Yes, I know little devil; you and Hilda make a pretty couple!"

Otto blushed and answered him, "Well yes. We have made a lot and we are happy for now..."

Elias continues, "You should see that she is an appropriate woman for you, Otto."

"Yes, I know, but..."

Otto answered disputing again the Germany problem, but Elias was like he knew what was Otto going to asked for...

"Mr. Elias, I'm very worry. We do not have enough money and I would like to see the possibility to negotiate the business loan... What can we do Mr. Elias? considering the friendship between you and the family, we consider you like another member of the family, what do you say..."

Elias, got quiet and look at him with some compassion, until he answers, "Otto, don't forget... Business are like that, it is not my fault; it is because Germany is a great looser... It is a very difficult situation... The only thing I can do is renegotiate. What do you think if we put now the properties as a guarantee and see how much time we can give you? Do not pay me for the next six months, and I will give a lower rate since we have the properties as a guarantee..."

Otto did not respond for a moment, "Mr. Elias, only my father can resolve that. I can't do that..."

Elias answered, "Ok, In the mind time do not pay me until your father comes back."

"I will talk to him."

"But the German are the ones that form this nation and the businesses do not recognize this."

Finished Elias with a very calm voice, "It's what I can do..."

Although Otto did not like that, there was no respond and none the less consideration taken for the close relation that he had with his family, making Otto very upset, "Elias, don't say that! I was there and I gave my life for Germany, for the nation. That is not a way to react!" And in a quick move he turns of his sight and got out of his office shutting the door.

Elias was astonished, couldn't understand why Otto was so upset and letting Elias restless. "He will be fine" Elias thought, "I will talk to his father..." meanwhile Elias asked for Otto's records to review how much he owe and to plan how to recuperate the money.

Otto was again confused, and he still didn't have an answer from his father. His father received Otto's letter, his father was very distress, because he had an idea of what was happening and right away left for Germany... But before he asked to his lovely Heidi Marie to remain in Switzerland. Arthur and Ana Marie left with his father to Germany in the first train of the next day. Leaving from the Lucerne terminal, Heinrich visible distress, say good bye to Heidi Marie and hug her like saying good bye forever... She felt the same and beg him, "I'm going with you, I beg you..."

And she starts an inconsolable crying.

Arthur and Ana Marie asked her to calm down, but when Ann Marie saw the desperation of her mother, she decided to stay. Heinrich did not know what to do... Comeback to his lovely Germany or stay in Switzerland where everything was in calm and in pace... He thought inexhaustible in that... "Ok, I only go and fix up."

In that moment, Abraham arrived to say good bye to Heinrich and tell him, "Don't worry, I will be in the process of, I know what is going on in Germany, I have written to my cousin to know how he can help you."

And gave him in his hands a letter for his cousin, Elias.

"I know my friend... We will be ready for anything."

After that he went up to the train with Arthur. The scene was very sad: his daughter, his wife and his good friend saying good bye to him with sadness and gloomy they saw how little by little the train leaves the station and going away.

Motionless, Heidi Marie without moving, told the daughter, "He is gone, I know we will see them again..."

Her daughter answers her, "Yes, we will," and left walking arm in arm.

Meanwhile, Heinrich on the way to Hamburg, was thinking on everything he has made, talking with Arthur of all his projects he had achieve, about Germany, but at the same time while getting closer to the German border, it was notable the change. When they arrive to the border it was terrified moments for both, they not seen their nation, it was a big impact, was looking like a devastating country, it was clear the problem in that moment was whipping Germany and the news were not stretching; were eliminating the little hope left, the newspaper was announcing the measure fill by the victorious countries, they were collecting the bill to Germany, the greater looser, that once was to be the most important economic power of Europe and to be better than Great Britain and France. Now it has a price, maybe the envy or the power hunger from England and the envy of those countries ended. The newspapers were informing that all the German market ships from more than 1.400 Tm of shifting and annual transfer of 200.000 Tm of new ships, to refund all the market fleet lost by the allies during the conflict.

The annual delivery of 44 million of Tm of coal, 371.000 heads of cattle, half of the chemistry and pharmaceutical production, the total underground cables etc. for five years. Expropriation of the German private property in lost areas and colonies.

The payment of 132.000 million of German marks-gold (for that time $31.400 million, £6.600 million) equivalent to $400.000 million of USA dollars to these dates, an amount that Germany couldn't pay and a lot of economists in that moment consider excessive since means more of the international reserves of Germany, that according with several authors caused the super inflation.

This situation for any country means the economic bankruptcy; the German town morality deteriorated, all the people were at the border of desperation and none less the internal revolts for the power in the new Republic confronted the extreme right and the extreme left to his maximum expression. Was when the confusion of the people made them to appeal to the propose that allowed them to be free of their problems; the Volks start to arise, the populism and the working class wanted to take the power since the nationalism was a productive land to make sprout lots of changes as well as people feelings.

In the middle of this fight was Otto, totally confuse since his interior was still not finish defining his conflicts of identity between being a hero, had been an aristocrat, had giving his live for his country and all these for nothing... Germany already forgot his sacrifice, his person did not have any value... Until he received a letter from Erick Fullman, who was his friend during his stay in Abwher. In the letter, he was asking Otto to join the provisional army in the intelligence line, in the recent formation and known Freikorps, because this new army power require all the specialty veterans, the most experts, of all knowledge to maintain the pace in Germany and contain the series of revolt happening in the country, the war was now Germany verses Germany.

The arrival of his father was close, Otto went to the station, he was nervous because he did not know how to see his father after long time and knowing what will happen when he tells him the situation of the business. His father and his brother came down from the coach to meet him, was a long hug like never, besides Otto took one of the suitcases and put it in his shoulder to start walking home. Meanwhile, Otto starts talking about everything happening on the farm; how he improves some things, how he built the irrigation canals for the higher zones of the pasture, explain the way he turns away part of the river to enter until their lands... When Heinrich stopped him to ask, "You did what?!"

Otto answers him calmly, "I made a canal from the river and took it to the high zone for irrigation."

His father obstructed answer him, "But Otto, you don't know what you are saying..."

Continue the questioning, his father was asking him very polite for his action, "And no one was telling you anything?"

Otto answers him very firm but at the same time confuse, "No... and I don't understand why should they tell me something."

"You should have consulted me for that Otto."

His father answers him very vigorously and continue, "Don't you understand that the water problem is very delicate? And taking the water out of its course to take it to the land... Ooh boy... I will have to see what to do about it, because we can have serious problems."

Otto was very surprised, and his father starts coughing, but did not stop crying out to him, "Ok, Otto, tell me what else have you been doing. How is the business manager?"

Otto answers him, "Well Johan is in charge; he should have the details."

By that moment, they were in the farm and were welcome by the service personnel, consisting of only the cook, Johan and two servants: Hans and Peter.

His father barely said a hello to them because his cough became stronger and couldn't have more interaction, he went to his room, but Otto insisted, "Father, aren't we going to see the pending?"

His father, in silence and visible upset left to his room. There was Arthur, who kept himself quiet all the time, but when his father closes the door, start screaming to Otto, "See what you do? Look how you set my father! Don't you have a conscience, beside who told you to come back here? You are a damned loser!"

Otto surprised fighting back the aggression, "You had better shut up!"

But Arthur came back to attack against his brother, "You are a damned cowardly, you escape from war, you are a COWARDLY!"

And the verbal aggressions initiated between the brothers, Otto did not wait too long in responding to him, "More than you, I don't think so."

"You got out of the army like a coward."

"I got out, but you do not know all I have been done, or what do you want? Do you want me to die?"

"Well, that should be better," Answer Arthur irascible.

In that moment, they lost all prudence and respect; a second was enough for both to start banging. They fell through the stairs between punches and falls. Luckily, his father did not hear anything since no felt exhausted from the trip and fell sleep deeply.

The screaming and the banging made the servants and even Johan run to see what was happening. Johan scream at them, enviously, but trying to control the situation, "But what is happening to you? Stop, stop!"

And trying to separate them while he insisted with an open scream, "Otto, Arthur... Calm down!"

And trying to separate them.

"Help! Hans, Peter, come on; Help! Come on right now...!"

Right away arrived to attend Johan petitions since were close by. This way, between the three of them to separate the brothers, since Otto was giving his brother a tremendous beating and on the floor. When separated, they help Arthur to get up and he tried to attack Otto again, trying to unload his anger, but they did not allow him to be in physical contact again with him, so they initiate a new series of insults, "You are an Arschloch (stupid)."

Otto screams to his brother, "Dumkofft (idiot)."

Answer Arthur, evidently abused and upset.

Otto enters in a mayor stage of anger and couldn't hold it, "The coward like you, are better out of the honorable country, Vexed!"

"You do not know what is honor! Johan, LET ME GO! It not worth it this pusillanimous."

Johan immediately attend the order and let him go, after that, Otto got out of the room, but before he told him, "Be careful, Arschloch! You don't know who are you messing with..."

Arthur was motionless, then he left to cure his wounds.

This was the result of an old grudge from the preferences of his father for the younger brother, since Arthur felt protected by his father, who is inclined to this one, since he always does everything he ask. Arthur has been working on this since long time ago and thought he has all the advantages to finish with his brother for good, and take him out of the business and keep all for himself...

It was late and Otto left the farm, he went to Hilda's house, where he spends the rest of the day and even the night; in a small house outside town, with her, he tries to calm down and told Hilda that came about. They were talking, remembering lots of things, and trying to find some answers; on the other hand, Otto very upset, shows Hilda the letter of his friend Erick, who was inviting him to induct to the military service, she holds her breath, look at him in his eyes and asked him, "And, what are you thinking to do?"

Evidently disturb put down her gaze and wait in silence some answer from Otto, "I have not considerate yet, but... He breath, but now, with this anger with my brother, I notice lots of things..."

"I don't know if I will be able to put up with this situation, I think everything is going to be worst after what happened. I do not know, but I'm sure of something: on any of my decisions for now on, you will be on its Hilda."

He took her hands and put her head up softly while holding her chin and looking at her eyes attentively, "How is that?"

After a long silence, without taking his sight off her, Otto answers her, "You have trusting men with your story and I know you also had have done this, your brother, and your father... You had said so isn't? a lot of problems in your house and they are trying to leave you on the border of everything..."

Hilda only watching in silence while Otto, moving his head continued, "That is not good, and you have had to accept the conditions... You are a brilliant woman and valuable, you have contributed lots of things to your father's business, but those brothers of yours have only abuse you, they do not leave you alone and they do not care about you, except when they need you. That is not right... They are so arrogating, understand that they are using you for their purpose and at the end they will never appreciate you. They are like that and first is their benefit and possessions and you are the last thing."

Hilda lightly upset answer him, "It's not like that, I have always hung on to them and they love me..."

"Mmmmmmmm, Is that love...?"

And he continued, "Look how my brother loves me and how he treats me when he sees I'm touching one of his interests."

"But Otto, what is that should do with your decision making?"

"A lot..."

He took her by her shoulders and look at her attentively, "I want you to come with me, let's go together; I will take care of you, leave everything, and come with me..."

But Hilda, with a broken voice, "Otto, my love... I can't..."

Otto insisted, "If you love me as much as I love you, let's get out of here. I won't be able to stay here for a long time and none the less with these things. I know is going to get worst... But do not answer me now, think about it and we'll talk tomorrow, we'll see you."

And left her standing with no words. Otto with his head looking down, got out very fast from the place. Hilda stay very absorbed and fell on her knees while he kept going away from there.

Meanwhile things were changing; Arthur on the other hand got up and the first thing he did was going to see with Johan the books of the administration. He reviews the expenses trying to find something to accuse his brother. Between a lot of restrictions and deficiencies, he discovers that Johan has been taking money from there in small amounts, but at the end were adding several millions of marks. Because the lack of family supervision, Johan took advantage of their absences and practically he felt like the owner of the farm and the business. Arthur told Johan while took him by his neck, "Sneak thief, you had been stealing from us."

Johan never thought he will be discovered, since Otto blind trust him and never reviewed the accounting books...

"Hooligan, traitor, disgraceful... Look at this, you did your own business by dint of us."

He took him by his ear and strongly drag him to a chair, he looks at him in his eyes and scream at him, "Give me my money back or you will be in jail... Or even worst: in a cemetery or in the trash..."

"No please, Arthur."

He was begging him very anxious, "We won't stop here, just wait for my father to know this and you will see what he will do to you."

In the middle of his anger, Arthur had an idea: What will happen if instead of taking this revenge, he takes advantage of it? his father did not know yet, Otto did not have any knowledge of it and no doubt he did know... He thought and thought "And if I do everything to come out well save and keep all these?" Let go to Johan and told him, "Johan, you know that my father is a very honest man, and he will never allow this..."

Johan interrupted, "But Arthur, I only took a loan, and will retune with profit without no one never knowing..."

"No, no, no, don't tell me that now, there is no doubt you are a thief, neither that you fool us... I will take you to jail immediately for stealing, fraud, breach of confidence... No, no there is no way out. And look, how Otto was asking for money if you took it all."

Arthur took with his right hand a letter-opener in a roman dagger form and softly hit the arm chair on the office where Johan was seating... He got closer and touching his neck with the dagger He got closer and touching his neck with the dagger said to him, "Johan, you have two choices: you must do exactly what I tell you or I hand over to the justice; I have the proof... And you can go to jail."

However, Arthur did not know that Johan was now part of a new Nationalist rebel party founded in München by a charismatic leader that was gaining popularity each day in the town, mainly between the working class, employees and subservient of the German aristocrats; situation where Johan was, from frustrated ex combats for losing the war, for all those feeling oppress for the aristocracy and were celebrating with happiness the fall of the reign. Johan was already an active member for that, but with the confusion and the threat of Arthur, pretended inheriting of the German aristocracy, a class that he hates for their origins, did not have any other choice but to cooperate.

But Johan had another plan beside what he had said. Arthur took all the incriminate documents and lock them in a secret place that only he knew, incase his plan fell he can attack Johan and take him to jail. They were two villain minds both with bad intentions; one for his ambition, greed, and anger against the German aristocracy and the other one for his greed and excessive ambition to keep all what his father made, leaving his family and siblings with nothing.

Heinrich came down to the dining room to take breakfast, and there were both, Johan, and Arthur, he was odd not seen Otto asking and questioning. Both already agree, comment what he knew of the Otto's inspected crazy actions y how he always gets out and does whatever he wants, for what the father answer, "Otto... I already saw a change in him, it's strange that he continues being the same, isn't he had enough with all the suffering? Ouch! he does not understand... Since life is charging high his stubbornness."

That reminded him how he had been the same of stubbornness as his son Otto and understood why his son was the same. They continue with their topics and after breakfast they start to work on the pending business of the farm and other details coming up without waiting for Otto.

Otto meanwhile, after his encounter with Hilda, he kept walking around town and watching how the movements of parties were starting to define; the communist very strong up north and the nationalisms down south, Otto started elucidating to which party should he join, since he belongs to the bourgeoisie and he always was faithful to the conservative extreme, just like Mark always inculcated; remembering this, went to the main central plaza, took the phone and dial to Mark in Berlin.

"Hello, good morning, Mark, this is Otto, how are you?"

He greeted spontaneously and with pleasure, "Otto what a pleasure to know about you, I have been thinking about you, and see you had called, so good! When can you come to Berlin? I must talk to you, but I'm not feeling good, and I cannot travel."

But Otto answers him, "My father has returned home and he is trying to save the business..."

"Your father? What a pleasure! I have not heard anything about him for a long time, tell him to look for me..."

"Yes, I will tell him on your behalf."

After a long telephone conversation, Otto took a new decision in his life.

CHAPTER EIGHT
THE CONFRONTING

When it was hopeless the conquest of Otto's ideals, things begin to change; his sudden change of opinion will have made his demons to come back with all the force of the pass. Why no return and confront all those insane feelings that he had manage bend by pressing and not letting them out of his mind? Things begin to bear, from returning to his house, the day after the confront with his brother.

Otto with a decision in his mind, went to his father, who had been reviewing the documents with Arthur and Johan; when Otto enter to the house, his father did not welcome him as effusive like as the first day, he was distant and absorbed than before, his father asked him to come in to the office because he wanted to talk to him. Otto thought was a talk of thanking him for all he has done: the irrigation canals he built, the pumps to solve the problem of irrigation in the tough areas, the arrangement of sales with the Dölling family, and the way he had rebuild the tractors and other machinery of the farm and business; even though he was worried for the divert of a lot of water to the farm... He even thought that was reason of the talk, but he knew it has a solution, but the real reason of his meeting left him astonished.

"Son, I do not know what we did wrong; we educated you the best we could... Point out each time with a strong tone of voice – We do not know, and I don't understand, but the war, your victories or maybe your new friends change you a lot... I do not know you, Otto!"

Astonished, Otto answered, "No father, I have come back from that inferno to not know any more about it, I'm back here and that's what I want…"

But his father answers him with a strong voice, "Explain to me then, how you have been stealing from me since you got back?"

Otto got even more astonished and answer, "Stealing, father…? I do not understand, I have dedicated myself only to support you," the distress was showing in his words, "Do not tell me that father…"

"It was not enough to be a war hero and you decided to defraud my name, my family…"

His father continues answering him, although Otto did not have an idea what his father was accusing him, was totally outside his understanding, but his father keeps going, "It was not enough to steal the neighbor's water… You also have steal from me."

There was when he got up and screamed, "That is not true, that's not true!" Raise even higher his voice and hit the table, "What is this about father? Is this a sense of judgment?"

Heinrich answer him raising his voice, "You are an unpleasant thief!"

Otto interrupted him before he could say anything else, he got closer to his face and look at him straight ahead, "What? Father don't call me like that," and with tear in his eyes he ended "it's not true, father, where are you taking that from?"

Heinrich show him the documents and show him all the expenditures of money on his name, "But is not true, Johan was the one who oversaw all the loans, everything, he keeps accounts of."

Was all he could state until his father interrupted, "Well your brother, Arthur, has reviewed the documents and we found this."

He asked shouting for Johan to come to the office, but this one did not answer and did not show up; like looking for him everywhere, Otto was restless looking all directions.

"And why do you want him for, here is everything? We already took care of that astute, I have fire him why you did not tell me that before. Now, your brother Arthur oversees this business."

Immediately, Otto tie what happened in his fight with his brother and felt betray and totally disarm, he did not have a way to proof anything, he was very upset, and he was conscious that he couldn't give his father more worries, since he knew the delicate of heart problems, which looks like his father inherit of his father, earl Friedrich von Münster. His father very upset, asked him to get back all the money and to leave the house. His father screams at him with tears on his eyes, "I never thought you would do that to me, Otto."

He touches his chest and set on the office chair. Otto knew that was his brother work, but he never thought his greed would go that far... As a last recourse outline the following words, "If you really love me, at least you should hear my version..."

But Heinrich bend, put down his head and fix his sight to the floor, he denies listening. He asked him to leave off his sight. Otto got out very upset to go and meet Arthur, but this one was hiding in Humbug with the excuse of negotiate the loan with Elias Hoffman.

Otto, desperate for all was gathering in his live, plus the situation of the country, exploded; meanwhile took some of his belongings and got out of his house, not before telling his father that he was doing a serious error which he will sorry after and screamed at him, "But I will prove the contrary to you."

Turning himself, got up in motorcycle and left from there. All that was happening in moments in which the new republic of Weimar was in total bankruptcy and the dollar exchange rate against the mark was 2 million of marks for 1 dollar, the unemployment was more notorious, lots of families were starting to lose all their belongings; in the case of the banks, like the Simmons, where Elias Hoffman was part of, were taking the properties as guaranty and they were closing them; same as the requirements of hold ups were daily, the German stock barely exist and was totally economical wipe out; the French, American and England, merciless collecting the counts of the lost war by Germany, that mount 40% of the fiscal collection of that country. It was an unpayable debt; it was cheaper to cover the wall with frames that the price of the cover paper itself.

Like condemn to be slave of these powers for the rest of their lives, only some Germans with miserable salary keep their positions, the German companies like Siemens had an unemployment level up to 20% of the normal base and every day making more cuttings, lots of young man left universities since they couldn't continue paying their studies. The existing of desperation atmosphere.

The population that depends of a salary to live was in serious difficulties since the prices of the food and basic services rises in each week, making impossible the savings. At the same time, the urgency to pay for reparations causes that almost all the available foreign currency in the market were in the government power, which prevent the average German acquire foreign currency to protect themselves from the inflation; only the wealthy bankers and notable industries had access to this given resource since were required to maintain the productive company of the biggest German corporations of that time like Siemens, Henkel, Bayer and the little producers like Dölling, and the Münster, from the area depended from the credits of the regional banks. For this time, it was the existence of the Notgelb (emergency money) same that Otto requested before and which he had to returned as soon as possible since the interest were for more than 10% monthly, something never seen before and used by the creditor.

Meanwhile and coming back to the family Münster situation, Arthur was in Hamburg negotiating with Elias; he received him and explain the loans situations of his family. It was such a surprise for Arthur that he called his father from that place to come immediately to Hamburg and see how delicate situation their credit was. Heinrich immediately travel to Hamburg and both meet with Elias. Been the three of them and after explaining the situation to Heinrich, he started feeling bad, cuffing strongly and a strong pain in his chest; it was evident that such an event was from the notice given to him. Arthur took his father to the closer hospital from there where he got the first aids, but it was eminent: Heinrich suffer from a heart attack. In his situation and no strength to talk, Heinrich took the hand of his son Arthur and asked to settle things with Otto and to take care for his dear Heidi Marie and Ana Marie. Whit almost vague words and difficult to breathe, in a desperate intent to talk, Heinrich die in the hospital, even with intents to reestablish his cardiac rate. Heinrich die at six o'clock in the city of Hamburg.

Arthur was mute and disconsolate, but Elias who saw everything happened, looked for Otto, who was by chance in Hamburg, in a coffee place waiting for his friend Erick Fullman. Elias got closer to coffee place where Otto was seating looking to the street by the Konich Strasse, Elias somewhat hesitating to encourage himself to cross the street and from there almost three metros of distance and as a kindness told him, "Otto, I know we are not related, maybe neither friends..." He stutters a little. "Bu... But letting you know that your father... I knew that he is in the central hospital and... and he got delicate right now, I... I... just letting you know..."

Otto got mute and Elias simple turned around to leave fast. Otto got up and immediately leave to the hospital. When arriving he ask in the reception, trying to know if his father was there; when from far he saw his brother, he got closer, and both look to each other in to their eyes, and leaving behind their feelings, like his father was bringing them together, without saying anything, their looks say everything; slowly got closer and hug to each other. At their contact both start crying and ask for forgiveness for what they did, feeling both responsible for what happened. In a long silence, both couldn't say any words, and suddenly, only Otto, got up and went to the chaise longue at the emergency room and saw his father dead.

Otto fell next to his father and asked for forgiveness, told him how much he loved him, following by an internal dialog established with him to say good bye forever. "There is nothing else to do father, forgive me..." In the middle of a silence crying, discreet and full of pain, kept himself for some minutes. In a time, he reincorporated and with his face down he left from there.

"There is nothing else to do brother," Otto said. "We must let our mother know and I hope she can handle this news."

After the bothers tranquilly talk and confess to each other their positions, ending in reconciliation. Arthur asked for forgiveness to his brother and told him all he discovers, he told him of his intentions, while Otto in silence and for the love he had for his father understood him and forgive him. A seen that couldn't be better for both; the settlement was made by dint of the live of his father. How live is! Heinrich died and left his working, love, and respect heritage, but his dead initiate the reconciliation that was imaginable between his two sons.

Here it's important to underline how the dead or lives of persons changes the stories; all Arthur plans had for his brother, Otto's plan for his brother and the family revanche; the inseparable changes of roles, in a few hours everything canceled, and the story change the curse in this family destinies.

For the ones who have love so much like Heinrich and Heidi Marie, this news was overwhelming, all in the family knew the importance between each other. During his farewell, Heidi Marie already predicted, the time he was out of the house, the phone communication was very close, they talked, but Heinrich never told her love one Heidi Marie what he saw when arrived in Germany, he kept the discretion and never told her the problem between Otto and Arthur, everything to give her a little dose of peace and only told her that were some little problems that can be resolve. It was such the respect and care of Heinrich for his wife, that he worries not to exalt her for nothing and when a problem was evident, Heinrich always try to attenuate the things, so she did not worry and take the problem subtly. Inclusive, Heinrich, before going to Lucerne, told her the possibility of his dead, situation that he already present since he was diagnostic with the same medical suffer that took his father, subject that always was predicting since months ago before leaving for Germany, in such a degree that Heidi Marie when he was parting, she did it with a believe she may not see him ever again.

Arthur, by unanimously between the brothers, was who gave the news of what happen with his father to his mother and sister, Otto on the other hand took charge of the death steps to prepare the needs for a deserving funeral of an earl.

They entrust on calling their friends, the few friends left; since some of them emigrate to other parts of the world. From the family only attend some cousins and some other relative. From the friends from the old and almost extinct aristocracy were some left, some of them politics, who met in the secrecy of the time from convulsive Germany; his good friend Mark did not forget neither all his colleague that still living in the Prussian army where he served. It was like 60 persons between friends, employees, and neighbors, besides of his lovely wife and her daughter that arrived next day of his death.

The arriving of their mother, was something touching, because when she arrived in accompany of their sister Ana Marie, were welcomed for the two young ones; in a family scene, unique they hug and together cry the loss of their father and husband. These may be the last time that the live allowed them to share the most intimate of a human being: the family.

Without preambles and in a religious ceremony in the Lutheran church was giving the sermon and fare-well of Heinrich body. There were present lots of friends and neighbors that arrived at the church to say good bye to such an important personage, were attending influent families of Elmsohrn, also the Dölling's, the mayor family and the retired civil authorities and mili-tary that still remember the earl, also there were present Abraham and his family. Also, Elias attended, who was distant in the reunion, since he knew what will happen with the economic problems they were about to con-front. Despite was an emotive ceremony which came out lots of things that give origin to a new part of live of each member of the family.

Otto and Arthur mount guard before the coffin of his father, they were standing all the ceremony like taking care of a hero.

The outline of this important character that gave life to many things, in the same farewell sermon to his mortal remainders, generated a series of changes in lots of people and provoke feelings that reach with actions that provoke action verbs in the web of connections that he was leaving when leaving his contact, it is well known that those connections left in recollection and these lodge in the person's minds and are there influencing in the person's acts and they received this influence, something like that happened with the Heinrich web, left a track and that track it normally manifest on the moment of detachment, since detachment of the deepest of the same is the track, to saying are feelings that can be positive or negative, any of these feelings are translated in more energy to the bond the web is forming in the persons that still connected, referring these to the personal relations of his sons, wife, friends and with the web he left, in a certain way the mental heritage that can directly affect for several years and mostly spread generations in the human being, it is reason why attribute of a love one leaves and at the same time stay already on his works or actions remain or are pass through time in conduct paths that sometimes good or bad are copy and pass to one person to another throughout the same social behavior, it's how there is old traditions and customs that while the human being exist on earth will remain forever, one of this elements that he left to his sons was the love for his country something that Heinrich was sure that will prevail, are heritage that he pass in the deep subconscious of their sons, this was made possible that come out in time.

As we know, the time won't forgive and days went by and months, there is new stages begin, always everything is new so the sequence always continue, the Heinrich past stayed as a legacy, but the continue of the lives of each of one taking different ways, some good, other unsuccessful, and other bad, but at the end the essence was left in his thoughts that allowed them to continue relate this novel since here it's not the end, otherwise continue forward.

CHAPTER NINE
THE RADICAL CHANGE

Otto, regarding the events in Germany, in November 1921, after the loss of his father, he has taken the decision to join to the Freikorps, who were dedicated to suppressing the revolts of the parties that were intense fights for the power. With the experience of pilot, Erick Fullman, Otto's friend, being his partner and with the denial for the Versailles treaty that the Germans couldn't fly airplanes anymore, Otto was send to Polonia to train pilots for a few months, for being part of a group of elites received a good amount of money, some that he send to his mother to try to save some of what was almost lost, meanwhile Arthur stayed in charge of the farm and the business, together with his mother were trying to save something.

The social situation was impossible; Arthur did not know what to do, Heidi Marie must return to Lucerne, the rebellion were routines and the nationalists agitators, did not let working, to a such an extent that Johan his overseer and foreman who was fired was already part of the NAZI party and start to attack to the bourgeois, he put his employees against them for taking him out of work, since he had power over the community, as they had the slogan of a socialism of the town and for the town, that as a German shouldn't pay the debt and the cost of war and he said, on the streets and everywhere verbal attacks to Heidi Marie that they should join to his cause, that was lawful and that will come out from the Jewish bankers stockjobber that were extort, Johan somehow slip because the negotiation with Arthur, the consternation for Heinrich death, after some days of absence, went back where the family was to return what he took as a loan, he asked for a disguise clemency, since his intentions were other and after a long audience with the family, obtain convince in a force or obliged way to be accepted again, taking advantage of the necessity of a foreman for the farm and the thousands of things to do as well as the compromises, it was decided for them to come back to work... He had his plans well-built and in that moment was not convenience for him to leave from a good position to continue with the work, it was not going to be the same, but he knew how to shake the guilt of his villain, as well as astutely saying to Arthur and the mother, "Do not pay anymore to Elias, they are only robbing you, let's put ourselves in suspensions of payments."

Heidi Marie answers him, "But Johan, how are we going to stop paying?! If Heinrich and Elias were very good friends and he had excuse us for a long time the debt and we pay as we can, I'm not agree."

Johan responds, "But, can you see? Those foreign are guilty for the way we are... They are only waring us out, the town is already tired of this, we, the nationalists are with the German town, they are not even Germans and at least call us gentiles and we do not count for anything, the only thing they want is not losing their money, but will be days like our leader says that they will be sorry and Germany will be like always was, the most powerful town of the world."

In that moment, Johan got up and left her alone, it was then that Heidi Marie puts two and two together of what Arthur told her, Johan withdrew amounts of money from the account of his family and was giving it as a contribution share of that insanity, it was evident how the ambient was feeling. Johan talked a lot about the famous Dolchtoss or stabbing to the country of Weimar republic, it was something very strong that was spreading in between all the Germans supporting of the NSDAP party of that time, as a party group the frontal provokes with the elite of the "conservator revolution" as according with their founders, should conduct to a new time where the groups got exile to the part which they were borne for. So, little people like Heidi Marie did not have this feeling, since she was more Swiss than German, so far that was her feeling, however Johan insisted and was verbally attacking the Münster, Dölling, Hass, Neuman, Hoffmann families and other contractors and conservative families from that area to such a extend that Johan start doing strikes in all the work places he could and threaten on closing the work place, Arthur was upset, her mother was dreadful and Otto was already far away working in something that his family did not know, but Hilda who he called her from time to time and in one of those calls he asked her to meet him in Berlin, in one of his trainings at the central offices of the Freikorps.

Hilda got courage and decide to go with Otto to Berlin, Otto was already giving instructions to legion of pilots in foreign countries, already belonging to the Abwehr (defense) and the recently formed OKW (Amt Ausland/Abwehr im Ober Kommando der Wehrmacht) Department /Office of Overseas of high-ranking of the arm force, which he enter in the radio communications special section, where the reason of his visit to Berlin for some months had been training in a secret Fullman and Fritz Meyer that along with Otto were part of a division being train in:

Ht: Intelligent techniques of the army, communications designs of wireless systems, operations without wires.

L: Air intelligent with air survival systems and improvisation.

While they were already some experts since were a lot of request of this knowledge's in emergent countries, one of them in Latin America, which have applications and the fame of this instructors and strategies spread from the old continent, was when Mexico army knew about this prowess, when by chance in Mexico in that time after a hard and bloody fight revolution, the country should be more controlled because the government instructed the army in forming and counting with a new and modern system of communication control codifying and other advances in this area of satisficed intelligence.

It was like this how a new government in Mexico directed by a general arrives to ask to this department for an application of services, thanks to the popularity and what have happened in that country on January 16, 1917, when the German minister of exterior of the time, Arthur Zimmermann, sent a telegram to the Mexican ambassador, Heinrich von Eckardt, with precisely instructions to convince the president Venustiano Carranza, that Mexico enter to the war to the side of the central impairers. As an exchange, the telegram promised to Mexico the restitution of the territory's annexation by United States on the 1847-1848 war by the treat of Guadalupe- Hidalgo. Such a telegram also suggested that the president Carranza communicate with Tokyo to get an agreement to make the Japanese empire go to the German side. The Britannic intelligence power intersected the telegram and easily decipher, since did not have security systems, this provokes the intervention of United States in the war. Carranza did not accept the offer since Mexico was immersing in the Mexican Revolution and was not in adequate economic conditions. Beside the leader was worried for the Punitive Expedition of United States. Mexico not only enter in the war; they even send Francisco Leon de la Barra as a high Mexican commissioner for the pact.

With this preceding, some Mexican militaries at the end of the first war and knowing that Germany was defeated, but not the experience and fame of their militaries assessors and experts that was well known were available for actions more beneficial and not implicate compromise with any country in that time of peace.

This situation was when Erick Fullman, who is the direct connection of foreign missions of the small body of German war of those years, received the application and comment to his immediate bosses, they were accustom to military missions and well pay, decide process that application and commented to planned the costs and the risks, since there were several applications from Latin America militaries who wanted to count with this support, it was then when in an informal conversation, Erick comment to his friend Otto, "How do you see, it is an attractive offer, they are paying more than the Polish and the Russians," and continue. "It's triple, Otto..."

He stays absorbed, "But where is that damn place?"

He took out a map of the world and found it, with his finger Erick showed it.

"Mmmmmm"

"It's too far away and it's not in my plans and I want to stay here in Berlin with Hilda."

Erick in that moment with a mocking laugh, "But Otto you have enough woman, ha, ha, ha, ha..."

The countries that he visited, Otto was already an adult and desirable of lots of woman, beside his money, also for his good looks and his fame of a prefect lover, he was easily scattering in some groups of women, continuing with the conversation Otto said, "I want to have a family and leave something good like my father."

Erick responded starting with a horselaugh, "You are not that type, and you will never be..."

Looked at his eyes and took him by the shoulders and said, "But Otto this country is going to hell, how it's destroying in between the same Germans, no Otto it is the opportunity to do some money, we are famous, Erick continue."

"Imagine yourselves in that lost country, where no one knows anything. Will be like gods over there and even pay us! Is liked to be a conquering of an indigenous town of lack of culture; of course, it has their risks, they are killers and murderers... But what have you done, seen, and heard...? Ha, ha, ha, we will change what we know for a fortune! It is a golden opportunity! Women, money, glory and then with the fortune in our hands, we came back to Germany; by then this had calm down, Hindenburg won't allow that Germany fall..."

Otto interrupted, "No, nothing like that, I have detected an information fissure very serious, and I'm telling you these in between us, there is a party that is moving lots of mass to the south, it is complicating things, where I have been in the last years and days in Polonia, there you can hear other things and I have documented."

Erick asked him, "What are you talking about Otto?"

Otto answers him in a serious tone, "Erick, understand the situation here things are going to be very complicated, the rebellion populist party from München is having a lot of war and we have been trying to contain and you have seen this closer."

Erick response, "Yes, I remember, that one name Adolfo Hitler, the one that had another nationalism party before of something else, now he named the NSDAP, yes of course, we have suffocated their manifestations and the Republic is worried. They are something else specially that maniac and their fanatics! They are crazy. Remember? Was…" And he stops and thinks for a second. "When we were in a military battle on 1916 in Alessia, I remember how one of them, Frank Holler, I will never forget that name, huff, he was perturbed, he throws himself to the French ditch rap in dynamite screaming 'long live Germany, and die the French…' Do you remember that, Otto?"

He answers him almost immediately and with a sarcastic smile, "Yes, of course, lots of us were to the point of doing that, it was something very strong, of course I remember, well those are the kind of people that are active, in fact, Otto took out a binder and some documents, let me show you Erick what just arrived, we have the instructions to stop at any way to these fanatics, the sympathy is getting everywhere, the bad thing is that the town is blaming the burgess of what is happening and beside Adolfo Hitler is promising give back Germany to the Germans, I'm not saying this, see these papers, see this investigations, each election is gaining territory in the congress, you do not need to be a wise for this and understand that soon will be a majority and what will we do."

Erick responds, "Otto, you are right I have seen it that way, now with more reason I must insist on accepting the propose, and I will do it."

Otto remain thinking and told him, "Erick, I will think about it. Is not the moment… Not now Erick? We have something more important to do… We will have time for that, we can focus better on this. I wanted to tell you something that we have now."

He took him to the dining table and asking to be seated, "Let's see how much you have learned."

The document was a newspaper of Berlin Zeitung, "Look, what do you see?"

"Haaa I know, don't tell me; the news of the day, Otto did not answer…"

"Beside seeing the news of the day and the adver-
tisements..."

"Don't tell me that you announce your marriage
with Hilda."

Otto answers him immediately, "No, no; that's not
it, look, take it, review it, read it..."

"Look Erick, I'm telling you that there are the
instructions, the maps and our work orders, documents
and more, would you believe me..."

"I cannot believe it; we achieve the creation the
code and manage the new system."

"Do not tell me, fabulous! That was what they have
very well hide, right?"

Otto answers him in an exited tone, "Yes, it is Erick,
we have managed to find the riddle of classified information, that is something incredible and I can't believe
we did it."

In that moment, they start the codification to each
other and summaries the codification and decoding
prosses, for this technique it was required to count with
three entity, the generator or translator of the code, an
interpreter of the code and a decode of the code generated, it was necessary to count with three entity for
security systems and not to get in enemy hands such
information in a way that any of the three knew who
was who in relation of each of them, so each of them
have their classification independently, but at the end
the message was transmitted radial or on writing and
the receptors at the same time had their codes of inter-
pretation, it was complex system that to obtain these
were years of studies, that for Otto's, Erick and others
luck as part of the team was an opportunity of their lives
to acquire a knowledge of more than 50 years of study
and scientific generation of this information system.

They were doing that, when Otto shows him the
code and both notice that Erick was the generator and

Otto the interpreter of the code, and both knew of the importance of what they were doing... As a studious of this matter, they test each other, so Erick tells Otto, "Otto I'm going to test you."

For this Otto answers him, "Go ahead friend let's see what is this about."

After some minutes, they consult their manuals and watch their notes; Erick brings out a code... 8-16-12-1,1-13-9-7-15, 14-15-19.1-12-1-19,z-y-.8-18-19. 5-14-5-1-13-.1-6-5.2-5-19-12-9-14, then Otto took out the manuals and respond to him. 1-6-9-18-13-1-20-9-22-15.1-8-9.14-15-19.22-5-13-19.

Of course, they understand and the translator send the code and decode with a machine of computation that generate the code and made the algorism that only have two codes of accesses z26 and change constantly in base a progressive algorism and chronologic that ensure the date, time of the message to certification and ensure the value of the code and avoid the duplicated, when inserted these, a phrase comes out on writing decode, "Hello friend will see you in 12 hours in the Berlin coffee... And Otto took out of the machine, confirming with a phrase "will see you there..." After hours and test applying a new element that was, in each message of each point of the message, it was a map, photograph or diagram, this achievement was thanks to a tiny camera sensible to the light of high definition that was basing in optical principals, that it made it possible to obtain pictures of documents immediately, this new machine when is place on the points of any document you can see with a special microscope that the translation machine has to detected, as simple to place the document on a microscope and you can see the image to advance for this time but with a valuable technology, too late for the Germans that they had lost the war, but for Otto and his team was his source of income since they used day by day in different fronts where they were send to advise or hire by the countries with a conflict, they never reveal their secrets since part of his formation was retain with this information since he knew that if he fell in some enemy hand could do a lot of damage, reason why a pact between the studious so that way the secret was never revealed since in 1917 had a great failure when the code was deciphered with the well-known and public telegram of Zimmermann.

Comparing the new system with the one before, that code was for kids or very simple, the new system was form by several elements that was almost impossible that only one domain this technic system.

Doing their work took the newspaper and review the content, they received the code in the news phrases of the heading of the day, following their manual they found the code that was translated in the following way in the title of the main page, Germany is in an economic collapse, save your selves; taking this from the coding from the machine said "Team, present in Volta Strasse 25 at 1300 hours to receive the work plan.

Read this, they refer to the codes of date and more detail from there, take out the information, then Otto tired of working a lot and thinking, he tells his friend it was time to leave, and both left the place at late hours of the early rising and like this for six months they kept doing this routine.

The next day, both met in the decoded appointment to receive the perfect classified instructions, one by one, in a book thrown on the floor, where in the first page behind the cover a series of numbers 18.5.22.9.19.1-16.1.7-y.v.-16.1.12-b-16.1.12-v1-u1,s1 so Otto, look on page 26 in the second paragraph the words that where indicated, he reads one by one the message, the same way Erick take the newspaper and read the politic page in the interior heading and there read the instructions, both like a perfect unknown person, finish and mentally memorize each of them their codes and leave in an independent way leaving the newspaper in its place and the book where they found it, there a curious, who was drinking a coffee, saw the book and started scaling off, getting interested he took it with him... It was impossible to leave a trace, no one could decode this, the most unrestricted security system, it was such a grade of perfection that by then Otto and Erick as well as a team of 200 persons can see messages and decoded even in radio advertisement, in the politic speeches and lots of ways, this was the beginning of a German communication system that will take lots of years for other people to decode.

At the end the message after all was that Otto and Erick must attend their closer works, in the instructions of the high power, they were send to a mission in Russia as an experiment and work in the field of all learned in their service, their incursion was very precisely, they must detect the moves of the communism of Stalin and locate the contacts in Germany, since the agitated search of a communist party in Germany that must be neutralized, for this, to get out of Berlin as an engineers in communications from a Blaupunk business to carry out sales of equipment of radio communications to Russia, situation that was their first work disguise, for this, they have a precise system of identity change, they will go as a harmless employees of a German business with their migration documents perfectly executed, they will arrived in Moscow in the Spring of 1922;

The situation in Germany was difficult, so they got all the necessary for such a mission, at the end of their activities, Otto already tired, leave to his live with the look to start in five days his mission with Erick, they say good bye and agree to meet at the date and time in Haupt Bahn of Berlin.

As far as Otto had a stable relation with Hilda, who had been living with her for a year, Hilda beside her beauty, she was very intelligent, and she knew what Otto was doing, one of those early risings, Hilda tells Otto, after a long waiting and a passion encounter of both, she tells him that she was very exciting and she admired him a lot, as much that she wanted to start working in the military special service, when Otto heard that, he gets up from the bed. He stands up in front of the bed and with an upset look and high voice... He prohibits to say that again, he was upset and asked her to avoid telling him that, but she continues, Otto interrupted and tells her, "Hilda, it is very dangerous, and you do not know what you are saying, I can tell you what I can, but is a lot, I won't risk yourself in this."

Hilda answer him, "If is dangerous for yourself, for me is mortal not knowing if I will see you again, if I'm not with you in this, it's better to leave you forever from your life, I love you so much that I can't think of the day I won't see you again, beside this I can stay with you always and if I die, it will be for our love, but I want to be with you, Otto I love you, you tell me that you love me..."

Otto did not respond anything, kept quiet and only looked at her immutable with no expression on his face, cold and with a lost sight.

Otto didn't come back and stayed at the general quarter, he thought that she will desist and will leave from Berlin to come back to her house, he didn't want to hurt her, but without knowing he was hurting her even more with his behavior, his selfishness, his pride, and his demons, his horrors that came back to his head, he was feeling suffocated, trap and the only way was to focus on his work, he felt the need to concentrate himself on something, because he was afraid to hurt Hilda, he loves her, but in that moment he couldn't contain his fears, he was not sleeping for days, only drinking black coffee to stay awake, he knew that by sleeping his nightmares will appear, he loves Hilda and he was not able to tell her... He was strike up, he did not want to hurt her, in that moment his life was taking another direction even though he loves her very much, he has to leave her...

Maybe that's why he run away from her... Or not been included, but he did not count with Hilda's firmness and obstinacy, at that time the women were not allowed in the military non less in the special missions since Hilda already knew some of the militaries that operate in special body and did not take much to get to the higher positions, Otto was very innocent to think that all will end like that and the relation with Hilda will end easily, in love woman at that time was able to do the impossible to be close to him, but as the love was very big, the obsession more than love became a delirium, a caprice, but the worst was not that he left her for other woman, that she was returning to her house with her family and everything is fine, she has everything there, she took another decision and there is how the rancor, the frustration start to take possession that Otto was leaving in that women. His heart hardens...

There she transforms in a lethal weapon that sooner than later she will find him, there was how she arm herself with everything and turned around from a loving woman, self-sacrificing, and merciful to become in the opposite cold, calculating, with no feelings, she cultured day by day, the first option was get out of that apartment in Berlin, transformed in another woman, been his objective to conquest, humiliate and finish with Otto, she has to plan very well and the best way was entering to the stronger and sacred of Otto... His lovely army, from there will start her plan to finish with that love for ones, that how she little by little and level by level between festivities, reunions she gets to the high-est, finally after months of escalade she got an inter-view with the general Friederich Gempp, introduced by Otto himself. Some of other festivities where she was seen without Otto's company and other reunions that the General organized. In one of those festivities and drunkenness the general found her attractive, but as a gentleman he respected an official from his team and did not do anything, even thought he was confuse not seen her with his usual couple, and that took his atten-tion in his interior, since the first time he saw her, he desire her, so that opportunity couldn't be better, the sixth sense of the women never fells, she knew what the General was telling her without words, but now she will take advance to achieve her assignment, and she apply for a hearing with the General, and when he knew her presence did not take him more than 20 minutes in receiving her, and when he saw her a conversation started between them.

"But my dear Hilda, what a pleasure to see you, what a great surprise you have given me."

Hilda with her charming voice, "My General. I'm glad to come to greet you, I have been trying to find the way to see you, I have a subject that I would like to talk to you, since you told last time..."

The General very attentive, he received her with a kiss on her hand, and asked her to take a seat, after that the conversation lasted more than 40 minutes, the general after talking ended inviting her to the mil-itary club to have a drink... After an effusive meeting and a long passion night, Hilda achieve her duty: to be admitted in the special power group, beside her intelli-gence her physical attributes and captive beauty, obtain awaken the interest of such a character, to such grade that she enter and by the end of the decadent German army a woman in that time can perform as an agent and couldn't suspicions interest for an average woman in that time, it was difficult the special preparation, but for Hilda was not like that, she obtain get in the list and train in the time of Nürenberg.

Hilda, very distance from Otto and close to the General and her frustrated love for a decision and scape of Otto, what most hurt Hilda that broke her heart, was the Otto's indifference when ask to be together, to be ignore and leaving her alone that evening in Berlin, but at the same time had the hope to find him maybe to give him her unconditional love or to give him her disdain, something was to happen since both lives depart from an adventure that will join them or separate them forever, already with a little doses of revenge because the treat and the luck of decision and weakness for her, the firmness, hard of heart, selfness for him, Otto had hard heart, his love did not bend him, soon everything was ready for a new battle that he will save, one the love, other one for the hate, other one for the absence and one more for the loneliness everything points and was to happen the moment when they see each other again, but things were going to be different for Hilda and Otto.

We can see with these, how the persons by their decisions and behaviors change or transform themselves since the actions and aptitudes modify their tilt, the course from their lives of all people, that is why nothing is said, nothing is mark, the day by day makes the lives and make the consequences of all the dos of humans. That's why that a second of anger, love, hate, a word, a movement... A thought, positive or negative or the minimum action to the free will, change forever the tilt of the persons.

CHAPTER TEN
THE NEW LABOR

While all this was happening, Heidi Marie and her daughter Ana Marie together with Arthur were trying to get ahead, Arthur visible tired of taking care of the business pine to dedicated to cultivated their garden and decorated, thing that was impossible since he must work, now with more pressure since Johan his ex-employee was a commissioner of the party NSDAP and he was asking for fees and economic help for support of the party, in a gangster way in case he was not getting support since he was oblige against of the German burgess, situation that the owners of business and producers couldn't escape, he has under control already all the promoters of the area and all the employees and workers with power and reason were on his side, without counting that the one who was not agree with his philosophy of the country with the country were not well seen for this group under treat of not getting the support will be punish with aggressive actions against their goods since they knew very well each families from the area, he knew very well that they couldn't deny this help whatever was the way or by protection or just being alien to the new social line that each day was stronger, the NSDAP (National Sozialistische Deutsche Arbeiter Partie) already in the German congress were more representing of them and little by little the German conservator party was minimize, the people were convince of their vote and these make Johan grow even more since not only on weekends was wearing his gray uniform, it was common seeing him every day in uniform and each day younger and older German workers were joining his party and each of them giving a fee convincing that Germany will become free from the oppression from the French, England and all who want to harm their country.

It was intolerable, Arthur was directed by Abraham from Switzerland, who called him to warning of a bigger risk, Abraham and his family knew of the tendency of these party and knew against who they were after that idea from the German people, but Elias, Abraham and Isaac met in Switzerland to talk about the situation and the conclusion of these was that each of them would leave Germany.

It was like Abraham telling the intentions of the party, to this Arthur worries to the point that immediately tells his mother and sister, they were still questioning if this was true, when in that moment, Elias called them to inform that their debt was unpayable and have two ways; lose their property or negotiate a new loan, he did not know if he could cover the debt, to this Arthur begs for time to think about it, situation that Elias Hoffman granted, same one that made the arrangements to freeze the case and leave everything hidden to new times, taking the risk of keeping the records outside the bank to avoid the juridical process that apply, this was the way they were helping the family to get out of this situation.

At that time, the unemployment index was very high, there were no jobs, the best that most people could do was to join the belligerent parties of the moment or get out of the country, some of them start to immigrate to Holland others to Polonia and some more to Switzerland, and the adventures were getting on ships like

hobos and embark to Brazil and some more to Argentina and Chile, these was thanks to years back some
adventure to those countries and have some activities,
the majority were farmers and cattle dealer that start
forming their own work in those countries.

Arthur was mourning of what he did and felt
guilty what he did to his brother, his brother was right
for leaving him there with all the problem... He regret-
ted, Arthur did not have the abilities of Otto, he couldn't
repair the tractors and machinery of the place, they
did not have any employees, the little cattle heads they
had, he has to almost give them away as an exchange
for food, he knew that Johan was close by checking to
see what can he does against him and even worst, he
had the opportunity to send him to jail because what
he discovered, but because his greediness and jeal-
ousy against Otto was greater, now Arthur was paying
the price.

Not much time went away, maybe a couple of
months, when Heidi Marie and her sister Ana Marie
determine on seeing everything lost and go back to
Lucerne, where Mr. Whent was waiting for them, he
was old and asked her daughter to comeback and finish
attending their business, Abraham Hoffman, the same
administrator, now worrier for the situation that Europe
was decided to leave Switzerland, and needed Hilda
to comeback with his father, that's why she took some
belongs she had and leave to Lucerne, meanwhile asked
Arthur to comeback to Switzerland, but Arthur denied it,
since he together with others Germans accept the invitation of Elias and Isaac to go to America specifically to New
York, where they were promising at least a decent job, it
was the opportunity that he was looking for to get out
of the poverty that was declared to his family, it was like
that how Arthur said good bye to his mother and sister
and from there get out to Kiel where he embarks to New

York to taste luck. All this happened without knowing anything about Otto, he was more than lost to them, for Arthur, Otto has lost already that fraternity that his father tries to arouse, no one of the family knew about him, even less the Dölling that knew of their relationship with Hilda, they did not know anything about him neither from her daughter and Otto's mother with all the pain of her heart never knew where to find him. Well, that is the end of the story of this family, that one's again break the unity and the destiny separate them now forever.

A tradition of a family from the German legacy divided by the war, the poverty, situation that the German country was generalize, only some of them could come out, the big industries were desperate looking for exits to survive, the heavy German industry had the minimum necessary to keep operating and like all in general must adapt to the new social change that was exploit, the Vaters Land was listening as a hymn to continue battling for the country, since was almost inexistent, this moments of hesitancy and disillusion for the Germans aloud to propagate more the Nationalism spirit between the young ones, lots of them in their desperation were joining more and more to the democracy movements of the Germany of 1925... The communist was already a treat to the country and the conservators losing power every day; was in this step because the frighten of the communist, lots of people opt to support to the German Nationalism leadership already by Adolfo Hitler, even though his proposes were not well define, in that moment of desperation for any German being able to recuperated their country, the scream of "Germany is first" and "Germany for the Germans," the resentful situation for losing the war give them more fire to the live coal and ashes that becomes later a fire, and inferno to all the Germans.

At this time, Otto receive the instruction to move to Russia at the town of Lipetsk about 300 km from Moscow, place where the Russia army aloud the German pilots create the aviation school as a part of the Abwehr that end and form the Reichs where commanded by Albert Kesselring, who also move all his communication structure, transmissions in a direct army of publicity administration for the Russian army being able to develop the communication technology codify and continue on the perfectionist of codify army information which Otto was already part of it.

When Otto gets to the base where he was going to work together with his partner of codify, Erick Fullmman, will say between them, "Look, Erick! I can't believe it, there are the Fokker D Xlll, look at them brand new! There are Holland, faultless..."

"Otto, looks like you are in a candy store."

"Of course, Erick, this is heaven, there are the Heikel, the Donier, no, no, no! Is incredible! How can this happen?"

Erick answers him, "Where the Versailles treat it not permitted fly in Germany neither to have this, but with this agreement with Russia, Germany continue preparing and generating the new era of aviation; Now will be LuftWaffe... That we belong now..."

"What an observations Erick!"

"Now what, my lieutenant?"

"Excuse me...?"

"Yes, didn't you Know Otto? You will be a lieutenant and will manage a group of trainings. We are the new bosses!"

Erick laughed and took Otto by his arm and hug him, "I can't believe it; I was not expecting this."

"Otto there are some other things that we are going to discover while you enter in this new world."

For that moment, the ransom of the bellicose power and German supremacy were in their hands, and them renew spirit very humiliated in the great war and aloud arise from ashes to impetus and hope of the German country, even these powers were in a temporal exile, the new Germany of the fathers of the country arise in their minds, passing this feeling from one to another German from mouth to mouth and from house to house.

In Germany, the banks continue charging victims in the Rothschild the Warburgs, the Weinberg and the Simons, which Otto's family owes then a fortune, but thanks to the deep friendship of the two families it gain suiting stop the process of embargo and freeze the case until be able to save in another way, this thanks to Abraham and Elias who support to the family in this difficult times, they have the majority of the counts and all these owners were Jewish and between the country couldn't understand why specially to them was unacceptable for those nationalist reveal, however in those days it was agitated the German country disquiet that beside being in the worst of depression of the last 100 years in Germany, with a monarchy dead, the aristocracy that always was wordship by the German army, since the army emanated from there and have their success because the discipline and organization that create the best army of the world and was because the inversion and development that the monarchy did in that moment.

Otto did not understand, until that moment, the depth of all that was happening, he was concentrating to enjoy else again the moment to fly, returning was his passion and everything was not important, in anything happening while he was military and now lieutenant and while he could fly, that was his new opportunity to touch the sky... He feels in the glory... Now as an instructor and preparing himself to receive instruction and arrange his loyalty to the country of his German parents.

In the next days of his arrival, Otto met Vladimir Kreshenko, his homologous for the Russian part, when he met him and shook hands, he felt a cold and freezing feeling, that made him remember his war times, with his penetrate sight and his strong alcohol breath, typical between the Russians, he felt he was a different man.

Once on the airplane field, Vladimir was also a pilot, and as a first stage of coupling, each took his airplane and took off to practice operations and some war technics in which each of them have their tricks, it was spectacular see how the sky furrow and how they made operations, each of them in their way, but demonstrating that both were similar and talented, the more airplane exercises were made between them, a rivalry started to arise between them and Vladimir had certain malice for Otto, like they did not make a chemistry and that was for a long time, at the same time in the communications in the interchange of information, the Germans were superior in the coding of linking and exiting information, but they reserved some other codes that kept them perfectly covered, it was like that, when they went out to their first mission, they had to suffocate in Polonia certain resistant to the call for a revolutionary of Stalin, it was how Otto is assign for an espionage mission, his first mission where he was going to be the observant and coding, Erick was going to be the preforming of decoding instructions and Vladimir as preforming of actions.

A cold morning, Otto with his identity as an engineer of Blau Punk, arrive to the communications center Katowice in Silesia, Polonia, he will did some repairs to the local radio system, that is how he entered in action placing some devices that select a frequency to intercept the communications at that distance, with the goal to obtain information sensible of the Poland resistance, that is how he took out the information, came out of the facilities and going to the field close to the city and there to prepare a transportation, for he already has an airplane ready, some that take off and a series of air photographs and maps that are translated in micro point, to comeback, that will be his transportation. He takes the information place in the message, he codes it and send it through the radio, until there were his instructions, so he finishes his interventions, then Erick received the information and decoded, he meets Vladimir in the center of the city, he leaves a newspaper, asked him for a cigarette to Vladimir and arise the preforming of action.

Erick gets close to Vladimir, "Hello, Good morning would you have a match?"

The dialog starts.

"Yes, here it is."

Vladimir and Erick are closer to the fire and in the moment of giving the fire, they exchange the newspapers, leaving Vladimir the coding one with the precise instructions.

"Thank you, have a nice day."

They both leave in opposite directions, Vladimir was being followed by another Poland agent to follow some clue, this one follows him on the streets of the small city and to a coffee place, there he takes a seat and calls the waitress.

"Waitress, an expresso please."

"Do you want it strong?"

He answered, "Yes, strong (that was the password)."

They couldn't have a mistake and the words were precisely; a mistake in the diction could put it at risk the operation. The waitress comes back with the coffee in a cup.

"Here it is."

In the moment of leaving the coffee in the inside of the cup, after drinking some, appear the number 1224 with the legend since... In the ceramic, this means that he must present himself at the downtown hotel and there, he will deliver the next instructions.

Passing all these Otto had already moved from the city and on his way to take the airplane and get out of that area as soon as possible, since he ignored the instructions of the other one, and the other one did not know the instructions of the next one, all these for not finding some link on the looking of clues, it was how Otto took off while he enjoys the experience of flying, he has to go up to 10,000 feet to avoid being seen or have suspect, but it was almost impossible that some one sees him, meanwhile Otto in between clouds and air was preparing his route flight and goes to Lipetsk to report himself to his official of the Reichwher, where he delivers his report and goes to wait his new instructions, meanwhile his partners waiting, for these times a new airplane has a speed of 180 to 200 km per hour and their autonomy was up to eight hours, while that was happening, Otto was dedicated to train the young German and Russian officials, they were in an instruction, when he saw Erick arriving from the air field and Otto go to meet him.

"Erick... How was it?"

He answered him, "I learn a lot, everything is fine. Was easy, right?"

Otto said, "Was easier than I imagined, but tell me did you know what was the ending of all these?"

And he answered him, "Yes, but we must be careful with Vladimir, that man is something else."

That was the only comment, he did not want to say more, and put himself to update what was going on at the base.

What Otto ignored was that Vladimir finish the job and eliminated the contacts that was in effect the execution of three agents, which end murder for himself, this made possible to end with a cell and proposed of the communism in Polonia and leave free for the Marxist revolution achieved their objective to take this area to their initiated to a great price.

When some days went by and Vladimir integrated in the instruction, they were giving another mission, now air, it was an attack in the south zone of Moscow where a revolt could eliminate to the air resistance of the czar, so they took off and only six airplanes go with an Stalinist emblem, in one of those goes Otto, in the operation, Vladimir gave the instructions and confront the air battle against four arm airplanes, then Otto goes up high in horizontal at 65 degrees ascending and collapse at 12,000 feet, the airplane nose-dive, Vladimir gives the indication of attack, Otto shot parts of airplane wings, joy stick and motor, a wise move in his target... The airplane was unused. Exclaim Otto, the drop of the airplane has been visually confirmed, the pilot loses high and attain to land, Otto according with his teaching affirm his military conviction, knock down airplanes and unused air fleet... According with his German military ethics and the Baron school... But he sees how Vladimir follows to another airplane and was already unused he continue shooting, not to the airplane, otherwise to the pilot, that Otto couldn't believe it, he was saying to himself but what is happening to this crazy man... And he knocks down and makes the airplane exploit and destroy the pilot with his grapeshot, Otto was impacted, then he goes back to base and he gets out very fast from his plane, he is walking ant taking off his jacket, his glasses and coat, and screams to Vladimir, "Are you crazy? What have you done? What's happening to you? You are an idiot!"

Vladimir, with a big smile, and not likening the comments, he answers him, "What is happening little German? Don't you know that is war?"

Otto answers him vigorously at the time that he hits his airplane fuselage, "You know that we are pilots! We fly to unused airplanes and air force; we are not killers and screams at him we are not butchers!"

Vladimir with his macabre smile said, "What is happening, you don't have the guts like us. We are superior."

Otto answers him, "There are not guts, there are orders and ethic even in this. You are a murderer. You are a coward!"

Vladimir screams at him and starts fighting, at that moment arrived the base general and some recruitments and pull them apart. Vladimir was hit on his nose since Otto strike him accurate and that made furious. Screaming he said, "Leave me! Let go!"

The base general of the base arrested them: each of them in a different shack for 24 hrs.

This was starting a grudge that wouldn't stop there, Erick and the other Germans, suggest that Otto won't get in problems, they ask him to calm down and leave that matter there... Then, Otto agreed, there he knew what a merciless Vladimir was, with his stingy feelings and his rock heart. The only important to him was himself.

The days went by, and the missions continue, there were battles, attacks and Otto try to keep his distance, but each time they see each other couldn't cut their sights like challenging one to the other one and behind each sight his macabre smile. Some months went by, the academy was more efficient and achieving the desire objectives.

That was the beginning of a situation that Otto didn't have plan, the atmosphere was tense between the Germans and Russians, but they must be there, they remain receiving orders from one to another side and they achieve with success all the missions, in one of them was to arm an airplane in parts and create a strategy of hiding to scape and a night fly, were the first system of communications and night navigations with a categorical success, both already train were an expert in the subject.

A year went by until September of 1926. Changes were generated in the organization and the course of the story gain finish with the fear of the communist wave in Germany, there were eliminated from the politic German panorama, that gave strengthen to the NAZI party that was not the preference of Otto and lots veterans to be against their aristocracy convictions and conservator. Beside Otto did not understand the reason of the new propaganda anti samite, this was a delicate subject for him since his father and all his family had a long referral, friendship, and fraternity with these persons, was such his worry that try to look for Abraham in Switzerland and was going to check how things were going in the family business over there, that's how he contacts by letter and wait for the answer to this subject.

While waiting for the answer, Otto continues in different assignments of special missions, until one afternoon comes to him like always between beers and cigarettes in a small bar in downtown, it was typical that after work going the tavern to drink beer and vodka in an atmosphere of waitress and of course women. Between beer and beer Erick talk with Otto, "My friend, once again they were looking for me, they send me a telegram, they want us to go to America Remember?"

Otto between laughs and very relax… Answers him, "What is that? I did forget about it; Now do they pay good? Should be a good pay… Ha, ha, ha. I do not think they have the money, so ask them for an advance payment."

Between a smoke of a French cigarette those were his prefer ones, a puff of smoke exhale… Continuing,

"Look since they are insisting... Ha, ha, ha What do you think if we return to Berlin in two months and if they are interested, make an appointment there? And let them tell us what do they want."

Erick answers him, giving Otto some claps in his back, "Of course, Otto. Will do; you are right, let's put down our conditions."

Both laughs, and continue drinking and made a toast, "For our parent's country!"

And lift the jar. At the other side of the bar were the group Russians, when they heard the toast, they turn and to accompany them they toast from far with their vodka.

The day's pass, they continue working and just like they knew return to Berlin to the central court, things were very change in the political, it was very notable the changes in Germany to the agitation for the national-ism was feeling everywhere, mainly with the youth, the new generations did not see the defeat of Germany in the first war.

Otto kind of surprise and feeling very cling to the pertaining tradition, continue with his military proudness, but he sees the others very aggressive with a thirst of revenge very remarkable and blame the Weimar governor as an indifferent and coward republic, instead the promises of a powerful Germany was the convincing of all days.

In those days, Otto was seating during his days of resting and drinking his coffee and his beer in a picturesque tavern and watching how manifestations of young ones in military formations go by singing the German hymn... Woman and even children with uniforms and a red band with a swastika in the middle. Otto gets up to watch that military march and as a difference of other formations and manifestations, he sees how the people stop and celebrate in between a war band and sings, generating a triumphal ambient... He was in that, when a coffee table old neighbor asks him, since Otto was the first time that he was a spectator of that movement.

"Look at that, so many youths and very well train..."

The old neighbor answers him while continuing reading the newspaper, "They do not know what they are doing, they have them hypnotizes."

Otto asks the neighbor, "How is that hypnotizing?"

This one answers him, "Yes, I was part of the German resistant at the first war, I saw the dead and destruction, these young ones are going to the abattoir for sure, the crazy man that they have as a size of what he is doing, he still looking for something, but even him know what he wants, he is sick."

Otto puzzlingly answers, "How is that?"

The neighbor answers him, "Yes, that Adolfo. It's filling with ideas to the people and is blaming the Jewish for everything; it's full of hate and thirst of revenge and wants to use our country as a trap to obtain his dark purpose. I'm telling you who has seen a lot... and all who does not think like him, he considers it enemy. God help us from that sick man, but our luck until now is only a show."

Finishing the military stop and the singing, marching and drums far away... Otto looks at him in between the newspaper, takes a seat and without looking at him says, "You are right, I have seen the same, I have been outside Germany for some time and you can feel an atmosphere like a holy day, but very dark, it doesn't scare me, but I predict that those followers do not know what are they doing."

The old neighbor, put down the newspaper looks at him and says, "If you are a German, you shouldn't allow it, at least the German that I have in my heart, is the parents German, for the work, future, respect, and freedom; I do not believe the story of that crazy man."

Otto answers him, "Yes, it is true, I do not understand what is he looking for, but if he continues like that, is not good for us."

The neighbor said to Otto, "You really are... It's the same. This crazy one is using the hunger, the disillusion, the desperation of the people, there is no job, and he is selling a change in exchange of blood. I guarantee it! The good thing is that I'm not Jewish and I better shot my mouth now, because if I was a Jewish, I will be thousands of kilometers out of here."

In that moment, Otto remembers his friend Abraham, he thought how his family was doing, but refuse to look for them.

He gets up and leave the coffee table, turn on a cigarette and say good bye to the neighbor, "Good luck and protect yourself."

And with a hurrah Germany, he leaves...

Otto was on his way to meet Erick in a restaurant, where serving his prefer food; Schnitzel with potatoes and sauerkraut... Since they were going to meet there and did not have any idea what was the reason, but for him to go there to eat a good plate and his beer, he was anxious.

Arrived at the restaurant, took off his classic hat of short wing, that he loves to use, since his hair starts to fall and his big entries in his fore head were hit by the sun. He gets near the table and found Erick with some foreigners. Very well dressed, with a suit and perfumed...

"Hello, how are you doing, my friend?"

Erick gets up and introduce the two persons that were accompanying him, "Look Otto, he is Mr. Alfredo Reichen and he is Mr. Gustavo Almada, they are coming from Cuba, well Gustavo from Cuba and Alfredo from Mexico."

While they were looking at each other, since the conversation was in German... Alfredo was son of a

German in Mexico and was the middleman who works in a German company and Gustavo contacted him, between translations and introductions. They sit down at the table and start talking.

The exposition was very simple, Gustavo Aldama was a representative of the Cuban governor and was asking for a training of their pilots and fly techniques in his country, they count with a good finance support and by chance they have bought some Holland airplanes, some that they knew Otto and Erick were instructors, these for the fame in the area, they were asking as a personal level.

Cuba at that time was betting on counting with an air force on a great level and opt to look for the best and of course they found them. Erick the astute one for the money took the negotiation and after seeing their plan and project, gets up and ask Otto to sit down in a separate table to outline the operation.

"What do you think Otto, look they are paying us for six months of training the cost of five thousand dollars per month... Is a good fortune and the best of all, now here things are not good, look they have us resting for two months, what about if we ask permission so we do not lose our nomination...?"

Otto answers him, "Of course... I do not see anything wrong, the only thing that I have distrust, is to know if is true or not, you know these foreigners are... Look, only if they pay us in advance, I will take the risk. It can be a trap if they can't pay us, but if it's in advance, we can go safer. Beside it must be clear that will be only flight instructions, and nothing of military or things like that."

Otto clarifies vigorously to Erick, "Sure, we will do it..."

They got up from the table, and go to the foreigners putting the offer in a paper... They analyze it, talking in Spanish between them, meanwhile Otto and Erick getting ready to eat and talk about triviality of them in German, take beer and Otto was enjoying his plate while the others continue talking in a language for them rare. Otto between joking was imitating the foreigners saying uproar to Erick.

"Bla, bla, bla, bla..."

"What a rare language."

And they laugh... While they were listening. Since it was very easy for them to make business like that.

After that, they communicate with Alfredo in German that was a fact, but they were asking them to be ready to go to Cuba in one week.

Situation that made both happy, but first they must give the money before leaving them, and in American currency, by then Erick had an account of time in Switzerland and tells Otto, "If you want, I let you deposit in my account or do you have an account?"

Otto remembers his mother telling him, "No, I will deposit in my family account; I will get it to you, I will give it to you when you have the money..."

After this, Otto now more than ever must see his family and he thought of them in that moment, since they must go on the other side of the world, and he was going to be out for a long time, so he was taking advantage to see his brother and family.

Starting a new course of his life, he goes to Elrmshorn to see if they were there, it was his surprise that no one was there, his house was a Nazis quarter and the biggest of his surprises Johan was the commissioned... When he arrives feeling as owner of his property goes to the enter and there were barracks where there living lots of children and young ones doing paramilitary practices and at the entry some young ones like guards, Otto secretly gets closer and ask to talk with their supervisor, to his surprise that the old Johan and Hans were the captains of the place, they become peal when they see Otto at the door... but they become courageous and with their gray military uniform comes out with six guards well arm to the door and start talking.

"Otto! What are you doing here?"

He asks while standing in front of the house and with an arm on his waist. Otto answers him, "Rather, what are you doing in my house?"

And he begins to get furious, while Johan eloquence and gibe tone said, "Your house? Ha, ha, ha... Has not been for a long time, of course since you are a coward you left all your family and you haven't known anything, but I'm clearly telling you. This is not your house! is of the party. The Zwein (pigs) Jewish took it off and we took it from them. Thanks, that they did not put in jail your mother and brothers, you should give me thanks, Germany recuperated..."

Otto couldn't continue listening anymore and tried to attack Johan. He did not do anything to defend himself when his guards had him down and held him, "Ha, ha, ha, Otto my dear soldier... You are mistaken; you always were when you were able you didn't prevent coward! You should had killed me... Ha, ha, ha, but the best is that I kept everything; I deserve it. Your father never thanks me... Ha, ha, ha."

Otto scream, "Let me go pig, Animal!"

Johan put his boot on his neck and says, "What do you say warm?"

And start to press down against the floor, Otto becomes red and starts suffocating; he laughs.

"This pig German, coward makes us lose the war and our country is like it is, all their fault... That's why, Germany will resurge from the ashes, and this animal's warms will be crush by the Nazi Germany. Look young ones to this coward, look all of you! These riche ones will pay their sin to the country."

While he was exhibiting him with a nosebleed because the fracture Otto did on him, he grabs his boot in his head, "Let him go. Get him out of my sight... Take him out of here."

In that moment, they pick him up and let out some dogs that start attacking him, biting on his leg and arm... Until a whistle of his owner, another Nazi but higher rank, he arrives scream, "Attention!"

In that moment, Otto gets up with difficulty, look at the corresponded boots to the general uniform... He looks at him up... and is recognize, "Otto?"

Otto shakes up, "Yes, I'm Otto von Münster."

The general and all his surroundings were stone. He asks to all of them, "Where is your superior?"

Behind him comes out Johan with the right hand greet, "Heil Herr commander."

"Who do this?"

And Johan answer, "He is a subversive aristocrat anti patriotic..."

When the commander gets closer and strongly hit him in his face.

"What are you talking about imbecile? Arshloch! He is the predilect son of our country, this man is a hero of Germany and you have humiliated! You will be detaining and be in jail according to our criteria..."

He whips him with a lash and make the guards to secure.

"Herr Otto, lieutenant; my apologies, this fanatic stupid is hurt, allow me... We require of the crazy ones to win our battle. Crazy people like this are the one who has giving us the position we have."

Otto incorporates himself and the commander ask to be immediately attended, he enters to the house and introduce himself.

"I'm the grandson of Mark, the best friend of your father. My father and my grandfather always talk to me about your family... I knew that unfortunately fall into economic disgrace, but don't worry Otto; Arthur is in New York, he left with Elias Hoffman and your mother is very well in Lucerne with your sister; they went back a year ago and she left the farm because she couldn't support it... Look things are changing..."

Otto afflicted say, "But this is crazy!"

"Yes, it is."

He answers him, "Oskar Henkel my name, grandson of Mark Henkel..."

He gives his hand and tries to explain to him in detail the exit of his family and before anything, he has the care to ensure everything for the Münster, "And what is this stupid doing here?"

Ask Otto to Oskar, "He is a fanatic and I left him here because he knows the area... The property is seizure by the bank, but mysteriously the payments can't be found... Ha, ha, ha a good play from your father's friends, no one can buy, embargo and even less keep it. The option was borrowing it for some time; once we a get the power we will have enough resources to have our own quarters..."

He turns around and says, "Otto, we will be collaborating maybe the day our Führer takes Germany to the victory... This time."

The dialog continues, "I know you are in the arm forces and a valuable person like you is the kind of military that we are looking for..."

Otto interrupts, "Yes, it is, but I am military by conviction, we are an institution of loyalty, first to our country oath and then to our lovely military institution. I can't understand how you join a party like this, you that has the patriotism in your veins... That is not what Germany wants."

Oskar answer him, "I know, but I'm beating to the young ones. Look around you, look at his sights, look his war spirit. They are a generation that is looking for hope, they are trying to forget that we are losers, the biggest losers... And you better that anyone else know it."

In silence and looking down the floor, Otto answer, "You are right on that, but I'm not in agreement with your publicity, but well... That's you. By the way I want to thank you for my family... I thought to find them here, but I must go to Lucerne. At least I know where to go now."

Oskar answer him giving a clap on Otto's back, "Take it easy, I will be on the look of these properties, like I told you... I promise to you mother."

After this situation, Otto goes to Lucerne, goes with his mother and after a long talk, he gets current on the business situation, he gets inform that his mother is alone, his grandfather was dead months before of his arrival, Abraham and their family left for New York and Arthur his brother was with them, his dear sister Ana Marie was still with his mother, accompanying and helping her in everything, They were in Switzerland and Otto ask them not to get out of there for anything in the world, that he was going to return from a job in America and give the 50% of his job to deposit in his mother account... She gets very touch hugging, kissing, and crying with him... Otto stays there with his family for a week, since his departure was ready for a trip and another new live that maybe now will be a separation forever.

CHAPTER ELEVEN
THE NEW WORLD

It was the end of 1927, everything was cordoned off, Otto moves to Berlin after being with his family and always carrying out in his compromises, pick up some things and according with his itinerary of his new trip goes to the port of Kiel, it was a trip by train, he brings some personal things since his departure in this occasion was to a new continent and was estimating to be there for six months reason why he prepare his suitcase with the essential to be there, in a cautious way, Otto pays the rent of his apartment for eight months and left there more belongings, since the pay was very good, he took with him a good quantity of cash for what will be his job in that land.

Very punctual like distinguish his style and work, gets down the train and in the central station, Otto sees far away his friend Erick that was carrying a heavy load of suitcases, between the vapor and fog of the machinery and the sound of the speakers that tells the departures and arrivals of the trains. He tries to reach Erick... He was at 100 metros, while he was trying to get closer, he suddenly stops but keeps watching his friend and Erick did not notice the presence of Otto yet. Erick stops with a person with a thick hat and interchange a cigarette and starts a conversation, Otto keeps watching that encounter and for Otto's surprise, that person was Vladimir, the same unpleasant Vladimir... In that moment Otto hesitates a little to go in or not, he decides to wait and continue watching, he sits in a bench, takes out a cigarette and waits to see what happens, Otto with the year of training can distinguish lots of things, the lips of both, the expressions and other things were giving the understanding that was about work, instructions and something else than a casual encounter, when Vladimir gives him a small packet to Erick and he takes it unpreparedly, in that Erick gives him an envelope to Vladimir, Otto verify the interchange of something, Otto starts to worry and his mind starts analyzing work and investigation, Otto ask himself, what is Vladimir doing there... Why is he interviewing with Erick? He didn't know anything that must be with the Russians, what are they plotting?

That makes Otto's perception before Erick, minute after, both left and see how Vladimir gets in to one of the trains going out, the destination of that like he was hearing on the speakers was München... In that moment Otto asked to himself München? What must this Russian in München? And see how in the opposite side they were doing the departure of the train and Erick walking faster... that left Otto thinking for a while, after that encounter, Otto gets up from the bench and goes where Erick was moving, and in five minutes Otto reach Erick and finds him...

Erick turns around and initiate conversation, "Hello Otto, right on time my friend."

Otto answers him warmly, "Hello friend... How did you get here?"

"Fine Otto, I just got out of the train."

Otto asks Erick, "Are you coming from Berlin?"

With a little doubt Erik answer him, "Oh yes, of course."

"How come I did not see you getting on?"

Otto question him, and to this Erick response, "Like you see, I arrive a little late, and I was in second class, Damn, I just made it!"

"Good."

Otto answers him, he didn't continues inquiring more, so we continue with the encounter.

"That's good, the good thing is that we are ready, look almost at the door of our new adventure..."

And both give a hug to each other. Meanwhile Otto continues, "Allow me."

And he helps with some suitcases that Erick was carrying; he puts them in his shoulder and tells him, "First let's leave this to the port, get register, then let's go and distract for a while."

"An excellent idea Otto! You are genius."

And give him a pat on his back.

Otto continues making comments, "Look, I know that we have lots of things to talk about, and I would like to talk about this as we leave."

To this Erick answer, "Of course, my friend."

So, they go on and do the agreement and, on the way, they are talking about what they did on their time off, Otto tells him what happened and his encounter with the Nazis when he was in Hamburg and in his father's house, so the same way Erick told him some other moments where he has talking very agreeable.

Otto, meantime was very attentive to everything he was saying and was trying to tally what he saw and was hopping to hear the moment where he mentions Vladimir... He was like that during the evening and that comment never appeared...

With this, Otto begins to suspect something, it was very estranged Erick's behavior, Otto feels some details in his speaking way and like he was different, this was enough for Otto to take precautions, the waiting time ended and they got up to the ship that will take them to such awaiting crossing in the Atlantic to the other side of the world, Otto was feeling like a conqueror, he sees people coming up and equipment and how they bring up the airplane parts, he gets more exiting, when the time to go, he goes to his cabin and from there see how many people in the port are saying good bye to the travelers, listening the whistle of the ship announcing their departure.

This was going to be a navigation in an open sea for at least two weeks of traveling, that will become in another learning, and each time the coast was far away and in less than 8 hours he was in the middle of an imposing ocean, the ship was passing for a calm area and the view was an immense sea to his surrounded sight, it was a truly view, there was nothing else than to enjoy the view while they can, like this was the first days, Otto comes out of his cabin very early and goes to deck in the extreme point of the ship and there he waits and sees how the dawn comes up in his back, it was an spectacular show, it was his favorite place during those days, in one of those days he sees a group of people talking in a estrange language for Otto, of course it was Spanish, since his destiny was the Cuban islands, he intends to listen and comprehend, but he did not understand anything, nothing, he gets desperate. These traveler's partners offer him a big dark and smelly cigarette... He looks at it with strange since the smell was not familiar, he was used to the French cigarettes, his favorites, so the exotic smell penetrating was making him crazy of intrigue...

When one of them see how Otto was strange of what they were smoking, he says, "Hey! Listen blondie... Do you understand me?"

Otto with signs try to interpret what he was hearing. He moves his hand trying to comprehend and say, "Ich verstehen es nicht... (in German he did not understand)."

"But listen my blondie Is because you are German? Look man, I have something here that you have not tasted in your life, this is pure life."

172

Showing him a cigar, and their partners gathering there were laughing of Otto's amazement and the guy says, "Look my blondie, come here, taste this, since it looks in intriguing to you, then taste this man, give a puff of smoke."

And he offers the cigar with his right hand, getting closer to his hand while with signs and mimics invite him to taste it, "Give a puff of smoke, so you will know what is good in your life."

Otto takes it, look at it and between laughing and strange, he puts it in his mouth and gives a puff of smoke, meantime the Cubans were watching waiting for the blondie reaction...

"Look man, what do you think?"

Otto gives the cigar a blow and cough repetitive, but doesn't let go of the cigar, he gives a second blow and with a smile kind of nervous and relax... Moves his head... to the Cubans...

"Gut... Gut... Sehr gut..."

The Cubans say to him, "It's good my soul, look you are red what's happening? Looks like you have like it."

They look to each other and laugh of the moment. The laughs won't wait, Otto in a breath exhale the smoke and his eyes become big, like trying to eat the flavor of the cigar. The Cubans gathering there continue slowly, "This is living, is life."

And Otto repeats, "Life... Ha, ha, ha... Gut."

He raises the cigar up. The Cubans say slowly, "Good. Is good Havana, Cuban..."

Otto tries to repeat, "Good... Havana Cuban... Good..."

The Cubans were celebrating that Otto was repeating in Spanish "Bueno... Bueno... Habano... Cubano..." With his German accent.

After a while his friend Erick came, that was more training in the Spanish language, he joins the group

that were laughing and exchanging words in Spanish...
Between them staying little by little and integrated in
the Spanish language that for them was complicated
and more with the letter was very complicated to pronounce, one of them was telling them that looks like
they have spiders in their throat... And all were laughing of their accent of the German in the ship... It was a
funny situation but at the same time a way to know little
by little that new culture call American, beside that they
were very different to them in their food and dress, since
the Cuban group that they met were the negotiators
and the secretaries of the most important company of
the island, for that time it was an island with a powerful
economy and located in a very important place in the
known world economy since their production of sugar
and other drift products were generating lots of demand
on others markets, these group of Cubans were powerful
economist and spend big quantities of cash in buying
what their bosses ask, cars, jewelry, decorations, furniture, glass ware, it was amazing the fortune of items this
Cubans brought, it was how they came to know each
other and by the middle of the trip... It was a comradeship
very strong, of course the dinners... The dawns and by
the nights, the talks with cigars and rum... It was a scene
never seen before and more when they knew that these
German were ex-combats, their image change and were
consider very important for these Cuban group that were
admirers of these great war aces... What made them feel
even more comfortable and safe of their destiny.

Otto and Erick were feeling like never... Admire
and valuable and even were attended like kings in that
crossing that was in days to conclude... And without
more, Otto in the deck of the ship, was anxious to get to
his new adventure. With all the talking about that exotic
island was very impress to wait to arrive to see with his
eyes what he has been told, the moment arrives, it was

almost six in the evening, it was a hot evening of the summer of 1927 the month of August, immediately you can feel the wind heat, the clothing feels sticky, Otto couldn't stop sweating, it was incredible that weather so different, he was feeling suffocating, he has a kerchief that be using constantly, but it was an incredible view, for first time he saw those tropical trees called palms, an exuberant vegetation, it was like a paradise, while he was getting closer to the port of Santiago de Cuba, place where this ship arrives and where they disembark will take place, a beautiful bay, never seen such a view, was his first experience in this new world and was about to disembark in a paradise.

Arriving to their destination, a welcome group of people very well dressed accompanying for some militaries, they were welcome by Alfredo Reichen and Gustavo Aldama themselves, the same that made the contact in Germany, it was like that how they were welcome and took them to a car to Havana, to accommodate them in the Regina Hotel, where was located one of the best casinos, of course a casino, never in Otto's life had imagine a place like that, never seen a lot of luxury and abundance, it was impressive, while getting out of the car a well dress bellboy like a military takes the suitcases, he get surprise by the color of his skin, he never seen something like that... It was very different, and it was mutual the differences, the bellboy ask him to follow him in another different language, it was English.

"Welcome to Havana, please follow me..."

Giving the welcome the bellboy, and asking them to follow and with his hands making the signs to follow him, to this Otto respond, "Ich verstehen es nicht... Aber Ich..."

Alfredo interrupts, "Follow him Otto, he is telling you to follow him."

This in German...

Not known by Otto, he was hoping to hear Spanish, but he was surprised to see that they were talking in that language, to Otto's surprise, Adolfo gets ahead and talks to the bellboy in Spanish and tells him, "Wait, my friend, these blondies are not Americans, they are Germans, let me translate."

The bellboy answers, "Very well my blood... I will be telling you slowly, so you can understand me, meantime keeps following me, because these blondies look like tired men."

Once at the hotel reception and after going by the casino, which was luxury decorated, from the hallways, with beautiful squirrelfish, the furniture brought from Australia, and the paintings like a museum, little by little, step by step were drawing in his face the admiration of that new world, that he never imagine, finally they get to the room 414, he gets in the room and after the bellboy leaves his suitcases in the room, he extends his hand, Otto estranged thought that he was very friendly and very kind, that he was giving his hand for dismissal, when Otto gives his hand as a sign of gratitude, but the bellboy while he was shaking says, "No, no my blondie..."

And with mimic indicates that he wants money... Coins, to this Otto indicates...

"No, no... No Gelb... No Gelb..." And took him out of the room with a smile. "Danke... danke..."

Closes the door and stays for seconds admiring that room.

Otto throws himself on the bed that looks like it was floating in the clouds and falls deeply a sleep... Until next day.

Very early about 7:00 and on time, he is ready at the hotel lobby, there he meets his friend Erick, and after a pleasant conversation and stories of their experiences of their arrival to this enigmatic and beautiful city of Havana and the most exciting, everything was new for them, in that moment the arrival to take them to their new job.

When driving by the city, it was evident the glamour, seeing lots of movement, coffees, restaurants and the beach, a beautiful beach with white sand with a deep blue, beautiful Caribbean blue that impact the eyes of these Germans before their amazement and beauty of that sea that never in their life imagine even though the temperature was evaluating, they were admiring on their way the vegetation, the palm trees and beaches while they were getting far to the air field, that little by little a esplanade was discovering in the jungle, like an adventure, there in that place you can see the imaginable the hangars that came out in between the jungle, decorated by the tropical forest, it was typical that the houses there have their roofs covered of dry palms leaf or something like that, so different of what he was used to.

They didn't let time pass much when they got ready in their new job, they are introduced to their students where they will be dedicated to train the next eight weeks of work, during the introductions was remarkable the importance of these instructors and anything had to be consider in count, it's like how Otto and Erick do their thing, because of the language, they assign Raquel Oliva, a translator that will work on interpreting to clear misgiving during the process of instruction, some that belong to Alfredo's team, and some that was well selected to work very close with them.

All this was a smoke courting, since Otto ignore the true mission behind this innocent contract of training, there was already an international organization supported by the new groups and operating current where the communist were and the anticommunist web that was forming an attack team in America, who has their base in San Antonio, Texas and they were supported by democratic current from the United State and England governments, in the other side was the group that was supported by the new born NAZI party same group that was left structuring during the Germany of the Keiser that intent strategies allied extra territorial and they can expand the Germany territories or having some kind of support during the first world war to stablish their bases in America and count with the great oil resources, which they will monopolize other countries and Germany was very attentive since after the Versailles trade was very limited and with big commercial obstructions for many products, so it was necessary to look for alternatives so for that reason they were dismember by the American group, it was like that weaving a new web where in this moment looks like they all were for the same team, but according to the pass years a series of changes and decisions were taking different ways.

It was not strange, that the translator, who has impressionable physical attributes, the first that captivates Otto, when he sees her, he gets mute, Erick got fascinating to see such an extraordinary beauty, exotic, her skin cinnamon color, her big black eyes, even her height was not unusual of about 1.65, her proportions were very different, with a firm breast and well form, her hips that didn't let rebound her African descendance with a mix of native, with an trace of Europe aristocrat that makes a sophisticated beauty, exotic and totally unique.

This woman in little seconds was the center of motivation, captivating in all the attention and the interest to learn the language of these Germans that were perplexed before such an unusual island beauty. Beside all her beauty physical attributes, she was a happy woman, cheerful and very intelligent since she notices that her charm made miracles on the men, that was sufficient to start a work adventure and a personal relation that will have their consequences.

It was how that day ended the journey after a hard work of training, in a theory way, there were some of the planes that will integrate the Cuban lane that were form of some military airplanes that were obtaining by the Cuban government, it was such a thrust in that time Cuba has, that was one of the first American nations on forming a commercial airline, this thanks to the big winnings that they get for the big productions of sugar cane, refineries and the most important the production of rom at industrial way, that make to break out a strong industry and economic growth never seen in those latitude, this attracts itself the industry of the casinos and all that goes with this kind of emporiums.

After that day, Otto and Erick go back to their hotel, but before they are received by their host an invitation to a party night in the same hotel, once in the hotel, Otto and Erick initiate a conversation where the first stage of the plan that already Erick had prepared.

Now in their language, in the lobby while they say good bye from the persons who took them back to their hotel and from the beautiful interpreter, "Otto, I was dying to tell you, did you see the interpreter?" Erick said euphoric.

Otto amaze, but more reserved in their comments, answer him, "Well yes, she is an imposing t, I never seen anything like that..."

Erick says to him, "You are making her restless, I told you Otto, see? We must take advantage, we are in paradise and the best, they are giving us a party, I feel very waterlogged."

Erick was telling and Otto answer him, "It's too good to be real, let's see Erick, I have been observing you, you know we are what we are, and you have not given me in all this time the real reason for this mission until when?"

And raising his voice he asks, "Tell me right now what's it?"

And he looks at him straight in his eyes, to that Erick answers him not happy with his characteristic mystery sight, "Do you want answers? Here we go your answer: Otto, I inform you, that I have been named commander, now I will be your supervisor, in a while you will receive your instructions. For now, you are no longer a lieutenant..."

He responds to this, "What?! Are you demoting me?" And in a joking tone continues, "What are you going to do? I do not have anything in writing and why was I not informed?"

With a firm voice, he says, "Otto, it won't be like that, on the contrary, now you will be a Capitan of strategies and you will be at the front of the group of foreign infrastructures..."

"What is that?"

Ask Otto puzzling, to what Erick answers, "You want answers? Germany has established a pact with the Russians looking to establish a secret commercial bond and protect the interest of Germany, we found that America will help us in this project, they are recruitment more elements that little by little will give us the power that our country is looking for..."

When Otto interrupted him, "But Erick, let me understand what you are saying... Tell me one thing Erick, Are you already in some party? Aren't we already under the order of the German Freikorps?"

Erick answers him, "Otto yes, we are to continue working for the Freikorps, but now the congress is majority of the NAZI party and we are receiving instructions and are changing our original plan, now we have a new boss, you will receive the new instructions."

Otto very opposes answers, "But those rebellious can't get one's own way... I do not agree."

Erick says to him, "Otto, you are military and belong to the arm force as an institution of our Vaters Land, now we must obey whoever it's to be, the nation is demanding us and if the country practice their majority of rights, that is our guide, what the democracy gives us we will be there defending our country, not important the color or faction, the important is Germany."

"You are right on that."

Otto answer and calmer, he continues, "Look Erick, we will do what you indicate, but the Russian are very strange, Why the Russians? And who is on their side in this operation?"

Erick answer him, "You will know... Meanwhile you will soon receive a coded telegram, there you will find the answers, more than I know, remember that a lot of information you will have and I will have to complete it, we must continue as a team, this could be complicated, we are not in our country and we must take care of ourselves very much."

"But come on Otto, meanwhile take advantage of the occasion, and let's enjoy it."

He took him by his shoulders and direct him to his room and between worldly talks and trying to distract Otto, insist a lot on the translator, telling him before saying good bye and prepare himself for the event.

"Otto, think in that Raquel, she has not stopped watching you makes her restless."

In between jokes Otto answer him, "Well, what do you want? I feel a goddess here... Will see, I assure you that won't go too far." And both laugh.

That night no one knows neither Otto and Erick what will happen to that party, since they will acknowledge, they were going to live, experiment and the decisions they will take will determine what course of their new lives.

Otto, when entering his room, discover in his room when to turn on the light a packet that was in his bed, Otto intrigued, took that packet and try to see the sending or something, this packet was not containing anything with a simple wrapping paper, so very carefully he starts to open, it was a wooden box with a key with a red ribbon in one of their plots and stick in it an inscription, logically has a code, which he immediately saw and started to de code and discover the message, this message says:

The high command of German Abwher and the new military institution has taken a new unique general control of command that belong starting the date of 22 of August 1927 to the dependency of the German congress, which dictated the obedience and respect to the air and naval German army forces establish in decree... End of message... Must open the contents of this box where you will find your instructions and new nominations.

After that, Otto opens the box and starts looking document by document and see the instructions of that information and where at the end is demanded to destroy the material and store in a code the important parts and eliminate the elements that were soliciting.

Otto follows exactly according to instructions each part, there he notice that what Erick told him was true and saw his work plan and his strategy was delicate, maybe was the most important mission he ever had and even more for being far from his country, Otto felt touched to know that Germany was entrust an important mission for his nation and he was feeling proud of such an assignment, that in this moment he will have the opportunity to show his loyalty to his country once again and now with the possibility to give exalted results.

Once he finish that moment, he destroys the information according with the orders, after that, he starts to get ready and take a shower to be presentable at the dinner at the hotel, which he was invited, didn't take him much time, when he was ready, gets out of his room and he was another person, he was preparing all his plan according to the instructions given and he was calculating all his movements that he will do, in his mind were forming scene and actions to develop his plan, walking more automaton and absorbed, goes down to the hotel lobby and stays disconnected, until suddenly he received a clap on his back, was Erick who was waiting for him. Otto was surprised and says to him, "What's happening?"

Erick answers him, "What? Aren't you here, in this paradise, look let's go to that party for dinner to taste the flavor, the room very popular here and the women... Let's go my friend, cheer up...?

After this short conversation Alfredo and Gustavo arrive with four beautiful Cubans among them was Raquel, the one dressed beautiful with a tight dress distinguishing her physical attributions since Otto was impacted, after an eloquent smile at each other again, they left to the dance...

It was a place with live band, with tropical music with a candescent rhythm, with the bongo, cumbias and Antillean rhythms, Otto and Erick were delighted in the place, everyone looking at them and greeting them and wishing them the best, the moment of the room and a good cigar and music was there, between screaming of euphoria and laugh heartily, the guest, the hosts, everything was a great happiness, it was a spectacular night, incredible an expected end crowning all that hit, rhythm, dance, botting bodies, kisses, ending on the bed of his room, where Otto lived the Caribbean experience passion love, truly hit, truly passion with no place for mantle, just passion, wild passion that awaken that beast that took the most sublime, the sweetest that Raquel youth gave him, being that night the most sublime that Otto have ever live that day.

Same way Erick, in his carnal unrestraint, was a carnal enslaved, a captive of Magdalena, the friend and partner of Raquel, that with Otto made him live an experience that will mark him forever, He never knew what love was, the passion of an Antillean woman to all his expression, the fire of their looks of the carnal desire was the one, the illusions of the sense took him to the limit until lost in his own worldly pleasure.

The night went by and the day trap them, awaking Otto and Raquel among the sheets, the sun that woke them up late like mid-day, Otto try to incorporate himself with a terrible headache, he gets up nude from the bed and in between the silk sheets and white pillows that make the contrast of the skin color of the beautiful Raquel, that lay nude over the bed... While Otto looks at her, she open her eyes and with an irresistible smile indicate with his arms to come back to her lap and retake their subject, the passion that still have pending for stealing the heart of Otto... Otto couldn't resist and they remain this Sunday together all day, they eat passion, love and lots of water and coffee... Until Otto fell deeply sleep.

That occasion was used by Raquel in the total unconscious of her recently captive prisoner of passion, she gets up quietly and start looking that mysterious box that Otto have receive, she takes out some documents and exchange them for other ones with other instructions, she takes photos of other documents and silently dresses up and leaves the room, it was night already of that Sunday. Raquel goes to the hotel lobby, and there was Vladimir, waiting and welcoming her with a kiss, she gives the information and gets out from the hotel together.

Next day, very early, Otto incorporates himself and sees that Raquel was gone, he wonders, with a hung over caused by the rum and all the excess he had... He tries to incorporate and after a good effort, goes to the shower, gets ready and prepares to be at his new day to his schedule activity.

Already at the lobby, Otto waits for Erick, which was in the same condition than him and both give each other courage to continue but not before telling each other how they did and the enjoyable and exciting of the night before, that was the talk during the way to the airfield.

Once on the field and after some good black coffee and hydrated, they prepare for a first practice in the Cuban air, for this Otto ask the mechanic team to prepare the airplane, but he will fly only to avoid some disgrace and must verify the conditions of the wind, weather, current, etc. It was how Otto prepare himself, dressing with his traditional uniform of the freikorps, without the official insignia since they were working for the Fokker and for other country. Once ready in his airplane, prepares his take off.

For those dates, they were tasting a communication system in short wave that he was trying to taste to receive air instructions, Otto who knew about this necessity prepared quick in the airplane, it was like that he prepares and start the transmission, logical this one come in German and logical in the radio he hears Raquel, and that motivate him very much.

"Here base, testing transmission..."

Otto answers, "Go ahead, strong, and clear."

"We are waiting for permission to take off, wait two minutes."

"Informed and waiting for permission to take off..."

In minutes is given the go to take off and Otto speeds up to take off, until that moment Otto did not have any idea the show was about to start, he picks up his airplane and like getting out of the jungle the airplane elevates and suddenly the most beautiful scene, the turquoise blue ocean with a green tone and the contrast of the beautiful white sand that contrasted with the white of the break waves in the beautiful reef and little by little takes elevation and Otto is amaze of the beauty of the place so he elevates to six thousand feet to do an inspection around the island and for more than one hour examining the condition of the flight, the current, but for Otto it was an incredible experience to feel the fresh wind with all their flavor, Otto was amaze to see that air show, flying and feeling the experience unique air in such latitude, since he kept like that during the flight until he receive instructions to come back to base and to take all his outcomes.

He lands in between the jungle in that beauty esplanade decorated by the forest of palms and to some metros from the beach, like falling from the sky Otto lands the plane.

When Otto arrives, he starts to transcript the information and start to code the maps that at the same time according with the instructions he sends by close coding by telegram to the base in Berlin where the information was received, Otto did this according to the instructions he has received, but what he did not know was that the code was re-transmitted to the same Leningrader, that Otto ignore it.

Meanwhile Erick according to his instructions goes to deliver a special information to the local agents, same that has the purpose to detect the possible risk of security of an eventual position of their work equipment, that they already were preparing in Belin.

Days went by and Otto as Erick initiate the subject of the training of the cadets and commercial pilot, in a routine process but precisely.

Not before trying the first amphibian airplane seen by them, was part of their mission, to do this test, review the engineering, the aeronautic and all relating with this kind of airship, incredible can land and take off from any aquatic superficies with less than 20 cm of wave, there was taste in a natural pond that look like a lake or river... All a success...

But at the end of each journey, it was a romance more than a friendship between Otto and Raquel, different than Erick that he has one after another woman... To such a grade that Erick graves from Otto telling him to have all the woman that he can while he can, Otto did not listen to him, was determined to continue with Raquel.

The time pass and that romance of both have become a real trap for Otto, he did not know what was coming, but before concluding his training activities, he was about to send his last packet of information in his room, when he notices a detail in the way of arranging his documents. Otto has the custom of arranging by position and size the same as well as some colors, situation that for any person should be indifferent the arrangement, but part of his training was to be very observant, in the last transmission, see that the documents were not arrange like he left them last time, he tries to remember and because his photograph memory and underline his memory remember that in fact they were always arrange different, he sees by coincidence the times that Raquel was with him... He always fell sleep and Raquel leaves, but remembers in dreams how she always before leaving she sits at his desk, looking like she was dressing up and getting ready, he did not take much interest in that, but when he sees that arrangement of his papers, took his attention a lot to such a grade that he says to himself... Can't be possible... I don't believe that Raquel, went by his mind the possibility that she could be interested in those documents... But he didn't stop there his normal paranoia because his way and the type of work, he laments and was hopping not being true what he was imagining, it was like that how he transmits the information not before placing a test of what he suspects.

Next day, Otto initiates his investigation and suspects, he doesn't say anything to Erick, since what he saw in Kiel and did not tell anything what he saw with Vladimir, that disquiet him even more, he was also knowing Erick's insisting with Raquel, like he prepares everything for Raquel to be with Otto, he has a lot of suspensions, and the detail of his documents alarm him. He arms himself of coolness through the end of the day, when he was getting out work, he comments to Raquel on his last days and he must work and was tired. Raquel told him that she will relax with him for a little while and will accompany him to his room, Otto agreed and aloud to pass all that dejected between them in those encounters, he simulates felling sleep and he locates himself in a way where the bathroom door had a mirror that was exactly on the documents that he has them already arrange in a specific form, but he change two positions and if it was taken and put it back, only knowing the position and the mark of two letter will indicate that were move or taken.

It was like that how Raquel enters and does her traditional arrogates, take pictures of the documents in front of Otto's look, he gets cold... But immobile he notices that Raquel is working for someone else.

She leaves the room, suddenly Otto incorporates himself and dresses up, secretly goes after her what out her knowing, Otto follows her... Secretly, Raquel does not know she is being followed, greets some people in the lobby and continues walking, Otto follows her, she gets out of the hotel and near a park across the hotel, Otto follows her... When she arrives to the other side of the park, she is welcome by a person... Otto goes in between the bushes to see who it is... and from far he sees Vladimir... Otto gets astonished... Once again, his suspicious were becoming real... He did not have any-one to trust... And go back to the hotel... Otto didn't sleep that night thinking what was going on, he was afraid the information fell on enemy hands, it will be his end... He applies the contingency, he transmits the last load of data and changes the password of the final security code and transmit an alternative emergency code, with this the central command will be advised that they are being caught.

Finishing his work Otto, next day he starts to say goodbye to all his Cuban friends, Erick was there, and he was not leaving until next week, but at last he sees Raquel, more beautiful than ever, Otto was looking at her and admiring her, seeing her his heart accelerates and smelling her perfume, the smell of her body that were his lots of times. He sees her different, bur feeling her more than ever in an encounter feeling of passion and betray, it was a horrible feeling for Otto. He couldn't believe that she stole his heart, and did that to him, Otto couldn't feel more stupid to fall to a such simple situa-tion of a delicate mission expose by his passion. How could I feel, Otto repeats to himself each second, how to justify the love he already feels for her and the pain for the betrayal where he was a victim of.

He is very serious, looks at her and hugs her, but doesn't tell her anything, he leaves in silence, Raquel wondering... Try to interpret his silence, Otto leaves the place and does not look at her eyes, he looks down and in the last intent Raquel stops him, he does not turn and she starts sobbing and a tear comes out from her face when noticed by Otto has discovered her. Otto walks faster and does not turn...

She screams to him, "Otto... What's happening? Otto! Answer me!"

Otto saw her from the side and says to her, "Forget me, do not make me turn."

She tells him accepting and understanding that she has been discovered, "Let me explain to you please, Otto... I know I shouldn't involve myself in my feelings... Forgive me..."

Otto answers her, "Leave me, I must see what have you involved me in, I can't think of the risk I have been in."

She continues following him, screaming at him, but Otto did not turn. Raquel continues trying to reach him and screaming at him.

"Stop! For heaven's sake... Stop... My love..."

Otto answers her almost running and getting up in the port to the vapor ship that will take him to Germany, "I do not know why you did it, you have your reasons, is better not to talk about it, I do not want to compromise you more... And I do not want to know..."

Raquel had stop at the embark door for not carrying a boarding pass, from there Raquel scream stretching her right hand like trying to reach him, "Otto... Please, listen to me!"

Otto didn't turn around, continue walking and got in the ship; but when he enters to the deck he falls and starts crying next to the embark door. Raquel continues screaming, but her voice at that distance was inaudible to Otto's ears. She screams in German, "I'm expecting a child... Your child!"

She repeats it and repeats while screaming, "Do not leave me, I love you. Forgive me Otto... I love you..."

Those were her last words that she said to him and when she finishes these, the ship initiates the open sea crossing to Hamburg. Otto cried for some hours in the same place where he fell, he stays there until the ship slowly crosses the Gulf of México and the Cuban island was far away. When it was crossing the sea, Otto left to his cabin, and he falls again until the arrival in Hamburg port.

He kept locked in all weeks, working on decoding and building a strategy to counterattack, he stays generating a plan to protect himself and his information and discover once for all the kind of enemy he was against and the consequences of the complot which he was already prize. During the traveling, he only eats the needed, he was morally destroyed.

He was settled to get out of the island and finish his mission: in betray.

Meanwhile, the days in the island pass with the absence of Otto: Erick was preparing all the plans to move to México, Vladimir and Erick were working for the secret service of Russia, which has an expansion plan to generate communism in America.

Even though Erick was German, he receives big quantities of cash to give information of the German plans: this intent to ally with México to obtain the resources most wanted: the petroleum, since a problem of blocking the supply to Europe, which Germany will maintain present in the commercial operations; giving information of the quantities of extract crude and it destiny's that Germany register to be able to calculate the moment needed and start their project; that in those days the congress should approve to make contacts and buys to México, and besides of the hiding intentions of being in America since there were expanding intentions from both parties, from the communist as well as the Germans.

On the other hand, Raquel continues her job, generating the sending information plan to the Russian agent team commanded by Vladimir; however, days after Raquel tells Vladimir that she is pregnant from Otto, Vladimir starts avoiding her and maintain exclusive job relation, since the news was not well taken. Raquel stays with the hope to see Otto again someday and while that happens, her pregnancy continues until she gave birth to a boy, which she names him Otto in honor of his father. She raises him by herself knowing that someday he will meet his father, their life went on until the time comes to give him that opportunity.

Meanwhile, Otto already in Belin, arrive to a new world, everything was different; the people look more tranquil, but still was the feeling the financial crisis that makes lots of Germans took their families to abandon the country and migrate to other places: France, Poland, United States, South America (mainly Argentina and Chile).

Otto delivers to his headquarters the detail information of his mission, making observations of the complot that he discovers and which the high-ranking officer were aware. Also, he delivers the microfilm of the island overfly, information of natural resources and the experience of the new airplane amphibious Fokker which successfully can take off from the water. This airplane was the pass version tested in Cuba and obtained for the first airline of this same nationality for commercial use, but the plan to create a smaller version of two markets, which does not deliver to the German air force, because the denial of the Versailles treaty. His reports were giving surprising results, this one, specifically include all the details of the regional operation, the where and how it was getting the information, Otto delivers the information seal and with a new security code, which was given to the General Walter, his supervisor of this operation and asks him, "Lieutenant Otto, or should I say... Capitan? Corrected, yes, Capitan. If you don't know, you have a new rank and congratulations."

Otto accepts the salute and thanks him saying, "It is for me a great honor to serve my country."

The General continues, "Things have change already in our country; I would like to set ahead a little since also will be changes in our structure because we have a strong resistance to lose control of our arm force, the NAZIS groups are pressing a lot in the congress, and they are doing some changes in the constitution even in the congress."

Otto asked, "What is this about?"

The General answers him, "I know you are loyal to the country, medal on several occasions and struggle for cause, but... We have changes. I will ask you a question," giving a pause, "Capitan," looking at his eyes attentively, "Do you know Heinrich Burning?"

After a moment of silence, Otto answer, "Depending what do you want to know about him."

The General says, "Just tell me if you know him or not."

Otto answers, "Yes, I know him."

The General answer him, "Well, he is an old friend of mine, and he is fighting to maintain the power in Germany; we are losing the battle against those reveals awful NAZIS."

Otto answers, "Yes, I know him, he was a friend of my father's family. He was born in Münster and is a great economy professor. What does it have to do with this?"

"Well, I just want to know what side you are on, there are changes and I want to know where to find and how to arrange my filing; I have lots of information privileges and there are going to be drastic changes in this country during the next five years. Be prepared, for now be dismiss, I can't talk more for now. You have two weeks off to rest and the country thanks you for your work."

Otto answers him, "I don't know what are you trying to tell me with this, but if it's better like this, there is no more to say."

Between the lines I understand the deep of this, Otto says good bye with the military salute and leaves.

The situation was very candescent in Germany. Otto was not only between two fires, he was in between three fires: the Russians, the conservators of the Weimar republic and the Nazis... all very dangerous. He gets out of his quarters and goes to his apartment in Berlin, after the crossing, Raquel's betrayal and now this news, Otto couldn't fall sleep and stays for three days again inside locked in and waiting for instructions of his new mission.

Without knowing, Otto little by little memories of the war came to him. The inferno that torments him starts to come alive in his head... And none the less were mixing with a frustration feeling for Raquel and for Erick, his friend. Try to put together the ideas, but was impossible, the nightmares start to fill his head. Trying to distract his mind, he starts to investigate everything that was happening, and he starts to discover that the worst panoramic was eminent, discover the real intentions of the NAZI party... Otto was astonished that much greediness and desire of power disguise with the laudable promise to rescue, visualizing a catastrophe to his lovely country.

It was how Otto culminate his deductions and possible exits since he was an eminent target. He starts to develop a schizophrenia that turn him irritable, accompany with a persecution delirium base on his deductions. All this make him to lose confidence in the people and ending on becoming a solitary man.

After several days of being locked in, he gets out and goes to a hiding place in a close forest of Berlin, in the city of Erkner. He dedicates to wait and think on what he needs to do. He stays there for some time receiving new instructions; almost uncommunicated with the world, except by his superiors, he did not call his family, even to his mother for the fear to be intercede or related, to protect his mother and brothers. He decides to maintain anonymous for a while, it was such a delirium, that he maintains that profile for the rest of his life. A radical change and permanent consequences in the conclusion of this story.

CHAPTER TWELVE
PHASE 4

After being retired and hiding for a while, Otto a little more tranquil dedicate himself to observe how the days went by in a small town of Erkner, to eat well in their picturesque restaurants in front of the regional train terminal, and was like a mechanic for some days, repairing tractors and several farm machineries, he did this to distract himself more than necessity, but attending the radio and the newspapers. Did not let go more than three days without checking the media, always to Berlin news, waiting for instructions, depending on what he should know when to present himself to his job again on the base. In this form, two weeks become two months.

In a picturesque town with a about 5 thousand habitants, but was very beautiful for Otto, but it was most beautiful in the evenings at the side of the river Flankensee, where he rows in a little boat and listening the ducks and birds. It was the only thing that calm his anxiety and his turbulent relapses; he lies at the bank of the river on the grass or sometimes load the boat and stays there contemplating the blue sky, remembering his passion: to fly. Remembering the beauty, it was to fly, and deep breathing the smell of the water that was rebooting from his boat, is was the most beautiful staying there until he gets tired. It was his way to find peace.

After some placid evenings by the river border by a forest that between the fable and the sounds evoke a symphony of a tranquil sound, with the branches and the soft wind that fondle his face. Otto closes his eyes and transport himself to his beautiful home... like this beautiful lake... Once tranquil Otto went in front of the small Rathouse (local city hall) that was there, bringing him memories of his childhood and that one time his father took him there to a property of the Hohenzollen. The aristocracy at that time was very distinguish and was familiar to be in one of these places. Otto only goes in front and lets his memories work in his mind... It was one of those moments, when news in the newspaper interrupts his tranquility: The 80 % of the German congress was belonging to the Nazis force. It was a matter of couple of years to finish with the conservative congress and parliament's traditions.

Otto hurries up, took his belongings, and moves to Berlin; boarding the train, but before with a sigh says good bye to that beautiful place. He turns and with a look gave a farewell that could be everlasting...

Once in Berlin, goes with the general Walter, when he arrives to his office, the secretary tells him to wait because he was busy, the form of attending in that place looks like mainly, like office lawyers. He sits in the small waiting leaving area, and while being there, he hears a familiar voice, when the door opens, he finds with surprise Erick getting out of the office, Otto was surprise very much and immediately gets up; the general ask him to come in and at that moment, Erick very serious extends his hand to Otto, but he did not receive and went by directly to the General while getting to the office. Otto was waiting for Erick to leave, but to his surprise the general asks him to stay, Otto couldn't believe it and being left speechless. Inside his paranoia, he thoughts that this was more serious than he imagines, he tries to contain his emotions and not showing distress, something he was well train. Erick gets closer and with not saying anything, but with a light smile in his face, was trying to tell Otto to take it easy, but Otto got in a defensive position. The general asks both to take a seat.

That scene was desperate: Erick and Otto together... Couldn't believe it.

The tension scene was interrupted with the general saying, "We must see this subject as an urgent manner. Otto, we can't permit this situation; we have the report of what you gave us, but even that, here is Erick."

Otto gets up and goes in front of the General and says, "With all my respect my general, I can't be in front of this betrayal man. And since he is here, we can manage in to the stablish process in the code and demand to be apply immediately."

Sit down for a moment.

The General answered him and raised his voice, "This subject, precisely, must be with this matter and let's get to the point: Erick in fact is working to detect the infiltration of information with the Russians, we have the knowledge that they are doing lots of movements in America and Erick is trying to investigate the origin of that..."

Otto interrupted, "I have seen him receiving money from Vladimir! How is that possible that you are not betraying us?"

"No Capitan, this subject is already made clear, he intends to pass as a betrayed to give and take out the information of the Russians that are the power and are finishing with the monarch period in Europe. Germany is frightened that they can invade our country; that's why we assigned Erick and because the delicate information we couldn't reveal this mission to anyone. Thanks to that, now we have the information of all the operations and the space web that are working in this organization."

Otto turns to Erick and complaints, "But we are friends because you did not trust me."

Erick answered, "But how can you believe that I would do such a thing? You were very involucrate already, I couldn't compromise the operation; you know what I'm talking about, I must allow you to see me with Vladimir. And you did exactly what we were hoping, now they all think that I'm on their side, (the Russians) I have the information that we were looking for and we avoided several rebellions. Otto, do you understand! I'm pledging my life for the country! Understand me, it was necessary to deceive the real enemy and I must protect you; thanks to the code change and other actions of the protocol we obtain all the points of contacts and their spy technics. In short words: we dismember the identity of this organization... Do you understand?"

Otto answers them very disturb, "But I do not understand how we are here."

And he starts to register the office to look for evidence that was a trap for himself. When with no notices Otto uses the word, "Respond me Erick: Valquiria 4466."

Erick kept in silence, looked at the General Walter and like if they were connecting to each other, and with a look of accepting, he responses to the code, "Zwanzig (20)."

After the answers, a total silence was generated in the office. Otto sighs and puts down his shoulders as a sign of relief, since he was very stressed.

"Volta 2."

Otto said, "That was the code of official confirmation,"

"I understand."

The General Walter, continues with the conversation, "Otto, are you understanding all now?"

He responds with more assurance, "Yes, my General."

Turns his looks to Erick and said, "Now I understand all... Thank you friend. Now I have it clear, you look for my reaction as a part of the plan... Look I still have a lot to learn."

Erick answers him, "Otto, if you were informed, you shouldn't react like that; it was necessary it to happen like so that everything came out in that form."

Otto interrupted, "But Erick, the consequences are serious... Raquel... Did not want that to happen."

"Otto."

Erick said to the General looking at him and agree with the look like allowing declassify the information and Erick continues, "That was not part of the plan that you fell in love with her, she did not take the sufficient precautions to prevent the consequences... But we are taking care of that; we will give her the necessary for the product to be cover."

"How could you, is my son... I can't believe you are telling me that."

"Otto is a compromise situation, you can't go back to Cuba, or do you want to risk Raquel's life and your son? Is serious."

Otto irritated, got upset and raise his voice saying, "I can't let that happen."

But the General gets up and interrupted, "Otto, are you in or not? There is not going back, everything is planned, you can't say no. It is on you to continue this project, it's the only way out."

Very tranquil, Walter took out a Luger pistol and put it in front of him on the desk. And said to him, "Otto, if you want to shoot us, there are three agents outside prepare for any contingence; we are just a simple instrument of a higher organization, we will be substitutes for others. The plan is going to perform any way, there is no way out. Or do you prefer someone else to take your place?"

Otto looks down and quiet for some minutes, Erick, and Walter cross looks and immediately after Erick gets up, place himself next to Otto, put his hands on his shoulder and gave him some pads in his back.

"Otto, when you enter, you promise fidelity to our cause, to this organization that more than the Country is something beyond. Now our interests are subduing to a more powerful group that rule our organization structure. There will be changes, but we will be permitting the necessary to achieve the control of the cause, our cause, the action of the biggest project of the German history. You should be ready to participate, even though now more than voluntary you are binding the destiny of our organization, their perceiving, and principals."

"What is this about?"

Otto responded, "Tell me Erick, what is the purpose of all this? Why more work? For who else? Who is behind all this?"

Erick responded, "I don't know who we are working for; we only receive instructions from Walter; who receives instructions from other superior; that he also receive them from another person that receive from other control... It is not a case to get to the deep of this, just concentrate to continue doing your work, show your obedience to the country and you will be rewarded... It is your decision."

Otto very upset answered, "I won't do anything until you tell me what it's all about!"

The General gets up and said, "Otto, either you accept, or you know what to do. We will never do anything against you if is not necessary; and decides refuse... The only way now it this... There is the Luger. You know what to do."

Otto tumble down again, in that place there was no pictures, ornaments, or decorations except for a triangle in the middle of the room behind the General. A couple of pyramids and two eagles... Nothing that can help him as a sign of the nature of that place. The general asks Erick to get up and to keep in contact, "Erick, it's time that Otto passes to phase four."

"It's time. Take him there."

Otto looks at him and said, "Where is that? what is this about? Phase 4?

Erick asks him, "Calm down Otto, it will be brilliant be with you in this phase, please follow me."

Erick, follow by Otto went down to the basement building and enter to a warehouse full of antiques, Erick asked Otto to put on some glasses like goggles used for welding, covering his eyes. Both put it on and went to a dark room apparently empty.

Once with the glasses in their eyes, a simulated door on the wall opens and a blindness bright light surprises them, Erick very calm ask Otto to follow him, so they went through a tunnel of light; they stop for an instant and could hear the motor and the chains that make them come down to that room (about 50 metros deep) since you can feel the descends even though couldn't see because of the blindness light.

When they got to their destiny, the light turns off, take off the glasses from their eyes and they could see an incredible structure of installations, people working in different disciplines, iron workers, construction, etc. Like it was a construction work of a building, but in a subterranean cavern...

Otto couldn't believe it, he was surprised, he never imagines that. Erick interrupts his amaze and start to talk what was this about.

The organization had a very secret center, where as a petition of a lot interested and the organization they belong to, training the agents in lot more specialties. It was a place completely dedicated to the education, formation, and generation of agents of high level. At the same time, they have lot of discipline that develop technology for pacific and bellicose purpose if necessary. At the end of the surprise space, they got to a room cover with white marble where inside there were some people with a dark uniform and others with white uniforms. It was waiting and called him by his name...

Otto, surprise and totally amaze, discover that was Hilda, his great love. But now, she was one of the persons in charge of that place. In that moment, Otto thought "Now it will be my end." After leaving her and ignore her for some years, he couldn't look at her eyes; he was feeling guilty and shame for what he did even though he did it for not hurting her. Or that was what he thought...

She, on her behalf looks at him directly to his eyes; the love for him never had ended, even with the time, she realizes the reason he had left her. Her love resists the time and never loses the hope to see him again; to such a degree that she knew that she would see him soon. But Otto was not conscience of that, he did not have any clue what happen to her, but she was there, more beautiful than ever, firm, present with her beautiful blue eyes, and her captivated smile, that in the moment it was a solid block of ice, he can glimmer in her beautiful face. Otto felt that he couldn't resist, but at the same time he felt a great guilt for what happen between them... Suddenly he confronts to his destiny, he saw her as a superior, his superior and solute.

It was explaining the reason of the light to enter the place; it was like a mental trick that practice a tremendous dose of intimidation over the persons who enter for some reason, being strange to the organization; were taking by surprise the blindness light, who came from a one metro size reflector and produce a sound that simulate to be an elevator. An excellent distractor to confuse and dissuade with a mental effect that involve inside a confusion that makes it easier to repel the invasion and capture of the invasion.

To be part of these group have strong consequences, since it gets to the deepest of the institution and be transform in the new member of the elite group; so, in that matter the room had an inscription in a white base with black letters a thought:

"The reason demand, for transcendental matters, to have a communion of the formal impulse with the material; this is, to exist an impulse of play, because only the unity of reality with the form, of the contingence with the necessity, from the passivity with the complete freedom the concept of humanity," Schiller.

Otto was reading them when suddenly the silence broke up; Hilda starts talking, "Capitan," referring to Otto, "First, to express you my best wishes of success in your new phase of knowledge and training, you have been selected for a superior mission and we are hoping for all your cooperation and understanding. We know surely that your performance is satisfactory and your qualifications are above the expected; we also know that you have surpass the crisis and is why we take the decision to integrate you to the phase 4."

Otto even more amazed than frighten, asked, "Phase 4?"

"Capitan, the phase 4 is the last step in the training to the most distinguish agents, is above the institutional election and is the work team that follow the precise instructions to the fulfillment of our superior plans."

Otto intrigue asked, "Superiors?! What are you referring with that?

"Are the interests by the ones who battle our country, created for the sublime porpoises of our freedom and our supremacy, that the regard of several politic events, we have to preserve to maintain our country always unify even in regard of the different interests that pretend divert the loyalty principals and permanency of the value of our society preserved by our group."

Otto questioned, "What group are you talking about?! What is all this about?

Hilda very astutely answered, "Your position now is not to question but to obey, be loyal and the loyalty is the most important in this moment. Capitan, there in not much options now: either be constituent part or already the Capitan Walter gave you indications of the way you can carry out your exit."

Otto stays speechless and very serious; he stays there quietly agrees with his head. Hilda continues with her intervention, "And like I was telling you, now you have to perform with training during two weeks under a strict anonymity; at the end of this training, you will get the instructions to be followed."

After this conversation, they ask Otto to follow Erick and he did it, more thoughtful than ever... Otto stop to view the halls that look like tunnels with rooms, all of them with iron doors and a green and red light. Look more like a jail than a quarter, that place was colder than others. After that break continue walking behind Erick; almost to the end of that hall they stop and Erick open the door for him and kindly told him to come in, "Come in, this will be your house for two weeks. Get used to it, it's better that what your imagined."

He took him by his arm and brought him in. Told him to get comfortable. Otto did not say any words. The looks between them were their communication, their body language was saying everything. Erick broke the silence, "Otto, we need to have a long talk, I hope you understand me."

Otto almost without talking agree with his head without looking at him. He sits on the bed and stay there. Erick left and closed the iron door. Otto absorbed on the bed fell on his back and stayed inert.

He was in a room with all the services, he had a private bath room and a shower with hot water, a desk and a small living area, all very austere but with the needs to be comfortable in a place like that; he has a water jar, towels and in the desk some pens and paper, in the side of that a reading lamp and notes with the work of Schiller and Kant, which he has a note that said, "You have three days to read this work since we have some questions about this subject..." Otto, odd, look at the writing and like he did not want to do it, he starts reading the notes.

After several hours, Otto gets up, got closer to the iron door, but he did not try to open it, and put his back while he hears a knock on the door with three continue knocks, Otto opens the small window on the iron door and sees a person with a tray and a food service cart... He is surprise...

"Capitan Otto, we are bringing your dinner."

Otto peculiarly told him, "How will you get it to me, if I'm locked in? If I am in prison."

The waiter responded to him, "No Capitan, it's not like that, just open the door..."

Otto opens the door, and notice that did not have any lock on it, it was a simple handle to open... After that he gets out to the hall, he puts his hands in his head... Like saying, "What is all this about, it is crazy," think Otto think, get out of this, after his internal dialog, I thought I was locked in and asked the waiter, "How come the cell is open?"

The waiter answers him, "Cell? What cell are you talking about?"

He raises his voice in the hall, "This grime jail... don't you see..."

The waiter answered him, "Capitan, I am sorry, you are confused... this is not jail like you said."

"But look..."

Otto gets closer to the iron door and touches it and with his hand shows him the hall and said, "What is that?"

The waiter simply responded, "I will leave your food in your room, and we will come later to pick the service up."

The waiter went in and left the food while Otto is looking down the hallway and how the waiter goes in very tranquil, got out and left saying, "Enjoy your meal Capitan."

Otto stays astonished, confuse, and totally lost in his thoughts; after some seconds, he follows the waiter, he saw a big door, that enter in to a big room, there were lots of people working in their desks... All of them turned and saw him and continue working.

At the end of the room was a withe room with a door... He continues and saw a big room where lots of people in a meeting were, like it was a conference. He got closer and saw how they were showing a movie of a NAZI propaganda, since the beginning until the center of the room can see some uniforms with that characterize clothes...

Otto continues with his traveling, in the next room to the big room he could see like a dining place, he sees how the waiter enters the kitchen and saw Erick seating in a corner of the dining room, drinking a cup of coffee and reading a journey. He got closer and put himself in front of Erick and said, "Erick, you better explain me what is all this about or I promise you I will lose my reasoning."

Looking at his eyes he responded, "Otto, what do you want me to tell you? You are seeing with your own eyes, instead you tell me what do you see?"

"This is a big organization... Is an information Bunker; is an operation center that I never imagined exist and all underneath my feet. What I thought was a simple military organization became to be more than that. I'm very disturb, amazed and astonished at the same time..."

"Friend, you are one of the few selected, you have the perfect profile for this organization, now you don't have other options, you are part of this family."

"Family?!" Otto responded shortly. Erick got up, took him by his shoulder and said, "Yes Otto, now this will be your family and now this will be your house, and all of them now are your brothers and sisters, at least will be for the rest of you days, and hope to be many," and outline a smile in his face, giving him a hand squeeze with his right hand in his left shoulder.

Otto understood, in that moment, where he was, in an organization beyond spying or the militia, he didn't know what was, he only knew that was an organization a lot more powerful even more, that transcendent in several social stratums and the barrier of several nations. It was an organization perfectly structure and with all the elements to ensure that was about something bigger.

After that revelation, Erick accompanies Otto to his room, on the way he was explaining to him the regent motifs and principals of the organization that he belongs and Erick simply call "the family."

This way he left him in his room, and asked him to finish the instruction given, starting with filling his stomach with a delicious shorn, mash potatoes, a good portion of Sauerkraut (typical German dish base on cabbage in salt) and a delicious bread cook by the excellent cookers. He dismisses him and leaves him there, in his room, but before in his presence, open a bottle of an exquisite red Italian wine to accompany his food. Erick broke open this one and after a taste, he serves the wineglass to Otto and cheers for him, wishing him success in his new stage. But before he leaves said, "Excuse me Otto, Should I close the door?"

Otto answered him more relaxed, "Well yes..."

And in a joking tone, Erick said to him, "Let me know when you want to get out," he smiles and left him there, more tranquil.

A week went by between psychology interviews and instructors on different disciplines, rigorous psychic, and technical training... He learns a lot of things at this time, some of them were put in practice in the moment, since the place have all the necessary for the practice actions of the received instruction.

After all this time of "voluntary" captivity, Otto cohabits with all the recruitment of the center and rarely sees between blinds to Hilda... He sees her each time more beautiful, but always with an immutable face, until one day he saw her in between the white room windows and saw how she lightly smiles at him; even the thought that such a gesture was a product of his imagination. To him came all the memories of what they lived and enjoyed time, he wanted to see her and explain to her how regretful he was, what he did... But it was not possible.

Days went by, between trainings, instruction, and practice; could build already a civil or military structure in the middle of nothing and for any necessary purpose. Obviously there, the identities of all were anonymous, no one can cross personal word, the psychological profile of all were similar: almost all of them were orphans or they have abandoned their families, the loneliness was a primary characteristic of them. They became in real beings of hunt that simulate being harmless, but they have a lethal load on their knowledge. They were formed to create big things, over the interest of a nation, but their convictions were already compromised with the internal rules that went from the loyalty to the organization above any interest, the fraternity between compatriot and members of this elite group and they obey to the cause of the organization. All that behind the patriot noble spirit that was rule by persons and interest that they couldn't identify.

It was one more evening of work and study, Otto went to his "room" or "cell" like he called it, since he never took out of his mind the condition of a prisoner. When he enters, he got surprised seen siting on his bed to Hilda... It was such an amazed, that visible stop in the entry, like he made a cell mistake, but she calls him by his name, "Otto, I was waiting for you," said with a visible smile. "Come in, close the door, we have to talk."

Otto responded to her, imagining the worst, "But Hilda, let me explain to you..."

But Hilda interrupted him, "No Otto, now I have to talk..." Hilda continues. "But first come and sit down here next to me."

Otto got closer and slowly looking at her took a seat. Hilda continues, with a stern look at his eyes, but this time with a different face than the first time they encounter, at the initiation of phase 4.

"Otto, I did not understand you and I was frustrated, I was an obstinate and I was confused; I did lots of foolishness..."

She started to narrate in a superficial way what happened, that she was the General Friedrich lover for several years "I started working with him as her assistant, his wife never knew, I was very astute, I kept a very friendly relation with her, the general knew to always appreciate my discretion. I knew that was wrong, but I wanted to get high; I did not know that once entering I will compromise to lose everything. It was how little by little I involucrate not only with the general, but with more personage to such a degree that I was the perfect lover. I achieve a lot, but the general die later, I got very

well related and enter to this organization... once inside
I understood lots of your attitude towards me and the
same as you, I left my family, I left everything; since it
was very dangerous and I could have the lives of my
love once in the hands of these persons. In fact, even
now no one knows what you and I had; only you, here
is the secret and while you do not express that we have
something, they will never suspect of you neither of me.
Do you understand, I do not have much time, I'm doing
this for you and if you want to know, I never forgot you,
I forgive you for leaving me, I understood that you were
doing it for me; how foolish of me not understanding
you. I completely lost my reasoning and with that my
will and my life, all to become in this that you see now."

In that moment, she starts crying intensely and
hug Otto, who was amazed without believing what he
was listening; the frighten invade him, because his suspects were even bigger: he was one more prisoner and
furthermore a piece of war, one more active. He also
exculpates with her and let her know that he also never
forgot her; that moment was a total declaration of both.

From the crying to the mutual comprehension,
from the comprehension to the caress and the affection, then the stolen timid kisses; the chemistry did
their work, and the hormone invaded their brains, their
hypothalamus react losing all reasoning. Their subconscious enlivens the join salivation action, the corporal's
fluids were intensification and the sex chemistry flood
their neurons reacting to the impulse generated, to
passionate kisses and to the unrestrained passion, that
was there... latent, hidden for years, in the age memories and giving themselves to the elixir of the sexual
urge repress from both.

The carnal sexual urge, empower them, the reasoning disappears, the place, the occasion of those
seconds... In an instant the sentimental tilt took hold of

them again, what leading in a river: The surrender of both in an out of breath uncontrollable breathing, that culminate in a passion game that both wanted.

After this intensive encounter, the shadow of the reasoning comes back to their minds, without saying nothing to each other were exhaustive in that bed what was the witness of their total devoting themselves wholly to... Something that will mark them forever.

Minutes later, Otto opened his eyes, since he fell deeply asleep and when he notices that Hilda was not there, he dresses up quickly, got out to see if he sees her, he bites his lips to repress the impulse to get out screaming like crazy and asked for her; but he stops, he contains himself and lamented, the reasoning took control over him, became panicky and got back to his room. He stays on his bed thinking of her, with an ardent desire to see her again.

He did not see her for several days. Otto was called to the central office and received the dialogues of his new post and was inform that he should read it.

Otto carefully reads it, point by point, accepting with his head the fulfillment of the obligations corresponding to phase 4. He stays there with the manuscript that demand his signature; in his hands; there was not going back. He wanted to ask for Hilda, but because of he already knew, prefer that no one knew about the encounter with her.

Otto got out of that place, in the Belin streets with his new name and his new identity, saw the new world and the sun light dazzle him. It was given by his new bosses, the instructions to remain in the city in a special apartment; where everything was luxury and comfort, like it was an adaptation week to the real world, with a spectacular view at the door of Brandenburg, it was the moment, the end of his new stage. And he remains there until he was call to a new mission.

CHAPTER THIRTEEN
AT THE DOORS OF THE SUNSET

It was the ending of November 1927; the world had agitation for a strong world reduction, affecting to all the countries, mainly United States that was in a crisis that transfer to Europe. Germany was a chaos inside this economic setting, A pact was writing, which Germany were in the necessity to look new markets while trying surviving to this crisis.

Otto was reading the news on the newspapers how the German congress were changing, where most of the integrates belong to the NAZI party. Looks like was inevitable that this party directed by who, several groups presume him as crazy, unhinge, and clumsy took the power.

A cold morning in November, Otto receives a certify telegram to present himself in the central office of his group. He was on time for his appointment and in that place, he received documents, money, and a suitcase with several devises for his use in the mission. After receiving instructions, he left, since he had only 48 hours to present in the pier 44, Sofia ship in the Rostock port. In that place, there was a big air base being built, but it also very secret (because of the Versailles agreements); Germany couldn't continue to be captive before the operation of their defeated.

He must present himself at that point, where he will find the contact who will give him the instructions of his destiny, however he didn't know who this person would be. Otto knew that from there set sail to his final destiny; he will embark to a new adventure; he was enthusiastic for this event and maybe trustful specially because all he had lived days before in Berlin. He couldn't forget his lovely Hilda, the encounter gave live, gave him courage to continue in the path to his destiny, that was about to un lease.

He arrived 12 hours before the indicated time to his destiny. The Rostock ports. At his arrival to Hauptbahnhoff (main station) of the city, he smells an odor like a mix of bread recently made and coffee; to an aromatic and delicious coffee, that was stimulating to get in and taste the bread and the delicious German dishes that were extend in that terminal. Very tranquil he starts to get closer to the place guided by his smell... Walking on the railway platform of the terminal, Otto saw his reflection on the floor, with the sun at his back and the shadow of his body, in that moment he realizes of his reality, he put on a typical hat of the time and got to the place to buy the cakes and bread.

He tasted with certain knowledge that maybe, this was the last time that he would take in these pleasures. Giving himself a feast with the coffee that allowed him to combine the flavors that he loves, he fells a great joy for his gustative papilla. He eats and drinks with a great pleasure and joy, like getting drunk with these flavors, soaking it in his mind, to stay there forever; like making a ritual of farewell with those smells, flavors, feelings, and joy that the land who saw him borne gave.

Once he concluded his ritual of farewell, a person came in closer to him with a leather suitcase in his hand, wearing a fine coat, who ask for a coffee, he seats next to Otto and said to him, "Friend, you know how to enjoy these dishes, you can see they are your favorites ones."

Otto responded, "Yes, of course, you can't eat this daily and, in a place, so special."

"Exactly! This is something that we can be very proud."

Answer this character and continue, "By the way... where are you coming from?"

Otto answers him, "Where are you coming from...?"

After an odd look, by asking instead of giving an answer, the character told him, "Take it easy friend, I'm arriving from the blue lake... And I'm going with my aunt Sofia who is here in Rostock..."

Otto stopped eating, look at him and without saying anything, he knew that the character was his contact; only then, he responded, "Well, give her my greetings, even I don't know her, I know something about being the lady of 54, right...?"

That was the identification code of respond. He continues eating and drinking, not looking at him, but placing his sight on his cup of coffee.

The character without saying anything, gets up from that place, cleans his moustache and told him, "Enjoy your meal foreigner, have a nice trip."

That was the confirmation code to deliver Otto's instructions. At the ending of this brief talk, this character gets up and left his suitcase, on the floor, next to Otto. Otto very tranquil finish his last drink of coffee, gets up and takes the suitcase. Got out of the station and went to pier 44.

After arriving 6 hours left for his embark. According to the instructions, Otto sat in front of the pier and took out the local newspaper.

In this city, located at the north of Germany, it was a Russian squad, that will be collaborating in this mission; reason was selected that place to do such activities, combine the access to this point was closer to any delivery. He puts himself to read waiting for his departure meanwhile in that newspaper was the destiny of his mission and once he decoded, he discovers that his mission was Mexico; a country not strange for him, since his incursion in Cuba, but at the end an American country...

Otto was very happy because he imagines that Mexico was going to be like Cuba. In the document was explained, obviously in code, that he must go to another stage of instruction, that he will be contacted at his arrival, and he would not present immigration documents and no one will ask him for any document, only his boarding pass, that was inside the suitcase. He follows the instructions to the tick went to the pier, embark, and presents his boarding pass, an official, who sees him indicated for him go to cabin 84, Otto passes on and prepares himself for his journey.

From his cabin, sees how little by little they were leaving the pier and how they were getting away of the port. Somehow his unconscious, was feeling that his body was leaving something there; he was feeling an uncontainable nostalgia, in such a luck that because his anguish, let go of all his memories from his childhood, his mother, his sister, his father, his brother... Everything in a spectral feeling that makes him feel an emptiness inspected in his heart. His breathing gets suspended like wanting to stop the time; split his soul for leaving behind his family, his people, his country... While seeing how each time was getting smaller the flag of his lovely country; the country of his parents that he was scarifying, like he was taught; the country of his parents that he loves and gave him a lot.

He was mentally to comeback some day with glory and with his head held high for his family and the people that he loves and redeem his name. He sees himself create in some place in his lovely land with golden letters the name of his family...

He stays like that, with the desire of his live and with purpose to comeback. He keeps with those thoughts until he falls sleep.

The time of the crossing was faster, went by almost imperceptible for Otto, since he dedicates all the trip to build his work plan and review his information, the contacts, the places, and everything that was in that suitcase. During this work, it was obvious the mark of the Russian team work that kept evident the presence in all the work structure.

Otto spends all the trip analyzing where all this was going, thinking in the different options he had... It was looking like to be a one-year plan and the pay was big, he was thinking in leaving that work and was looking the way to end with success to come back to his land and concrete his plans. Meantime his mind was wondering those ideas, in some moments he distracts himself daydreaming and seeing himself with his lovely Hilda.

It was a trip of lots of work, planning and concentration, he must memorize lots of things, schematize all his ideas to concrete and perfectly execute the plan, just the way he was taught.

Time went by, and in an early morning of winter, finally arrives in Veracruz. Otto already prepare with his luggage, he got out to the deck to watch little by little how it was getting closer to the coast and how it was reveal his eyes the picturesque port of Veracruz, with its buildings and white houses that stand out at the border of the littoral, each time closer, to a light of a beacon that even at the first morning was giving the welcome to the ships that were coming from the open sea.

As soon as got to the place of disembarking, Otto got out of the ship, an official from the port only ask him for his boarding pass, there was no one else to ask him for his documents. He came down with a trunk and a suitcase; there were all the belongings he brought with him. When he arrives to firm land, he receives help of some men with a wagon that offer him the service to carry his luggage and belongings to which Otto agreed. The Spanish it was already familiar to him and with another accent was understandable for him. In that moment, he asks them to take him to the 34 Hidalgo street; place where he already arranges to stay there and where he will receive the rest of the instructions.

When he arrives, his presence was unmistakable; with his hat, a coat and a scarf on his neck, his skin stands out and become evident his aspect of foreign in the middle of that place. All the people that were moving around the port were looking at him and greeting him, but between themselves making comments, looking at each other and evidently that he was foreign; some of them thought that he was Polish or Russian, since very often visitors from those countries. The people were very kind greeting him either with words or with a simple bowing his head, to which Otto responded in a similar way and with a small smile drawn on his face.

Like that was all the way until arriving to the place where he will stay for some days... he thought to himself. The porter of the place received him, she told him that she was waiting for him and took him to his room, that only had the essentials. There is Otto already use to it, gave some coins that have prepare for such a purpose to the loader who help him.

It was a silence travel, Otto started to feel the heat and the humidity of the place while the morning went by but remained in his room until new news; he was estimating 8 hours more according to the plan, to received his new news, meanwhile he laid on the bed and rested for some hours.

Exactly at the exact time, Otto received a telegram from the porter's hands, who came to knock on the door of his room, Otto immediately attended, and she gave him the telegram. Afterwards, he opens, decoded, and prepare to get out according with the indicated there. He went to the central plaza and sat in a bench, it was close to 7 in the evening; between the clamor of the people of the place, you can hear a joyful dance.

Between marimba, singing and dancing he stays sitting there, waiting for his contact and suddenly he saw at the side of the plaza how a particular gentleman was getting closer, that was greeting the people and with some ladies he took his hat off and smile, while others simply allude with the body. Little by little was getting closer where Otto was, he went next to him and like asking permission with the sight he stop in his side and making a sign asking if he could sit, after that Otto agree with his head and the gentleman sits there, dressing very elegant in white, from the hat until his shoe. He had a cane putting it between them like marking a space and resting his hands in the cane observing the show that was going on in that plaza. Like talking with himself and with his sight stick on the dancers and singers, he starts talking in German.

"How was your trip friend? You are coming from far away; I hope to be worth all... Well."

Otto, for a little while was quiet and the gentleman continues, "Look, we have a packet that has to be noticed the coffee place over there in front," with his cane point to the place. "Look it will be very interesting, I only have to tell you that... The fourth table when you enter to the left."

That character, annoying got up and tells him in Spanish, "Enjoy your meal friend," and left.

Otto got up five minutes after the man in white left, he went to the coffee place of the parish and place himself exactly on the fourth table of the left and there was a person sitting... He saw him and put him a chair... Talking to him in Spanish, ask him what he wanted to drink, but he asks for a strong coffee for him. The waiter came and from high he pours the coffee almost to the half of the glass and after that he pours the hot milk, letting fall from high touching the glass; the effect generates an abundance and smelly foam of coffee with milk, a spectacular acrobat that Otto never seen before and cause him charm and smile visible surprise.

The companion was Juan Garcia... A retire lieutenant from the Mexican marine, who welcome him and start talking to him about the subject they have pending; they stay there between cut Spanish, signs and more until late hours of the night. At the end of this encounter, they both left, but before Juan Garcia gave Otto a packet with the following instruction: "Show up in the ranch *La Esperanza* with Carlos. You will have there your next instruction."

After that, he has a small map and the way to get there. Next day Otto shows up in that place and was welcome by his contact, Carlos, a business man owner of the coffee processor in that area. When he arrives, he was conducted to a warehouse, they show him the communication system and Carlos left him there... With no words he left.

It was a hiding place in the middle of the forest vegetation, with thousands of insects, mainly a cloud of mosquitos. Otto couldn't believe such a dimension of swarm (unbelievable), beside the suffocated heat generated there... He must invent a netting for his hat and put on oil on his arms to repel the mosquitos. Otto knew of the pandemic illness of the area, and with a better reason, he opts to protect all his body, scarifying to support the heat that was there.

He starts to work, he stays there for two days until he finishes building a complex radio system; he builds by himself and configure the communication, since they already have installed a big antenna. He initiates transmitting and perform some test, at the left the codes or opening to be operated by his relief. Otto left from there and went to let Carlos know. They spend a couple of days talking and tasting the best thing of the place... The coffee that he loves.

Afterwards, Carlos tells him that he was married with Maria, and have three kids and that he was very happy there, financially he was very good, and told him the wonderful life in Veracruz, however, Otto time was short in that place, since he must leave from there the next day and move to the capital of the country. In regard of that, Carlos mentioned his experience about the matter, "That is the most beautiful city that I have known, at least for me, is the most beautiful."

Otto got very enthusiastic by what he was told. He went to pick his belongings up at the apartment, but when he got there, it was under his door a telegram that only said, "Greetings friend. V: V:"

When he saw this, Otto knew who the matter was. He quickly prepares his belongings and immediately move to the bus terminal to travel to Mexico City.

During the traveling, all the people were very kind, since it was evident his foreign origin, the people generally saw him with pleasure, like it was a very important visitor, his face feature, his walk, his clothing... It was visible different. Lots of people, mainly the women, coquettishly smile his way. For Otto was something new and make him feel very good, a feeling that motivate him to continue in this land so different and exotic.

Unlike Cuba, in this land, you can feel a great poverty; it was full of flies; there was a lot of mud on the streets; stinking water; like the drain comes out to the streets, the people were asking for charity everywhere, the children were swirling around him to get some coins or bread... This surprise was a lot to Otto and asking to himself, how can they survive in this place so hostile? But came to his mind the memories of those battle fields, where the smell of rottenness and the horror abound.

In that moment, his old demons catch him while walking, he had an anxiety attack, even when he had had lots of years controlling them. Those scenes let fly and took him to a panic, he left from the streets and got in a lonely alley, near a stable, where he vomits like a water fall. The people were looking at him when walking by him and thinking that he may be sick and leaving.

Otto deeply breathe several times, like trying to recuperate his breath; he recovers and incorporate; he cleans himself with a scarf he had on his neck, a mandatory item for him because the sweating and heat, that have him almost always wet; he continues his way, but for that moment all those memories where in his mind that terrify him and his fantasies began to revive his inferno.

Around those places, unhealthier than poor, was making his way, he sees how the women were very exotic, lots of them with babies hanging on their backs with rags, others with loads and more with those bundles of infants that moan all the time. There cinnamon color and their mestizo feature than native, were getting his attention; the dark eyes; the food very different; full of flies everywhere; eating corn mass in everything, at the beginning the flavor was not pleasant for Otto, but little by little he starts finding the taste.

During his traveling on the bus, Otto was treated a stranger, everybody looking at him, it was complicated times for so many revolts; lots of them avoid him, because there was a recent partisans between government and the catholic church, there were lots of people in other countries trying to allay the devastating attack between themselves; some instead, offer him food, offer him drinks and even offer him their sit, maybe because of fear, attention or as a sign of submission before him as an evident foreign he was.

Otto never feels uncomfortable in a long time, with a smile on his face, trying to simulate the tension of the observer on his way, he arrives to a market, where you can see the buses that will take him to Mexico City. He only saw a written sign by hand that said Mexico, he got closer to that bus and a person on the bottom of the door indicate him to pay his ticket, he gave him the money and go up to look for an available seat. When he enters, a sweat smell, food and who knows what else hit him, but he was doing his job, he must support all that, he places himself in an empty spot and his suitcases where place in a work basket on top of the diesel bus, that by the way the steam came out everywhere.

He shares his trip with all those people, exchanging words and learning more about their life style. Otto was very surprised for this new adventure, little by little he adapts to the atmosphere, so the trip went on between mountains and big cliffs, strong winds and wonderful views of the valleys of a country that he thought was incredible contrasting: beauty, poverty, unhealthy, kindness, submission of his people against a minority power, a total corruption of the country and a stinking government.

The traveling went by and finally arrive to the capital of the country. At his arriving almost dismiss their partners of the trip as his friends, even some of them offer him to stay in their home to rest, but Otto has already a reserved place. Did not pass to much time when he was welcome in the bus terminal by a character that use the December season to dress up his typical Russian hat; between food stands and thousands of people conglomerate in the streets, it was an impact encounter. After traveling of amazement and comfortability, to see Vladimir, his relax face disappear, came back to his cold and rigid character, his face decolored in his usual paled color and begin the most challenge conversation of his life.

"Otto, friend, is a pleasure to see you... Come here... Friend, I thought I would never see you again."

Replying cynically in German with his strong Russian accent, opening his arms like trying to give him a hug. Otto simply gives him his hand to greet and looking at him, Otto said, "Look you love to leave your trace and signature everywhere, in everything... Is that the telegram for... I was sure that was you..."

"Ha, my astute friend like always! but do not entrust what you look for sometimes you can't find and what are you following is sometimes an illusion. You know that you can never hide from me, luckily, my friend, we are now in the same team; rather, let's go to celebrate, here is a giant lustful! Well, in this forget the world, friend, is a pleasure to see you."

Otto, not very convinced, got closer to him; well yes, Vladimir was right, he has instructions to cooperate with the Russian team of Phase 4, there was nothing else to do.

"I came to work and let's get to the point, we do not have anything else to do, but to follow the instructions given to us."

Otto, annoyed by this character, he concentrates to accompany his new partner of mission; meanwhile, Vladimir was giving him a count of how the situation was in that country.

Mexico was disturbing for a recent partisan between the church and the government for the control battle and power of the country, as well as the changes of ideologies, reason Vladimir was very please since his Marxist tendencies. He was very aligning with the communist independently of the work in phase 4, that he was convince in support.

Although he took more time on the description of the facts than the travel time to a house located next to the Roma neighborhood, Mexico City; there were waiting other Russians that together will be collaborating in this new mission. Within none of them could confirm which was the formation or the purpose of the mission like pieces in a big puzzle. But each of them must do their part in a group and individual way according to the case. Otto, each time was getting lonelier in that job, to such a degree that will leave him to his good luck in some months, but not before he coordinates with the rest of the members of Phase 4.

Like that he spends his stay in Mexico City, with the mission to carry out some communication test by land an air, as well as to taste the communication with the assign contact in Veracruz. The codes were managing in an individual matter, that way any member of the team knew what the other member did, because if they were caught by any authority, will not exist connection or facts of any relation between them. This guaranties the operation.

Otto and Vladimir were not agreeable between them; on one occasion, very early in the morning, Vladimir evidently alcoholic, complain to Otto what happened with Raquel in Cuba, he was surprise that he knew about that subject, he was bothered and confronted to each other, since Raquel had had a relation also with Vladimir, and he couldn't forget him that she has a child with Otto. Vladimir in his drunkenness confess his hate to the "bastard" a term that he used about Otto's child and cry out in his face... The discussion ended in a beating up. Luckily the other two partners pull them apart, and Otto understood of that hate they have for each other was controlling him, he decided to leave before exploding in anger, and compromising the operation.

Quickly he left from that house and went in to a hotel located down town of the city. From that moment, he continues with his work and avoid Vladimir as much as he could. Five weeks went by when Otto conclude the communications and left from there by train to Guadalajara city, and suddenly from one day to another, Otto was in that city and on his way to his next control point.

On his way, the control center asks him for a major discretion, because in Guadalajara city had existed more violence because the social and religious reveals and fights. He arrives to his new destiny as a mechanic of the train services company of the city. After 12 long hours, Otto was very upset with his fight with Vladimir, he was thinking of that child that he mentioned and which he did not know but he would like to know him.

He was asking to himself the reason he had left him and his mother Raquel; but at the same time minimize his guilt remembering that he was not responsible for how all this ended like that, after all, was Raquel who betrayed him and hide the detail of her pregnancy until the end. Nevertheless, otherwise, he was worried about that butcher Russian to harm to any of those two and his anxiety invaded just to think the destiny of both. After lots of thinking on that matter, he decides that in the first opportunity he had, he will come back to Cuba to fix that matter but meanwhile he couldn't do anything for that matter.

After more than one nightmare that attack him and his mental disturb situation that afflict him. Otto arrives to the new city. It was an even more dramatic encounter than the last one, this was a smaller city than Mexico City. When he arrives there, just getting out of the car, what was his surprise... Between the vapor of the machinery, the fumes smell of estrange food and the penetrant smell of corn cakes and some others smells of bread freshly made, that for a second he was transported to his country, but in those same seconds he came back to his reality... He saw from far away the obvious figure of his friend Erick.

He was waiting for him, Otto immediately reported, and Erick took him to the Jardin hotel right in front of the church of our lady of Aranzazu. The travel to the hotel was not very effusive like last time; the atmosphere feels with some hostility, the only inter-change words between them was just for greetings. It was evident that the friendship relation between them was ended, but for work reasons he continues there with an open channel of communication.

The communication between them was corporal more than oral and the postures let you see and ended when Erick left Otto at the Jardin hotel so he can rest, since next day hard work was waiting to be done.

Otto arrives to his room; he seats on the bed, put his hands on his front head, like holding his head; he rests his elbows on his knees and stays distress for some minutes, and this occur with Vladimir and Raquel, couldn't take out of his head the uncertainty of not knowing about his son and what could happen. But there was something that made him feel a distress even more, it was something that he couldn't decipher but he was feeling it; he tries to calm down and breathe deeply to tranquilize himself, but he knew himself and those symptoms only appear when something serious happens. His premonitions until that moment have never fell; he felt a tingle in his ears, he felt his tongue-tie, he couldn't pass saliva... But he couldn't understand what was accumulated to his worries and pending. What was that he had to carry?

That night he was awake while thinking and string together, cases, persons, situations, and moments to try to build that puzzle of feelings and information that was torment to him. He remains like that until the wariness of the trip and all that train of new experiences defeat him and falls sleep.

The next day, when he got up it was almost noon, he had under the door a telegram; he took him from the floor and gets ready to get out and did not open it until he was at the small bar at the front desk and after he ask for a cup of coffee, and having the cup in front of him. Very calm he opens the envelope to read the content, it has a code ready to be decoded.

The order was to go to down town of the city to the Arms plaza, a place where he will be contacted. He follows the instructions and sits in a bench in front of the kiosk that was in the extreme right side; There more tranquil and with a spectacular weather or at least it was for him, since he didn't have to fight with the suffocating heat, he waits with his white hat very common for that place, he was watching the people walking and notice that the people were different than the ones he met in Mexico city, these were more like the Europeans, even the Indians features avail, outcoming a very special mixt.

He was immersed in his observation prosses, when next to him sits a tall man, brunette; wearing a dark suit made of wool since was winter season, his suit looks like military, but without emblems. It was the Capitan Modesto Ramirez who came in and giving him, signs ask him to follow him and took him to a coffee that was in a building in front of the arcs next to the plaza; there was Erick sitting waiting for him.

Arriving, already with a mayor dominion of the Spanish language, they introduce themselves and indicate to Otto that the Capitan Modesto will work for him, that he will be available for Otto's needs and for the moment he must present to work at the train terminal where he will stay for a week in the maintenance area, so Otto can keep a low profile and not have suspects, since the city was full of foreigners, belonging to the intelligent team from several countries. After that, the Capitan Modesto himself will oversee giving him all he will be required.

Next day, was Monday of work at the central train, in between what he can understand and what he can express, Otto discover that from the 10 units in service only 5 worked, because the other ones couldn't be use because of the crisis; this situation came right on for him, since he was an expert in repair under shortage conditions of resources, just like he did it some time in his country.

Otto feels sorry for all the operators and mechanics that couldn't do great things because their educations and aptitudes were very limited; he saw that the persons were very depended to each other, so he took the initiative on such conditions. He needed to be very busy to avoid being suspicious or intrigued and, he must be ready for what he was hire, he puts hands on and check thoroughly all the units, analyze his way of operating and after some days of studies, start to work directly in each of the trolleys. After the amaze of the garage boss, he gets to put in circulation all the units without the necessity to buy any parts, he repairs each damage part, he replaces mechanics parts with the old and forgotten motors in a warehouse and re-build with parts from one and another part to such a degree that all the mechanics were amazed.

It was such an amazement that he causes, that the case travel to the ears of the municipal president of Guadalajara, that when he knew this news of all his trolleys working, he went very fast to see with his own eyes such an exploit and to meet the author of such a prowess. The save that represents and the benefit that was given the city were enough matter for the venerable Luis R. Castillo to meet the author of this work; He asked for Mr. Jorge Arámbula, thinking that was him since he was the responsible of the garage, but this one indicate that the one he was looking for was a German that was hired as a mechanic a week ago. He couldn't believe and immediately ask to be introduce to him. However, when they arrive where Otto was, he was already gone from there, they couldn't find him anywhere, no one said he left... The Capitan Modesto, who was around there, said the following, "I saw that foreigner getting out, he was going north, but then I did not see him anymore."

The mayor and his team were very contradicting for the result, but at the same time very happy because the people were waving and giving thanks to the mayor, because the service was reestablished. It was an incredible result, and the mayor did not let this occasion pass, so he took side and gave instructions to try to maintain as much as possible the work of the service. And the German man was left as a legend there.

For Otto's part, he never knew of this event, he arrives to his hotel, where a young girl was waiting for him and was trying to tell him to follow her; it was a young one with a very native style, a native beauty, cinnamon color with black hair; she was wearing a coquette fit well dress to her waist and long to his knees; she has some sandals with the same green tone as her dress, that can see her feet showing her small toes very fine delineate; her face was adorn with a deep black eyes that laugh along with his mouth; very cheerful and because the difference of the language, she makes signs to Otto to indicate him to follow her. Otto puzzled sees her and she respond to him with a smile with a tenderness that he never saw before; she insists and tells him with her hands that it was urgent to follow her. Otto couldn't understand what was going on, but he decides to follow her... During the way all the time behind her, so he only sees her back and can see her long black hair that shines with the sun and was all the way to her waist.

After all this insistence, Otto ends following her several blocks until arriving by the Miguel Blanco street, until stopping on the number 34, in front of a large house; they enter to a hall and after ringing some bells a maid came out that was asked to come in at the same time she was opening an iron gate that was there; the women asked to be seated, the young girl sat in a chair almost in front of him, she smile and ask him by signs to wait for few minutes, that the person for whom he was there was almost there... Only some minutes went by when arrived, almost running to the gate door, the Capitan Modesto; between the three of them look to each other and the Capitan said, "My daughter I'm here! Thank you, now get up and go away".

She got up at the order of the men and quickly went out of the place, to the inside of the house.

"What happen?"

Otto aske to the Capitan, "Don Otto, I'm glad you followed my daughter."

"Your daughter? And why is the urgency?

The Capitan answer him more tranquil, "Don Otto, my job is to be at your service, and we have to take care of your integrity as well as your identity; what you did causes an emergency case in the operation and I have to change some plans."

Otto said what do you say happened?

"Well, happen that you did a prowess that did not have preceding, they had the trolleys out of order for almost six months, the municipality did not have the money to repair then and you in a week put them to run... Don Otto, that got a lot of attention and couldn't be good that these persons find you."

Otto was in state of unconsciousness, because the fast talk of the Capitan Modesto, he couldn't understand anything he said, he moves his head and with his hands intent to communicate at the same time he was talking. Then, already disorderly, he said in German, "I did not understand anything. Where is Erick?"

And he repeated in a strong voice and with a tone showing the accelerating he was "Erick... Erick..." While they were trying to comprehend each other, Erick entered the house and yelp at Otto from the outside or the gate.

"Otto takes it easy, let me explain to you, I have been looking for you for a while, but now Modesto took care of everything."

Otto asks him for an explanation, telling him all he went through, Erick was thinking for some time and analyzing all the information giving by Otto, he elaborates a quick mental plan and agree to his plan.

Erick explain that in base to the plan, he shouldn't do what he did, because took very much attention since he shouldn't make himself notable, and ask Otto to keep himself to the border of everything they ask, Otto more tranquil, said, "I understand, but why don't you give me more details once and for all for not to be like that and be able to cooperate in this?"

Petition which Erick agree, and both went out of that house bound for a place outside the city, close to a field, that looked like a landing field, waiting to pass that agitation. Once there they start to develop the detail or the plan.

Erick explains that he must elaborate maps and draw route from this city until the Pacific Ocean, which implicate to do 12 flights in the early morning and 12 flights more in very precarious conditions since they must leave enable some landing strip and apart from all this, the mission must be finish in eight months since the time was requested.

This job implicates a lot of discretion, situation that result impossible and even now after being obvious in this community, for which must add modifications to the plan.

They devote to restore the plan and during several weeks they did not get out of the property, during this time they receive everything through Capitan Modesto, however, this one, was helped for several women in between them was a lady called Doña Cuca, relative of the Capitan; a girl with the name Marta and a young girl that always accompany Doña Cuca, and who Otto follow in Guadalajara, this girl each time was seen more present in the place, since she was very curious for this foreign men that were different to the ones in that area.

While the time goes by and working, Otto and Erick learn to eat local plates, like the tortillas that Otto did not like much, saying that taste like dough, he prefers a bread with a salty taste that was elaborate in that zone, he love it for the not traditional flavor that he was used to; as a different for him, Erick prefers the tortillas, that he love it.

Both were well attending, but the socialization was not given, except at the supper time and dinner time, little by little they were knowing better in between the foreign and the hosts, to the point on developing certain familiarity and mutual sympathy.

Each day were closer to them the two younger girls: Julia the daughter of the Capitan Modesto and Marta, Julia's cousin. Both were helping to do the labor of the house, or better said bringing and taking all the necessary for their work; this did not go by for any of the fourth, the time and the cohabitation will bring consequences.

After several weeks, Otto and Erick received the parts of a light plane to perform the required overfly to be able to continue with the mission. When finish building the small plane, they proceed cautiously to carry out the test in the place away from the city, in a camp close to the train way to Chapala. There they cover a makeshift shed where they were working to finish the plane.

The day arrived, they were ready and have every-thing prepare; an early morning of December, Otto took off while Erick does control operations in land on his radio system. This new experience of flight was trap-ping each time more to Otto, he got lost in the just dis-cover of Mexico's sky and while he was getting higher to the south east, he imagined that he was flying over his native land; he saw the beauty of the Cajititlan lake, went up to pass the mountains to encounter with the majestic Chapala lake and stay stone with the large lake, the animal life, specially the bird diversity. Otto was so thrilled to see the beauty of the place, that decided to go around the lake, went up to four thousand feet of high and took advantage of such a position to look to the deep of the horizon and appreciate clearly the two giants; an active volcano that was emitting big fuma-role and, on his side, a big mountain with snow... It was a spectacular different to all he has seen, it was beautiful to see how the clouds form under the foothill of those natural monuments; just spectacular.

The overflight, aloud him determine that the place was not far from the Pacific Ocean. Otto got back, verify the landing conditions and with no notice came to his head the idea to look for another zone more distant; immediately thought in the enormous lake and consider inspect the zone to find a place more distant to establish his base.

When Otto land, he met with Erick and start developing the views and the closeness, however the curious and other people that saw the plane start to come closer to the camp; Erick did not like this; so, they prepare everything to move the landing zone to a place more distant, far from questioning and from persons that could alter the plans. This way, Erick gave the order to keep looking for another place to establish; Otto according with his air sights, suggest moving to investigate the high zone of the Lerma River that flow in a great lake, since he detect that when he went by the lake, this one was acting as a big mirror for the radio waves, which was ideal to place such a system and use it as the base work to conclude the plan. Moreover, point as a benefit that there the transmissions were a lot better, with such arguments, Erick did not have another option that to be agree, of course after thinking over for a minute.

Immediately, they went to Guadalajara and by means of Capitan Modesto Ramirez contract the workers crew that move and dismantle the improvise hangar to put it in wood boxes and store it until further notice.

Meanwhile Otto spends sometime in the place, resting and knowing the zone; he always uses his white hat and after worse he starts dressing in all white, like remembering the personage that he met in

Veracruz, besides that he feels fresher. The time went by since the incident with the trolleys; situation that allowed him to be tranquil walking on the city while Erick accompany him.

Such a situation starts a small romance between the German foreigner and the two young ones that assist them. There was no day where they were cohabiting, as much as Erick and Otto were not well seen in the town; Erick as an English teacher was popular with the girls, it was well known that he gives English and German classes and besides he has the peculiar characteristic that the third class ends in bed with their students... He was such a character in downtown zone of Guadalajara. On the other hand, Otto was more reserve, but none less known by the girls, however there was one in special that did not let him alone for a minute... This helps him a lot to domain more the language and fall in love more for this new land.

While this happen in America, the high command of Phase 4, was receiving instructions to postpone the project for six more months, at which times they will receive the corresponded pay for their services. There were no more orders, and they must be in attendance to the new instructions, in Germany, the NAZI party took already the power and was asking to intervene in the Phase 4 structure, however, the high command of Phase 4 prefer to keep the secret about their activities until farther notice. That's why in a certain way Erick, Otto, and their team kept in an inanimate for some time.

This plan time promote that Otto discover that one of the young ones was very interest with him, to such a grade that Capitan Modesto got upset and one evening he demands that, they not to look for trouble with him, since he will have consequences and it won't

matter on rank and missions; that if they have something going on with the young ones of the house (specially his daughter), they will have to marry them by the
law or do not see them again... Such a word has a strong
impact on Otto and Erick, since they were very comfortable in that place, they were feeling like kings and
this episode came to torment them. Yet Erick agrees to
keep one of them and Otto seeing this, decides to follow
his example.

"Otto, look, at it this way, you and I have enough
women, these young ones are capable to do everything
or what? Are you waiting for your Hilda to come back?"

Otto answers him, "Don't say anything about her,
Hilda is everything for me and I'm not capable to do this."

But Erick answers him with a big laugh, "Ha, ha,
ha, continues laughing, but you even left a baby in
Cuba! And you are telling me this..."

Otto, taking a serious look, interrupt, "We are not
sure about that, could be Vladimir or anyone else. Erick,
I'm sure that if was mine she would tell me..."

"Ok, calm down, what are you going to do now?
will you continue with women to women, or will you
settle with one of these? At the end of everything this is
only for some time don't you think so? I wouldn't take
it seriously and you will have the permission to do anything in this dirty country; with their 'laws' that they are
not limiting me for nothing."

Otto stayed thinking and answers him, "I will
think about it, but about the laws, I don't care either but
in regard staying in this country: first dead than stay
here. Ha, ha, ha...

After this dialog, they talk to the Capitan Modesto
and arrange the papers to marry in secret to the young
ones accordingly. It was such a cultural shock between
them that even the communication base on signs and

mimics, the girls please their low instincts to the grade of being scared after several months of cohabit.

Months went by and meanwhile Otto dedicate to look for an ideal place to conclude his mission. He moves around to Chapala lake shore analyzing all the possibilities, he couldn't use work material, since all operations were temporary stop. Meanwhile Otto dedicates himself around those places to help the people in altruistic way while he was looking the best place to install the communication system and the previous plan by Phase 4. He went by Ocotlan where the poverty did not let them cultivate, because the high price of parts, the people look for the German don Otto to such a degree that he was like a legend, since Otto took care of himself hiding anywhere for more than a month. He repairs a lot farm machinery and charge in a symbolic way, accepting what the people gave him as thanks.

Such thanks reach to a greatness, that Otto accumulate several cattle heads and even horses, which he gave to Don Modesto so he could exchange that for money, that same person kept it in camp that was the property of Mrs. Cuca in a secret place that they only knew. His happy days of prosperity were known all the way to the ears of an influential General and ex-president of Mexico, who knew of the German exploit, he asks to meet him to help his property in Jiquilpan.

Don Modesto has an intimate relation with the Zuno family, who were helping the local politic movement, Otto was well seen for this group that Don Modesto belongs and such a relation allowed him to move within this group of persons, that thanks with good amounts of money and projects of irrigation of land very interesting; in what Otto was an expert.

In June of 1928 a meeting with his friend Erick, in a small restaurant of Gunter Hans, a retired old German that has a restaurant that was called "la Alemana" in front of train station and behind the Aranzazu church; in this place was very typical to find lots of Germans, some for work reasons, other residents of that city that like to taste the beer made there, very German style and the German typical food: the Schintzel with potatoes and Sauerkraut, also German Chamorro and sausage and plates made with a local flavor but keeping the delicate and essence of Germany.

Being in that relax environment, Erick came closer discretely to Otto and ask him to accompany him, "Otto, I have to see you urgently, come with me..."

Otto left his beer and followed him, "What happen? Is the mission back on? Tell me!"

"Calm down Otto, is something personal, more complicated... Hilda is here..."

"How? Where?! What happen? Erick tells me..."

"Calm down Otto, this is very delicate".

Very quiet they left the place, to meet in a new point of meeting: the house over Miguel Blanco street. Once there, enter to the interior hall; where some day in the hall, in that living seat Otto was sitting. Breathing deeply, Erick took him by his arm and told him looking at his eyes.

"Hilda wants to talk to us she is sick from her stomach and wants to see us. Calm down, we will enter the room; she wants to inform us herself of something... My friend, we are together on this... I know about you two..."

Otto amaze without saying a word got up and enter the room where Hilda was laying on the bed.

There a deep dialog starts between those three, they were talking about their distress and the Germany situation, but Hilda stopped both in an intent of creating a compromise between the three, which made them responsible of the destiny of their loved country, it was then when they notice were supporters of very different ideologic current: (and was a fourth one that will change the destiny).

The first current was the German conservatives, that continue giving money to take out Germany from the poverty, recuperate the German proud with work and demonstrate to the world the authenticity of their promises of a pacific and working country, but aristocrat, where the social class were generating according with the capacity of each person and not for a political corruption with the cost of power that oppress the country. In other words, the directing will be those more capable, prepare and with resources to do it, even the idea of standing for the work is for the ones who generate work and only with discipline base, effort and ingenuity can get ahead, looking for the good of his national identity: Supreme Germany, this was the same line of the nobles, aristocrats and the vestige of a monarchy that keep this region by vigil in harmony. To which Otto was grasping.

On the other hand, it was the socialism current, what Erick commune, a truly follower of Kant, Schiller, and their fundamental pragmatic philosophies, without felling on populism and libertinism where the democracy and the common well was his maximum which Erick was attached and he sees for the good of the German country and his biggest grudge for the great defeat of 1917. That grudge impulse him to work in favor of any cause against the nation enemies.

And at last was the third current institutional, where by means of the totalitarian state, that rule the country destiny; where the industry and the commerce are property of a unique destiny: for the country and by the country for that only end. Which Hilda support. She was convincing of her ideals for her Marxist influences;

same that Germany, in that moment repudiate totally to such a degree that were evident the mutual hate between the supporting and the different politic lines.

The three of them have different ideas of what they want for Germany, but even though they were out of their country, which make them an easy target for any of the tendencies that would take the power in the new nation.

But there was a current that was not commune with none of the three, it was supporting the best of each of them, but was taking to the extreme the worst face: it was the Nationalism Socialism current; directed by an insane and his partisan that were taking advantage from the hate to the communism, the fall of the monarchy, the blame of another for the defeat of 1917, poking the fire of the German country where was more vulnerable: his identity. Line the biggest looser, the greater defeat, the thirst of revenge, destruction and the grudge become in hate to the other countries and races. This explode inside a lot of people that did not have anything to lose; since they lost everything, even the elemental that was their identity. It was in that moment that was used for that group of "lowborn" like they were known in Phase 4, reason they were looking with all means to close the way to this current where you can visualize the destiny of a perverse plan of a self-worship leader.

In such a scene, the three of them, respecting of each current, they must collaborate at least to take care of each other and protect their common interest: Germany; in a such a way that if one was betray, will avoid the other one to fall and on, they took the oath on Phase 4 and they kept it on their own to at least protect their love ones, since now Otto, Erick and Hilda got married and form their own descendants. Therefore, they must avoid the punishment of the betray or their oath in

Phase 4 fell on them... They were analyzing that point when Otto thought determinedly and just ask Hilda, "You are married, right?

Ask Otto intrigue to Hilda; she responded, "Yes, but the baby girl is not Schmitt's, that is all I can tell you."

"How old is that baby girl?

"She was born in May of this year, for your information, you must understand what I'm going through... Just imagine why I'm appealing specially to you..."

Otto kept silence, thinking on what happen before leaving Phase 4; he kept thinking questioning to Hilda, "Hilda?" Otto took her by her hands and looking at her very tenderly in her eyes... Like talking between them, in an absolute silence, it was a deep connection with her; looks like they were talking without making a sound from their lips, it was so deep like their feelings. Their thoughts were aligning and their breaths where synchronizes for a minute, without saying a word... Otto put his sight down and told Hilda. "I understand everything..."

She let out from her eyes a tear that fell on her face and immediately change the subject to continue giving details of what was going on.

Hilda told them that now she was responsible of the first American web of implementation of the system of information expansion from the team of Phase 4 and has information of the plan that will go on depending of the current which they will incorporate. While she was showing the decoding plans, she indicates of the need of five years of hard work, where she needs to hide.

When she organizes such a strategy, she looks for support in all the agents, but she decides to look for the only two hopes: Otto and Erick; since she knew the risk to expose that she has a daughter; which was born in her native city and hide her existence, with a temporary leave permission for health reasons, she expose herself to the worst, but she avoid being discovered, she left Germany as incognito and arrive in Mexico in the same way. She begs them that Vladimir shouldn't know any detail, she asks them for an extreme discretion, since she could hold up anything, they could do to her, but not to her daughter...

She begs them to keep the secret, since soon she will find the way of taking care of her daughter. As Otto and Erick look at each other, the three of them took their hands and made the pact of taking care of each of them for the rest of their lives, until the descendant last; that is how Hilda gave then the documents with the information on what is coming and ask them both not to be in danger, to hide for some years and they will hear from her, they accept all and each of her conditions and receive their instructions.

The three of them warmly say good bye and each of them left on different destiny, Hilda stays there for a few days in Guadalajara, for her daughter, leaving her in the care of a family, which identity Otto and Erick agree to keep the secret and at the same time keep an eye on her. Hilda left to South America where she was forming the first divisions of Phase 4 in south America, since it was considered the place more secure to develop their activities discreetly, but as soon as established there she will meet with her daughter.

Otto thought it was impossible that a mother leaves their daughter in such conditions, it was inadmissible for him, but in the circumstances in which Hilda was perfectly comprehensive. Otto assumes all the responsibility and it was like his own daughter, because it was and he knew it; Erick, also understood everything, he was agreed and consent to keep the secret and support both in this painful but necessary separation. Erick and Otto kept it until the end this secret.

The girl was place in the middle of a Mexican family that gave her protection and lots of love, the years went by and she grew up living a princess life, Otto, and Erick watch over her always, to a such a degree that Otto's wife couldn't stand that reality and repel the girl in all the forms that were possible; Otto never told her that she was his daughter, but he sees her like it was and he always introduce himself to her as her father. This ended in a serious conflict that increase the distance between Otto and his wife.

Meanwhile, Otto was attach to the indications and together with Erick select a place where they start their work requested by Phase 4, which was a lonely camp for everyone else and strategy located in the best place of all: the camp of Cumato; a very small village, with a population of ten to twenty families, close to the town of La Barca and to a small-town call Briseñas. There was selected by the means of Don Modesto, now Otto's father in-law, he had an excellent relation with an ex-president of Mexico who had lots of farming land, some complete forgotten and some half cultivating, however with the ones he cultivates had to generate a wealth equally to the production of all the Michoacán state.

This relation gave the elements that by the means of Don Modesto, the middleman, Otto can obtain a land giving it by commission of irrigation, under the look of finance project by the federal government, appointed to generate a central pumping from the lake territory to the towns.

In less than a year there had 20 crew workers, a total of 200 rural coming from other states and under the temporary workers; some that were taught the reinforced concrete, several technics of vaults, concrete constructions never seen in the area, a special technic, to such a degree that were constructed more than ten thousand square centimeter distributed along in three labels in a one single year; all that to a the meters deep, such a construction was develop in a total clandestine before the amazement of the few people of that place, that was known as "the little white house of the wheel."

It was a sophisticate construction with tunnels of internal irrigation that were working as refrigerates since the deep where they were, the temperature was very high and was giving ventilation and the air was circulating in the interior. It was a work to shelter more than 100 elements: everything was plan: cabins, bathrooms, kitchen, communication center... Including has an energy center, since for those dates they transform several tractors in power generators to such a scale that they have power in all the work and provide close to 200 homes with power and public lighting, situation in that forgetting place it was impossible to imagine. The structure was equipped with a deposit sand which capacity was almost 25,000 liters of diesel and gasoline, which was designing to work underground so couldn't be seen to the public and the objective was to generate electric power to be able to operate the center, since they must finish the work no later than 1930.

After of conclusion with this work, all the crew were dismissed and everything was cover with 2 meters of dirt and on top of this was build a warehouse where was place the materials for the irrigation system, that was the apparently purposes.

While all this was happening, the life of Don Otto, like was known in the region, was very simple; he was a mechanic well known but estrange at the same time. Otto changes the perception of this country and their people when he sees the poverty and the forgetting town where they live. During some years he has the experience on cohabit daily with the town people, they were very simple, with little or no education, with a struggle they have access to basic services, they were like stop in time, accumulating years of slowness, they rule by the popular knowledge like basic knowledge to survive...

The time was attracting feelings of envy in him, mainly by the workers of the place, since they see how "Don Otto" was capable of resolve situations that the cacique of the region that by convenience they did not want to be resolve. Don Otto opens their eyes to the people of the town and little by little they leave the depended of the yoke that were subdue, Don Otto touch the interest of these powerful little kings that were just hoard of seeds and ambitious speculator dress like trading that, in conjunction with the authorities and cacique operate to the people taking advantage of their ignorance and total dependency. They have the town to their mercy, they force then to work in a force march by two or three rich families from La Barca or from Zacapu, inclusive for the General himself, they squeeze as much as they can, some cases until dead in the job, they never gave them the money of their work; they were like slaves...

Don Otto spread his feelings, to the oppress town, indirectly incite those persons to realize that they can get out of that situation and be free on their own of that tyranny. But instead, they receive retaliation for their freedom and Don Otto was not the exception, he was constantly threatening, and order him to leave instigating the people, but Otto was a man of arms and did not scare him, he went with Don Modesto and told him what was going on and immediately order to fence this zone by soldiers at the service of the general. As a result, Don Otto receive federal protection in a 20 km all around him, and as an exchange he build the biggest work and in favor to the community ever made: he detour the Lerma river and their branch line to the highest zone of the general Cardenas land, technic that he learn long time ago; he did it for the first time in his own land in Germany, now he was doing it again and couldn't avoid to remember how upset his father was, even he was trying to help, however this time will benefit to a whole community, the high lands were receiving water all year long with a new irrigation system by pumping and channels only seen in Germany for that time. This bring more prosper land that produce tons and tons of sowing from there. Was as an exchange of this favor that the General allowed Otto to continue with his plan and keep it in anonymities.

While this was happening, Erick was getting three more agents to work in the installation of the radio transmission tower, such a signal had too much power that allowed them to communicate directly to Berlin, such a power was because they knew how to take advantage of the reflection properties of the Chapala lake, which sometimes made as a mirror, allow them the reflect of the radial waves. That was create a hydro port, making the dredge from the entry of the Lerma river with the Chapala lake an ideal place at the side using this point to embark the machinery and transported by plane in a complete signal, but the most impressive the high degree of sophistication that the technology had in this region, since this work of equipment arise numeral of inventions: the mud pumps, like were call by the locals; the mud dredge or the mud eater that were very common in these systems, the grates mud eater was call the Loba that extract and dredge big quantities of sediment to a such a degree that crate a deep of 5 meters in a week, all that material was taking it to the General's land and was use as fertilizer, since the dirt produce iron, hydrogen and lots of minerals that guarantee the sowing for years, it was a good-nature in the zone.

It was call "the little Germany" but was not suiting to be known and none the less to the General, who receive secretly an important amount by the German government. It was a corruption pyramid by the authorities that allow to do this work, while they make themselves "pretend not to see," because the German interest were base in the conclusion of this operation center which propose concern only to the high command of Phase 4, however all the indirect benefits overcome were to use in the General's land. It was necessary to create a new screen to dissemble the deceit activities, reason it was pretending an irrigation project and construction of a hydroelectric in the region, which the federal electricity commission was taken there to install over the pump center; letting justify the presence of the soldiers that gave Otto and Erick the protection that they required to be able to continue working on their project.

To be able to continue in this project, it was put on Elias, a young engineering guy in front of the work, who was selected for such a job, mainly to sign all documentation needed, serving more like "name giver" for the equipment of Phase 4, that as an engineer. Elias did not know such some circumstances; he was only informing that were hiring some German engineers that will support the work. Otto and Erick gave the blue prints with the specific of a small pump work; Elias Gonzalez was put out to the project, and he never knew for real what he was working on and none the less of the activities going on during the night in the work he was in charge.

In the same year start the use of the hydroplane to implement the test and the over flights of localization for targets and conclude the map draw that goes to the pacific zone. Once finish the blue prints, the information was coded triangle it in "Gelbe Netzo" or gold web, that was contemplating Monterrey, Mexico City, and Chapala lake and sending everything to Berlin by codes; all this information was gathering from the years of 1930 to 1935. Therefore, the things will change to a hundred and eighty degrees and this time will be final.

The lives of Otto and Erick was a relative happiness, but this was only an appearance, their personal lives with a total signal, such a theme was a total mystery for the world. On the other hand, Otto kept his purpose to continue helping the people, he tries to take them out of the ignorance and share with them what he has; on his free time, he dedicates to work on the tractors, trucks, and general machinery out of order that were a lot in the zone. Make him remember that at the end of the war, he lives the same, but in this place, even without a war, it was like living in a forgotten ambient and margination... His altruist activities were expanded from Ocotlan, Jalisco to Zacapu, Michoacan; in several occasions had with him helpers, young apprentices, motivated by his philanthropy taught several young ones to repair and modify pieces, so the need of parts wouldn't stop them and keep the tractor running or repair them if was necessary.

Otto must be discreet and avoid the outstanding work, this way he completes a team of almost 20 mechanics that even they were his students, some of them were capable to repair machinery by themselves.

Otto's contribution to the community on the generation of an irrigation system by channels and pumping, the creation of channels for the vent of dams, which some of them were used to transport materials from Zamora to the Chapala lake.

The most beneficiary for this infrastructure was Don Modesto, since his role as intermediary between the agents of Phase 4 and the authorities to facilitate their job, ending in giving him the ideal position that allow him to traffic with the waters. Similar practice was giving some power in the region, since he demands payment for the consumption of water; it was a very lucrative business, but highly risk, this creates lots of enemies. Lots of them greedy of the excellent hydraulic infrastructure that Don Otto created, but with the eagerness to maintain himself in anonymous, he allows his helpers to take all the credit, some of them more astute, ambitious, and dishonest, start selling and repair the pumps than Don Otto taught them to build, since they knew very well that at the end Don Otto by his strange profile as well as his desire to be always unnoticed in between the people, he never claim anything in his business.

The business was so productive that three or four of his helpers, that with difficulty had elementary education, had the audacity to repeat and learn by memory the parts and technics needed to build same pumps as Don Otto; his mentor teaches them the form to detect breakdowns just by the sound this one emits, this way the people start looking for them instead of Don Otto, since he was barely there, so these characters took advantage to become famous comparing their work with Don Otto. After that, the presence of who was their mentor was not pleasant; these persons taste the like of the money and did not have the intention to let it go so easy. Full of greed, envy, and hate.

In the middle of this ambient, Otto intent to educate his kids of Mexican ancestry under the values that he was transmitted at home, but his efforts were completely blocked by his wife, that even he has the right to do it, avoid at any cost that were educated according to his German custom. This upset Otto in excess and ending on abandoning his intentions before the obstinate stupidity of his wife. To this relation, the communication was null, they even speak the same language, they did not understand each other, and there was no cohering, except was about sex, however

252

it was a rape relation more than marital encounter. To a such circumstance she reprimands him to an open scream that the only thing he wants from her was sex, that he has always rape her life and that he was an animal... Otto never understood what she yell in that occasion, none the less what was happening on his wife's head, so she dedicated to raise their kids at the ranch custom; but in the worst conditions and with no considerations even though were kids of a brilliant men, it was painful for Otto to see how his kids were barefooted, eating from the floor and disregard them, because their mother became cruel towards them with the purpose to pester him.

This relation lead on Otto, a feeling crisis, and resentments against the race which he procreates his descendance, which at the same time make him to remember what Hilda, Erick and even Vladimir some day they advise him: "The mixes are not good, be careful in getting involve with other races, the blood calls and can't be to your favor..." There were six descendants of nothing, at the end he must leave her, confining himself on the installations of Phase 4.

The cultural crush was such, that Otto couldn't leave with his wife and his kids, he concentrated on giving what they need to live; take care of their safety, which left in charge of it to his helpers while he dedicates totally to his job in schedules of 14 to 18 hours a day, but without his wife and kids were less interfere with his job.

Otto got discourage for the situation, that stop insisting on giving them an education like he ever had... So much careful of his father, Heinrich, and he felt totally frustrated and shamed for not doing the same with his kids. With time, the selfishness starts invading him each day increasingly to a such a degree of losing interest in the subject and leave everything in a second plan; he left his wife on the forgotten and create an image of her as an inferior being, obstinate, "stupid" and retrograde, with customs proper to the region, so confine, that for him did not have a remedy.

But for Erick was another scene, he assists to his Mexican family, he takes care of his wife which he married; she was a teacher from Guadalajara who accept and assimilate his culture, she adopts lots of German customs, the German was the language used in his family, she did learn it to be able to communicate with his love one. Also, they belong to the local German community where he oversaw cultural matters, giving the opportunity to his kids Martha and Kart possess a private education in the German cultural center that was located on the Hidalgo street, very close from the cathedral; they join during the evening for cooking, dancing classes and other traditions of their father country, to such a degree that "the Oktober fest" was organize for this group. Otto was always invited, and he usually attended by himself, at least until the little Hilda became his official accompany.

Otto, to almost losing his biological family, he concentrated in who he considers his adoptive daughter and which the jealously of his wife, turn them apart, since she couldn't understand why he was so worried for that "rowdy youngster" or "insolent." At the regret of that, he continues watching her closely, he always took care of her and did not pass a week without knowing about her. On her part, she calls "Opa Otto" and "Opa Erick" (dad Otto and dad Erick) since both always stay close to her safe and wellness and every time, they can be visiting her in Guadalajara. She was the happiest girl in the world with the family she was placed, she did not feel the need of her mother since that family gave her the love that a child need. She was so happy that Otto constantly give presents to that family, as well as all the needs for the support and wellness of the little one. As a difference of his own kids, he could leave some basics of education in the girl; between them were speaking in German, she likes the typical food of her country and very often they tasted in the special restaurants for that...

The years went by, and Otto shared with her all the time he could, and that made him very happy, because each day she was looking like her mother.

CHAPTER FOURTEEN
THE PASSION OF A BETRAY PLAN

The intrigues between the power groups each day were more frequent, and the constant confronts between them were very serious, to a such of degree that the first victims start to come out from the new internal order: It was murder in Buenos Aires, Argentina the lovely Hilda... This event was well-aimed for Otto. He finds out that when was interpreting a cross message of the Russian group and the German group; Hilda had defended her lovely country, but the ambition of power of the new command changes all the strategies and the first effect collateral was this brilliant woman.

Close to 1930, the nation that saw him born, was now a Nazi Germany, totally consumed, the delirium power and the predictions of the three of them ended, as a part of Phase 4 they still in Mexico waiting for instructions from the central command, now Otto, Erick, and all the work team in Mexico belongs to form part of the "Ober Kommand of Werhmacht" and must be present. In these dates, two proxies went to Mexico City, where they met the 36 members of the Phase 4 to adhere to the rest of the team, conforming in a total group of 186 active elements in the country to receive a series of specific work that will endure the plans of the now call third Reich that assume the total control of the operations in Mexico. One by one were interview in Mexico City, they must show the original plans to be modify by the new government regime.

This way, each of them receive their instructions and were inform of the changes to the plans, during the information came out that the new commissioned for the manager of the American operations was Helmut Kpoohler commander. This was surprise to Otto and Erick but at the same time standing on end since they knew of the preceding of this men with no heart and ambitious; the power and the money were his motives, he had lots of links in the black market of oil and iron between Mexico and Germany, as well with pirates that help him to concrete his business from Africa until several countries in Europe in a clandestine way. In the down world was known as "the Red," because his physical aspect so characteristic since he always wears a red beard, of his tendency very fascist.

Mexico, where the government declare in an open war against the religion, the fascism has a great popularity and lots to adept of power; in a corrupt country in to the path, these circumstances become excellent for Helmut since allow him to do his cruel activities of merchandise smuggle. He creates a real Mafia in his world, that soon become his empire in Mexico thanks to ambitious of power of many "dying of hunger" name that he baptizes to the Mexican people. It was very easy to corrupt them, they were mentally weak that let to seduction for some gold coins... In between them were lots of politician, contractors, state secretaries, civil authorities, and military that were working with him... In exchange he made great fortune with his business. The money ruled.

Helmut in his role of commander in chief of the zone, acts as a first action to finish the details of infrastructure work that were in process in Mexican land: the installation "der Adler" or Eagle; the Springer tower in Monterrey and the operation center of the Roma area "die Brücke" or the breach with his annexed in Veracruz.

This works was finance by the German government through chancellors and approved by the congress, there were resources call "works of cultural approximation and delimitation of war" and they were part of the conditions of performance impute by Germany after the first world war. Like this several years went by which, Helmut gets excellent incomes thanks to his dirty operations, that of course were additional to his well "pay for his country services" that he receives from Germany, the same as Otto and Erick. Otto was sending part of that money to his mother in Lucerne, Switzerland through Erick, the other part of the money was to maintain for his Mexican family and the rest for Hilda's daughter, since he considers her another daughter for him.

That same year, Otto received a telegram from Berlin to report himself at the central command; he dreaded this news, but there was no doubt, it was perfectly coded since he has in operation the communication center more advantage outside Germany, beside the equipment provided by German companies Blau Punkt, were the most sophisticate for their time, combine that was already develop a new security code that beside being numeric, work in base to a new logarithm of calculation that only they can decoding with a new code processor that has the particularity by telegram and special combinations form a unique system in the world.

The day of the meeting arrived and in February 1934, Otto arrives in Berlin; it was different and the total nature of the Nazi party was one of the evident elements. He couldn't believe what he sees; the Nazis sustain that absolutely all the greater achieves in the pass of the nation were associate with the ideals of the national socialism, even before the official ideological exist, while all the cultural creations like literacy, music, painting, history, and science must be subject to the censure from NSDAP. Phase 4 was taken from them, who dictate all the Germans must accept and believe, controlling each aspect of the life of the country, including young ones, kids, old ones... And Otto was not the exception, even in his deep, he has another ideology.

The Nazi publicity was looking for the consolidation of the Nazi ideals and the success of the regime of the "leader" or Führer, Adolf Hitler, who was photographed as the presumed genius behind the success of the Nazi party and saver of the nation, a supreme leader who did not question. Hitler has the capacity to attract the attention of the public through his powerful speeches and helps him to win a cult to the personality in behalf of his followers.

To intimidate the state and the other political parties, the Nazi party depended from a paramilitary force, the Sturmabeilung (SA) or "assault troops" that were used mainly to attack the leftist opposition, to the democrats, the Jews and other minority groups or the opposition. The violence of the SA causes before 1933 an ambiance of fear in the cities, to contribute to attract a great number of unemployed young ones to the Nazi party.

The Nazi made their own concept of Grossdeutschland, or the "Greater Germany" so they consider the incorporation of the German cities in one whole nation being an important vital step for his success and prosperity, without caring to attack other nations: they justify the doctrine of the "vital space" (Lebenraum), where the Nazi assert that Germany needed more territory to develop plenty and for that, appeal the supposed right of Germany to harm other nations with the purpose to obtain more land.

This situation obligates the team of Phase 4 to deliver information of all the land intervene by this organization, however, delivering only the necessary since Phase 4 in total secrecy, since attempt against their interest and principals. This idea the regime Nazi demand to concentrate in only one state (the Third Reich) to all the individuals of "German ethnicity" of Europe, even if they were disperse in other countries, in contraposition, the presence of population of German origin it was a Nazi excuse to increase the German territory; happen with the annex of Austria in the Anschluss or the destruction of Czechoslovakia after the agreement of Munich; in the first case with the objective of join two nations of the same ethnic origin and the second with the excuse of "protecting the minority German ethnic" that was living in Czech territory.

Finally, this ideology takes to the extreme to project the colonization of extended areas of Poland, Russia, and Ukraine with German workers, which will save the native population and then exterminate or deport the individuals "exceeded," with that, Otto was astonished, he couldn't believe what was happening and he never imagine that Germany to act that way.

Otto was escorted by SS agents to the central command of Berlin, directed by some young that pretend to dominate with his site, like demanding reverence to his uniform of General of the new team of Phase 4, who was seeking eliminating and turn in to an information and organization to achieve control of the foreign territories with German presence, which plans, the new directing to inform with lots of anticipation.

Thanks to Helmut Kohler they were informed of all the advance of this team, mainly of the ones located in America, but making emphasis in Mexico; this ensure his position as a part of the GESTAPO, since the new generals and leaders of the recent group of crazy fanatics and unhinge members of the SS argue to have a necessary unification of powers and criteria of all these experts, reason why all the members and agents were confident to present before the new authorities to dictate his new plan of work. All were confident, except for the Russian team, since as a communist they were not welcome in this new scenery.

Being in this ambient, the General in charge, Gunter Schmitt asked Otto, "Capitan..."

Otto salute him like he always did, the way he was use do it: with his right hand in the side of his front head... However, immediately he receives a reprimand, "What are you thinking stupid? There is not the way to salute! piece of shit, our leader, the Führer deserve respect."

The General raise his right hand to the front, forming with his extended arm an angle of 45 degrees, while he bangs his boots with the heels at the unison with the scream, "Heil Hitler." Demanding him to repeat in front of him and screaming at him.

"Do not forget, stupid, that is our leader, and he is the only one that will take out our country of the indignation before their enemies... Repeat it Capitan... Memorize it in your head or Do you prefer a piece of lead in your brain?"

Otto did not have a choice but to do the effort to repeat such stupidities... He did it and after that, the General proceed. "Capitan before these dates, you are removed of the missions that you were doing in Mexico and you will receive a new instruction packet that the Commander Messer will send you, according to the new plans of the third Reich."

"Yes, General," Otto simply responded.

The General asked him to leave and present himself with the convoy to meet Messer, but first do the salute Nazi for dismissing. Otto with no words, left the place, to where they were waiting to give him of the indicated.

When arriving where was Messer, he saw a room, apparently an auditory or something similar; very extensive, full of Nazi flags with a picture of Hitler in the middle of the room, guard by two big eagle sculptures in bronze, one in each side of the image. It was very impressing the quantities of swastika they had in a room. Such a room looks to be unwise to the training; it has a high platform, like for the use to give speeches.

On one side were projecting, continuously from movies where were showing a German army very organize marching; the film was accompanying the choir and Mozart, Beethoven, Hendel music, as well as some known marches, such as the Valquiria; that have an impressing moving effect on the spectators. Same way, showing lots of people happy, working, building, cleaning the streets, decorating the cities... Like it was a great scene of an anticipated victory, standing out the values of the country, their people, their customs, and notaries the white Saxon race, all this in harmony and touching the deepest sentimental of the German country.

The biggest looser, that won't accept their defeat... Otto was astonished. He still was with his civil clothes on, he was taken to the audiovisual room, after 2 hours of information about the Nazi ideology, was giving the "Mein Kamf," but before receives a full literary description, and must read himself during the time he stays in the induction. After the brain watch, he went to a bedroom in front of the salon, it was a changing room and inside that room was a tailor that ask him to come in to take measurements, while he was waiting his turn for the new image change... And ideology and life course.

After three days of induction, he went with the General Messer, who meticulously did a personal interrogation, which objective was to obtain information from him and his family of his ascendency Aryan, their customs, and behaviors. When they were in that interrogatory, they show him photos of an attractive woman, "Capitan, do you see this photo? do you recognize it?"

Otto in silence, affirm with his head, "Yes, I saw her some time, on my first concentration, she is a Russian agent... I don't remember her name, who is she?"

Messer didn't respond to him and instead he said, "Now see this photo..."

Look like a face of something that looks like a woman, where you can see only the rest of her face worn out, "This happens to the traitors of the country, to the traitors of the third Reich."

"What is all this about?" Otto visible disturbed, ask him.

The General, with an authority voice and high tone, told him, "This is an example of what happens to the traitors; however, it is fitting to say that the photos are not of the same person; the first one is a traitor, the second one is the photo of how her mother was left... We pretend to notice that the traitors do not finish with the traitor dead, but with a prolongated mental agony that feels the worst fears, and the traitors end in a continues torment until consume themselves on their own horror and end with their own dead by their own hand."

When Otto heard this, he remembers what he lived on the first world war and became completely pallid, but he maintains firm and quiet, even his mouth was dry and couldn't emit any comment. Simply look at the General and trying to keep calm he says, "What else do you want to show me, General? I very well know what you are telling me, but I'm a patriot and for me, first my country before my life.

The General when hearing those words, outline a smile, and told him, "That's what I wanted to hear!"

After that, he asks him to leave. But before doing the formal salute between them. Otto left from there, with his uniform of the special foreign legion; which was a black uniform very impress, with bright red in the lapel and with some insignias of the Nazi German; with his official German bonnet, with a small but visual insignia of the eagle of the third Reich in the superior part of the bonnet.

He was given campaigning uniforms, lots of measurement instruments, new elements of codification and a sophisticated communication system, but he must change the codes used by Phase 4 for codes given by the third Reich. Was impossible for Otto to assimilate, since the new code has lots of errors and was not trusted, but even like that it was superior to the ones existing in the world to this moment. This result in a great advantage for Otto because he has thought to implement a code of Phase 4 to prevent at the time to honor the alliance with Erick and Hilda.

While he was preparing for his return, Otto has a free week, which he uses to go and see his mother in Lucerne, Switzerland. He went dressed as a civilian and try to go by as unnoticed as possible; it was a time where Germany was fair, since lots of suspects to intent to attack their neighbors. Even like that, in a fast way, he went to see her to know her situation.

He successes to arrive the small city, pacific and full of work as always. He went to look for his mother, who has a severe respiratory problem, she saw him and try to hug him, but Ana Marie, ask him to be prudent since she has delicate health. Otto sat at her side and try to explain to her what happen in Germany; he informs them that Johan took all their material by order of the state and the land was taken for Nazi purposes, this made his mother very sad, but she consoled herself saying that she did not lose them, simply were attach, and can be taken from that crazy government end.

He told them that for nothing in the world to go to Germany, since Johan was capable to send someone to kill them or do anything so he can have those lands; after saying such arguments, that his mother sadly accepted.

Otto did not mention that he already has a family in the foreign land, to avoid any risk; in case they were interrogated or investigated, any fact could be given by them, since there were not known and avoid risking their loved ones. Otto knew the capability of these individuals and he knew what they could do if they knew about that family. In the other hand, he asked his brother Arthur, to keep far away and do not come back to Germany and even less to know that he was working in a business with Abraham and Elias, which they ask all their cousins to do the same, but some did not want to understand that was very dangerous to stay in Germany...

Otto persuades his mother to never mentioning that she was friend or knew the Hoffman family, since it was for sure that they will get all the Jews in Europe. This put his mother very nervous and his sister, but he calls them down and obligate to compromise to maintain that secret forever. For last, he got sure that his mother has the money he has been sending, since for that time, they live only from that money, and they were administrating very carefully since all their business and fortune were lost with all the economic problems that they had.

At the end of those days, Otto says good bye to his mother like he was not going to see he ever again, he cries for a long time by himself when knew he wouldn't come back and in that moment, came to him all his memories of his father, he felt the destiny crave; proud of his lineage, the heritage of lots of life... He saw how everything was becoming dust.

For a long time or maybe forever, he says good bye to Germany, remembering all the happy moments of his childhood in his lovely country; leaving his mother and his sister there, with no more than the hope to be fine even knowing of the horror to be unchain over all Europe. At the end, all hug and Otto got out of there to Hamburg.

The day arrive and Otto travel back to Mexico, the time was pressing, when arriving in Mexico City he met his new work team in the house on Roma area; there was the Command Helmut, the German ambassador in Mexico, Georg Nicolaus; besides a twentieth Germans, all of them in charge of different areas. Now the property of Abwehr (army) dictated by Ober Kommando der Whermacht (High Central Command) from Berlin.

They were all perfectly inform and knew why the mission in Mexico was a priority: the obtaining of their minerals, oil, natural resource and the strategic closeness with United States, since they did not know the position that this one will take before an eminent conflict and for consequently, the have to keep on eye, including they have a plan strategy in case United States enter to the conflict and this consist on distracting with a creation of a chaos controlled in their south border or in Mexico, depending of the necessity.

The initiation to repair of specific missions, Otto got his and with that was given three thousand American dollars in cash; a big amount for that time. Such a money was destiny to the mission he has commanded.

Otto achieves to identify in this moment that the Russian team was not participating in this occasion, that feed on Otto, the doubts. This time he was not alone, he will be accompanying by three new officials, which identity he did not know yet, but they will arrive to find him at his operation center in two months. This allow him to do some changes to allow him to be well prepare for an internal war that he knew will come in Mexican territory; he feared for his family and his loved ones.

Then, the first thing he did when arriving to Guadalajara, was to directly look for Erick; both were taken separated, that elevate even more suspects. They met in a small coffee shop in front of the Guadalajara cathedral. Otto was visible nervous for his temple and Erick was not behind. A dialog starts on his language, simulating they were watching the cathedral.

"Hello Otto, how was it? are you thinking the same as me?

Erick asked him in a worry tone, "If you are talking about that we are fuck, yes."

Otto answered, "Friend, I already start to make movements and you should do the same..."

"What have you been doing? Tell me!

Erick answers him in a code, more than in German; gave him the understand that he took his wife and his two kids out side of the country.

"I'm afraid for them, for their life and I do not want to risk them, I'm sure the new bosses are going to do anything to carry out their purposes. I do not talk to anyone here..."

Otto got quiet again and agree with his head.

"I do not have where to send them, beside I do not have the way to tell my wife to leave or take my kids out of here... She and I won't talk. I do not know what to do..."

Erick intervenes about Hilda, "Hilda the daughter or our pact... I did some proposes; I told the people that are taking care of her, that we are not going to see her for a long time and to say that she is their daughter. Besides, Otto, we must leave her well economically protected so she never has a need..."

"But what have we done? For the country, now we must leave our kids, family... I can't understand, I'm full of doubts. I feel very annoyed and desperate, but you are right, I will do something about it. Count with my support, only let me say good bye to her and my family, I will see what can I do."

"That is not all, Otto, I have to tell you about Vladimir: he is no longer a friend…"

Otto got astonished but kept himself sure and after a strong breath he told Erick, "I imagine that. It's going to be very complicated. We must prepare for the worst… In fact, I have a plan that I want to share with you, Erick… it is base in an error of these new bosses, do you know that they will not use our codes in Phase 4? They will use a develop one by themselves, but they have a lot of errors… We will use the Phase 4 ones but with the last updated, the one Vladimir did not receive, remember?"

"Yes of course, respond effusively Erick, anyway, we do not have a choice… So, explain me what will be the plan."

After a long talk, they share the information that each of them must see where will be the strategy of the third Reich in Mexico; both were key pieces, being each of them in a privilege positions, but at the same time in case one of them couldn't progress, it was a strategy target. After any of these two options, the possibilities were against them, they have a lot to lose. Their position was almost secure, but they must arm an alternative plan, aviation maneuver and other actions to keep alive in this mission.

Two months went by, and both were working on the internal communications, they were hiding in the Cumato, Michoacán ranch, when they identify a code where they were talking of a rebellion against the team of Phase 4 and they have the instructions of arrest three elements for conspirator against the third Reich. They identify the signal coming from Monterrey. There they have two colleagues working, they were communicating and retransmitting to Berlin, when enter the Phase 4 code, that the Nazi couldn't decoded, but Otto and Erick did. This message said: "Sabotage, sabotage. We required support..." In the message described their escape to the north, close to the border with United States. The agents were intersected by members of the SS in the desert, but the message continue: "We have privilege information, we have facts of the Mexican authorities to we have bribe, and we can make it public."

The message ended, they intent to contact again, but they did not have any answer, they continue working on that, when they received instructions from Berlin and a message coded that they interpreted: "we have evidence of some traitors to the country in the foreign front of Mexico, we have been located and they are being taken by agents directly from the SS to the operation control. In brief, the rest of the team will receive, not assign agents anymore, but a personal from the SS for all the elements of the operation are willing to cooperate with their new supervisors."

Otto and Erick were afraid, since they knew those words were very delicate and those persons did not touch their hearts, they were extreme inhuman and even more when they were doped; inside this regime it was practically mandatory to use the Parvatin than rather to make them valiant, they were a mental disturbed, a real demon; nothing stops them. Reason Otto and Erick deny taking it, in all their missions with no exceptions. Suddenly, they look to each other hoping to know the date of arrival of these new bosses, when Otto listens the message on the radio, of the invasions of Germany to France: they already took Poland, Austria... That scare Otto even more.

"What do we have to do now?!" Asked Erick to Otto.

They receive instructions to overfly the pacific and to send the coordination of the locations of ports and delivery of merchants and military material zones. Otto had 235 hours to do such activity. He asked Erick to hide somewhere else and for him to keep an eye on each other. Meanwhile, he left to a place where he had a hydroplane hiding, to prepare his flight mission.

Otto got out of his enclosure, but when he was out, he met Don Modesto, his father in-law, who was arm, and visible drunk, stagger and very aggressive.

"Hey! You, jack ass who do you think you are? My daughter... Listen very well..."

Staggering his body and trying to walk towards him continues with his screaming.

"You are not going to leave her there! Less with kids. Damned... Damned insolents! Maybe they are not even yours, damned asshole... that you leave her! You are a fuck..."

Suddenly without notice, he points with a 45 revolver and demanding screaming, "You better take care of her. What a Jack ass you are! I never thought that you were a fucking shit... Damned shit German!"

Otto understands part of the message, probably the most important, put his hands up and he tries to explain in Spanish the circumstances. In a little fluid language, he achieves to sign.

"I can make your daughter to understand... Me lots of problems, understand lots of danger with me... Not good for her to be with me..."

"Don't tell me those damned things or you pre-form right now or you die right here, damned stupid. What were you waiting for? I knew that you only want her to sleep with her, hot ass!

Otto was insisting at the same time he was getting closer to him, while Don Modesto continue cursing.

Otto continues his closeness; slowly but firm, step by step, he was not nervous, but did not let watching his movements of his drunk father in-law. Don Modesto was very drunk, with his lost side, but he was a danger, because at any moment a shot can came out.

With his hands, up and with his poorly dominate of Spanish, Otto insisted, "Look, Don Modesto, let me explain myself... Please. What you want me to do... But let me, explain."

In that moment, he was almost in front of him and with a quick move apply a technic of disarm: he took him from his arm, gave him a turn and throw him on the floor. He has him on the floor with his trap hands and took advantage of the position and throw the pistol from a quick, he put a knee on Don Modesto chest, he contains him with one hand and with another one he took him by the neck.

"Look, don't understand that is war... I'm in war! My country is fighting! And I'm dangerous... I do not want to harm you and your family. Sorry that I have family! Now you take care of her. I will leave soon from this stinky place. I won't be back! You will soon know of people worse than me... You better listen. You don't know what you are getting on."

He closes his speech with a hit straight to his face, which made him loose conscience for some time; then when some women arrive and some workers to pick him up. Otto got up, puts his finger on his face and screamed at him, "I never wanted to do this again, and if do again all your family will pay. Get out of this place! And do whatever you want, from now on you have to take care of you."

Otto took him by his neck while looking him straight to his eyes, "I tire of this people, and their customs and race!

He growls to his father in-law, pushing him he took him outside the gate of the ranch and order him to one of his arm guards of the SS that were send from Berlin, do not let this guy close to neither of their family; he throws him on the floor and Otto left walking without giving him his back until he loose sight of him...

After this accident, at the small ranch starts the rumor that Don Otto became crazy, that he fires his father in-law and hit him, this got to his wife ears, that immediately went to confront him in person, but with no results, since from that date Otto never came back and did not allow himself care for his wife and kids, that by then were eight kids... This resolution causes them a big pain and the mother use to take them out of there and move to the town of Jamay, where they stay with some relatives and don't see Don Otto any more since he became crazy.

The reality was other; Ott by that action, finally could take away his family, he was saving them from a danger of death. He must act like that, against all social norm that exist in the family community; it was a great pain also for Otto, but there was no other way to do it since he couldn't explain his family what was coming. His family could never understand this actions and Otto could never explain. After this, Otto started his last flight of recognition, he prepares the hydro plane, he did the flight like they were asking in Berlin, the information was coded and was transmit by radio to the central command.

Was given the instruction to supervise the clandestine delivery of fuel oil to Germany, this one was sent by the Manzanillo port and was going by Panama to arrive all the way to Germany; this route was implemented since was no possibility to send fuel oil and the other raw material by Veracruz, since the United States did not like that Mexico sells to Germany, since the boycott that was... But Germany was paying lots of money to officials of the recently state oil company from this ones allow to take out of the country clandestine the barrel of fuel oil... This situation was kept for several months, until were intersected by Vladimir...

Otto receives a message coded from Erick, who was under supervision of the SS in Guadalajara, Erick achieves send the message to Otto using codes form Phase 4, without the agent's notices. Otto received it and transcript immediately: "Be careful, Otto; Vladimir is looking for you and myself. We have to act immediately."

Otto knew that, if Vladimir has that intention, it was not going to be good.

Since that moment, he prepares good and implemented some prevention actions: In a perimeter of five kilometers round, by the way that he knew Vladimir will take to intent locate him; he places dispositive of radio signal, forming like web sign that will identify by approximation sounds of Vladimir to his implements. He obligates the agents that he has under him to move to the Eagle; a cover place by the warehouse of the CFE that was where he has the special underground of transitions, gave instructions to keep there until a new notice. One person can keep there for more than three months hiding or making activities in a self-way in a complete seal and total anonymous.

Meanwhile, Otto prepares the quick boats and left them ready for in case of need, he can use them and escape.

Three days went by like that, he couldn't sleep and dedicate himself to attend to the radio, checking if Erick gets to transmit any message, also to be pending of what he must say to his central command. The situation was very confused in that moment, he was very attentive of what was going on in Germany and on the front, and he was receiving instructions according of what the central command required.

The information that he was receiving was very precise and the Hitler politic of add neighbor's territory to become with Lebensraum ("vital space") that include Austria and Czechoslovakia annexed to the Czech part and establishing a government in Slovak get to the stage of the second war world on September 1, 1939, when he attacks Poland. Otto was with his nervous breakdowns, he couldn't concentrate on anything, there were quickly hours of sleeplessness, and he has the responsibility to maintain on the position, ready for any requirement, since they were in war at that moment. United Kingdom and France declare the war to Germany. At the beginning Germany has military success fast (from there the term Blitzkrieg: "fast war") and achieve the control over the low countries, Belgium, Luxembourg, north and west of France and later over Denmark, Norway, Yugoslavia and Greek in Europe, and Tunis and Libya in the north of Africa. Also, he has firm alliance to the Japan empire (who was doing their own invasion on Asia and Oceania) and Italy (that they already invaded Albania, Ethiopic, he controls Libya along with the Germans and attack Malta and Britannic Egypt). His alliance, or better say vassal, were the Vichy government (the French south part controlled by the marshal Petain and some of the colonies African and Asiatic: Morocco, Syria), Finland, Slovak, Croatia, Hungary, Romania, and Bulgaria.

Other states must collaborate with the Germans for not having retaliation and not been invaded, so their neutrality was clearly manifested, evidently to be surrounded by German territory, did not have many options, these states were Sweden, Andorra, Monaco, Switzerland, Liechtenstein, San Marino, the Vatican, and Turkey.

While in Mexico maintain on the margin and continue supplying crude oil and iron to the Germans in a clandestine way, the Russians have the doubt of something not well with Germany, because they have the certainty that the alliance with the communist was only for conveniences of the German power. The Soviet did not wait to intervene, and Erick been consent of those, let Otto knew that it was evident that the Russians were alliance with England and France, giving place of the expected for many and not ignored in Mexico.

Vladimir did not arrive to look for him in that moment, everything was a constant scaping, but Otto couldn't be tranquil at any moment, his days went by in between his hidden place in the deepest of his operation center, the furtive exits to check his communications installations were operating correctly, the constant corruption of the authorities that each time were demanding more money to continue protecting him...

At the beginning of the second war world, they were not well seen in the community, when he occasionally got out, people scream at him, "There is a Nazi!"

Which bother Otto a lot, since he was far to be one of them.

After a time, Otto stops not answering the messages send by the front of the south of United States and having a specific information about that country, that he knew that did not have anything to do with the conflict, so he starts to fragment and sending then with restrictions or incomplete; however, it was detected in Berlin and immediately, the agents of the SS were trying to locate the erroneous information source. Erick and Otto were conscious that this will happen.

An August evening in the middle of a torrential rain, the operation center was threatened for a huge flood never seen before, the river was carrying lots of water that start running over putting at risk the close towns. It was such a risk that they can lose the installations of the Eagle radio, situation that Otto has foreseen, so he applies all the pumps to all their capacity to avoid the flood. Doing this he did not count that the water was all the way to la Barca, that small town was threaten for an increasing that was taking everything on his way. Seen that, Otto quick move to a pump station that was close of there and intent to divert the course of the flooding, but the eject got stuck because the branches and the mud. The only way to make it work was to get in to manual clear it... Otto did not have other option: to close that eject or the whole town will disappear along with his installations.

He knew that by closing this, the pump could extract faster the water and avoid a major flood, he has to do it since his installations were at risk and also he will avoid that the small towns were taken on this flow; it was how he tie himself in a post and got closer little by little where the eject was stuck, he left the control on so the eject close, while his body and arms take off the branches and mud from the doors so the eject can close and the pump can start taking water to another channel. With this all the flow was diverted to the high lands and the rest was send to the Chapala lake.

It was a great exploit and the people that live knew that Don Otto saves the town of a disgrace, so a great number of persons run to help him, acclaim, and thank him what he did for that community. The matter got to a such a degree that a reporter from Guadalajara made a note that place it in the first page and the title said that a German (Don Otto) save a complete town from a flood...

His hydroplane was taken with the strong flow, it got drown and was destroyed in pieces, the flow took everything even the Chapala lake where everything got lost, that became a fortune for Otto, since means less evidence on his behalf, in fact he was thinking in disappearing the installation since he was afraid to be discover.

The news was the order of the day, and the attention was directed to Don Otto, what was enough for Vladimir to know where he was, opening the way for the great finally.

He barely sees his family, since he knew the risk that it could cause if they were related with him; he only sees Hilda once a month in Guadalajara and in the middle of an extreme caution, the girl sees him and is so happy, in one occasion Otto told her that soon he will take her to Argentina, a country where he was thinking to move, since the situation was every time more chaotic. Otto and Erick were very compromised in the illegal operations of Germany in Mexico, and their partner from Phase 4 in Berlin where looking for a way to take them out of Mexico as soon as possible. The SS took the total control of everything and it was a war against Jews and communist; the persecutions were eminent, he inclusive had receive precise instructions to stop or inform about Jews in the work team of phase 4 and to report any relation direct or indirect with this group, this causes to much to frighten Otto since he has a lot of friendship and close work relation with his administrators and family's has lots to thank them, the situation puts him in a dilemma and he was trying to hide all that history, but he felt that the Nazi and the SS already knew... He was waiting for the worst, since he was the one, they suspected, they were treated as traitors of the country.

It was the worst fear, and soon the news that were waiting arrived: Erick in a message, asked Otto to meet in Guadalajara to talk about a serious matter, they agree on the appointment and proceed carefully as always. It was mid-morning of October 19, they arrive in "La Alemana" restaurant.

There was common exchange of news, it was saying that the new politic of Hitler, it was the foment to the arm industry and the state wasn't paying the reparations of the war, that the employment was down from 6 million of unemployed in 1932 to a 1 million in 1936; this was something very amazing. They were saying that when the war explodes, because the rates tax and the resources obtain of the occupied countries join with a freeze mandatory prices, the income of the state allow Germany to stable the economy until the end of the war, this makes the Germans proud in the alien and allow to take certain companies of success, but Otto and Erick, because the information that they manage in Phase 4 knew that there was a dark bottom.

But the economic status and the unemployed in Germany was the least worries for them, when they knew the fact that Germany invade Russia the same year, since they knew of the operation (Unternehmen Barbarossa, name in a code given by Adolf Hitler), beginning on June 22, 1941, required of the contributions that the team of Phase 4 could contribute, since they have a fundamental information of the Russian front, obtained during the time when they were alliance in the Republic of Weimar. Giving this information means a great hard hit for Phase 4 because the violation to the confidential principals that has suitable by the Nazi party. Making use of his power on all ways seek and eliminate lots of members of the team Phase 4 with the purpose of obtain the information and use it with their old alliance and implement his invasion plan of the Soviet Union by the axis forces during the second war world. This operation opens the Oriental front, that become in the theater of one of the biggest operations and brutal of the arm conflict in Europe.

The Barbirroja (red-bearded) operation means a great hit and high trade of their alliance; the Germans seal his own dead letter and Otto's and Erick's fear about Vladimir stay base, they did not have any idea what will happen, but they knew the range of the information that Vladimir had thanks to his operations in Mexico and even more because he helps to arm the web. It was evident that Otto, Erick, and Hilda were in a danger risk, especially when was announce the knowledge that the Germans unprepared massacre to the soviet forces: a truly traitor, because such a butcher was possible only thanks to the classify information that was exclusive of Phase 4. The hate was based on the German traitor and their team of traitor, leading for the crazy they have as a leader...

Otto and Erick have classified information, which they have safe that the communist, for the first time, they will join England; something never seen before, but will happen, because the gravity of the German traitor... The soviet suffer strong loses and lost big extensions of territory in little time; nevertheless, the arriving of the Russian winter finish with the German plans of finishing the invasion in 1941. During the winter, the Red army attack and make null the hopes of Hitler of win the battle of Moscow, the operation ended on December 5, 1941, with the retreat of the German army.

The damage was done, now they have the enemy over them and the beginning of the German hunting in Mexico... Vladimir send messages coded by Phase 4, they did not have escape; Otto and Erick desperate, ask for support to Berlin explaining that were errors in the messages security by radio and asking for the change of coded telegram. Their petition was granted in exchange of give part of the classify information, since as part of the protocol, all their movements were documented, becoming the documentation on inevitable evidence of all their subversive activity in the foreign country. The Mexican authorities were not responding to their petitions of protection because they were being exchange for high amounts of dollars that Vladimir as well as the England agencies offer to the Mexican corruption as a change of revealing the activities of the Germans of Phase 4 in Mexico.

The hunting start, Vladimir has already the contacts bought, while Otto maintains in a complete total alert, he has a second base located inside the communication center, about 500 meters from there. One afternoon, Otto heard some noises and abnormal movements of the people of the ranch, he sees the people running from one place to another and at night, when the movement ended he went to check the operation center for the inside of his bunker and when he went in to check that his partners were there, he did not hear anything; so he went in the middle of the total darkness, to discover little by little the horror that immediately awake all his delusive when he was in the battle: his demons came back when in front of him saw his partners totally dismember, everywhere and there a blood message coded from Vladimir on the walls: "Otto, you are the next one."

It was too much cruelty and the rancor of Vladimir that Otto was almost paralyze of fright, but he reacts immediately, got out of there like he can; on his escape, he hears shutting and makes him run even more in to the sowing nearby, he jumps in to the river and let the flow take him until he gets close to the dock, where he grabs his boat and got in and very fast went in to the Chapala lake. When he was escaping, he saw like ten people on the border of the river with arms, that were watching him leave... He was sure that Vladimir found him, the things were going to complicate even more for what happen to his partners there.

Otto was crying of desperation and did not have any other option than leave to the Chapala town, trying to take advantage, and look for Erick with the hope to know what to do and to take and exit.

Meanwhile this was happening, Vladimir and his people, start the cleaning of the place, they took the bodies and took the documentation, the codes and all they could; they put everything in suitcases and boxes, they open the doors of the basement and flooded. They have the support of the army and the authorities, since the money and the corruption was higher, they oversaw burying the bodies in commune graves, on eliminate completely of all the related to the operation and destroy the communication tower; ones realize this, dynamite the walls of the bunker, making the water flood the place and less than a day disappear all the installations of Phase 4. This unravels, at the end of all, represent certain benefit for Otto and Erick since such installations clear their existence. Combine to them, the village notice of an unusual movement in the place and were afraid, avoiding getting close to that zone, reason there wasn't witnesses of anything. All was looking too easy for Vladimir.

Unfortunate, Otto didn't totally protect the information there, inclusive the most secret one was hide in his refuge, to 500 metros of the destroy base, it was a small cabin, however he must comeback there to conclude his job and erase his trade. He had a plan, and he will do it step by step that how he arrives to Guadalajara, it was night, almost early morning like about two in the morning. Otto and Erick previously were agreed that in case of being trap or follow, they will meet in the basement of the house on Miguel Blanco 34, since he has protected information that compromise Phase 4.

Otto arrives to the address, but before advice of his encounter to Erick, by a paper with numbers on it, that he left outside his house after ringing the door. Meanwhile Otto was waiting on the train station, sleeping in a broken train, but early in the morning went to Miguel Blanco, but when he got there, he discovers that the door was open, he enters the false door that was for the basement and discover Erick very pale and very nervous with lots of documents in his hand and shaking.

"Erick, calm down, we have to think well all things, we have to concentrate, this is serious, but we cannot lose our heads."

They have some technics that apply to lower the pressure in crisis moments that they learn in Phase 4, since they were expose to this type of ambient in a constant way; this consist on breathing deeply, sit and concentrate on oxygenated the brain, they control the breathing and with a mental effort to focus in happy events, they achieve to calm down, then take a sugar lump that they leave it on the mouth until dissolve it with the saliva. This way they got tranquil and can think.

They start the process to decipher the Vladimir plan, since he was plaguing Mexico of United States, England, and Russian agents. It was evident his culpability and knew the punishment in case the information fells in enemy hands. Phase 4 was totally compromised, so they write a communicated to the dome of Phase 4, where was asking for specific instructions for the manager of the crisis, they send it with a new code by radio, so they can obtain an immediate respond; but the message was detected by Vladimir team, however they couldn't decode... When Vladimir notice got furious and ask the Mexican government to turn an order of apprehension and search against of those two foreign that they were in Guadalajara. Otto and Erick interfere such a message and notice that it was public for their search.

Not just Otto and Erick notice that, Don Modesto in his behalf, finish discovering what was happening with Otto and finally understand the things and the danger his daughter and grand kids were exposed, reason he moves to Jamay to pick her daughter up and her grand kids and took them out of there to shelter in Cumato; in a very small ranch in the middle of the sowing to avoid being discovered. At that moment was all Don Otto words make sentence and discover, that with his attitude, he saves the life of his daughter and his grandchildren.

Therefore, Otto and Erick start the plan "disappear" that consist in the destruction of any evidence of the existence of Phase 4 in Mexico; to achieve their goal, they divide the activities. Erick was the most expose, since he was recognized in the city of Guadalajara, so he must stop going out to the street, fortunate, he already sends his children to the city of San Antonio, Texas, who now, used the last name of her mother, he already says good bye, however he wishes to communicate with them for the last time...

Was that moment of feelings that the phone call could be intersected by the Vladimir group, which immediately, gave notice to his division in United States and a week after of the phone call...

Erick omits mentioned to Otto the phone call to his wife and both concentrate on their work and destroy all documentation they have. Erick was almost finishing burning the information that he has to destroy, only was a part of secret codes left, when for his misfortune by order of the high command, appear the amounts of done operations; of the clandestine shipment, the delivery of money to the politician and the names of authorities that give protection to Phase 4 in the country, as well as the American agents that work for both, when he feel a presence in the darkness, but he continue throwing papers in a burning barrel that was expelling fire.

"Erick, do not turn around... I'm here for you."

"Vladimir," said Erick to the human figure that can see in between the shadows projector by his small fig tree.

"Yes!" Respond mocking and making resonate his laugh.

"You believe to get one's own way... Really? You can't with my cleverness and my intellect, I always win!" Affirm Vladimir.

"If you are burning that information... He made a pause, leaning on the light of the flames and from behind of him, he shows him a photo of his children and his wife tie up... At the end it's not matter... Throw the photo to the fire... At least we get an agreement...

Erick was astonished and without looking at him, say, "What do you want?"

"Only want names and facts... That's it, that in exchange of your family".

"I do not have more family than Phase 4."

Erick responds accurate; however, Vladimir continue, "They know that you are a traitor..." He shows the picture of his partners on Phase 4 dismember on the bunker. "Yes, they know... by the way what an inhuman you were...

Erick lost his control and scream, "Is not true!"

Then he let go against Vladimir, but this one got him by his neck and after struggle three persons enter and hold him, tying him, and put him in a chair.

"Ah! Erick, shit little German, always a looser, the world most stupid, you thought that your damned country of shit will protect you... Let me tell you that Phase 4 now is with the Americans, Russians, England, they sold to the best bidder and your damned leader or shit will end like you: hate and forgotten. Ha, ha, ha, cut to the chase: I give you a choice, but you know I don't like to play. I would like to see how you suffer with your member in pieces, but first is first and then comes the pleasure..."

Erick kept immutable, did not say a word, only breathing each time stronger.

"I want you to give me the information, each name one by one! And for each fact you give me, is a part of your family body that I will respect. Ha, ha, ha, we will start on the hands; give me the name of the rats of the Mexican government that sell...

Erick did not respond, and Vladimir continue with the "persuasion," "The feet; the name of the army people that help you. The head; the name of all and each of the agents of phase 4 in Mexico and United States. Please..."

He grabs him by his hair and pick his head up until leaving his neck uncover, he put a dagger and flourish his skin; immediately he starts bleeding, he flourishes the skin on his front head and all his face was bleeding. But the cuts were over the skin, Erick was conscience and Vladimir continue to torture him, like this they were for two hours, he couldn't finish to burn all the documents, but Erick keep himself firm until the end...

Vladimir ended decapitate and burning his body with all the people that were in that place. At the end, all was like an accident like a fire in the basement of Miguel Blanco, when the authorities arrive gave certification of the unknown dead white man, and look like a vagabond that fell sleep and accidently the place got fire... That's the way Erick die and never came out to the public his existence.

Vladimir took the rest of the information with few names that were left on and try one by one to locate the rest of the members of the team of Phase 4... Otto was on the list. The end of Erick's wife and children was tragic, according with the official reports they die in a car accident when they were traveling to Houston, Texas, and there was no surviving.

Vladimir was busy trying to decode the little information he has on him and during those weeks, Otto comes back to Cumato, to the same cell where sheet by sheet he burns all the information. Otto took advantage that Erick gave him to ensure of not leaving trace that bind them with Phase 4, however until that moment there was an order to arrest against all Germans who were in a Mexican land, and took them to Veracruz, since that was the way Vladimir arrange it, who extortion the Mexican authorities to obey such a required instead of following the process formality; German, Japanese or Italian citizen, all of them were enemies for Vladimir and his team.

Also, there were offering a reward for any person for any of these nationalities, inclusive only with the suspect or presumption. This way was applied to achieve that the people and authorities of the place capture, so Vladimir could avoid such a work. The authorities of the respective countries did not restrain or gave Consular support, since those nations have war declare against Mexico and did not have individual guarantees. Lots of foreign that did not have anything to do with searching of Vladimir were imprisoned to take declarations even if they were not related. This was part of Vladimir's plan to discover the members of Phase 4.

Otto was alone in a place totally forgotten for his Germany, he thought it wasn't worthwhile all the loyalty to his country, the land of his parents, the land of great man; since now he was there, alone and forgotten by the whole world... It was a feeling of a totally humiliation, pain, sad and disappointment, he was feeling traitor by his country, his German proud was down to the floor. Now it was evident what had told him: Germany was the greater looser and he was living it himself, not for the first world war, neither for the second one, but for passing for all of them and did not learn anything... Were moments of totally isolation and darkness in his mind while he was burning each of his memories.

For each paper he was burning, he was going little by little erasing his story, he was feeling like he was seen his ancestors leaves on the smoke one by one. Each time he burns a photograph, a document, a paper, revive a fragment of his life, of his great father, his grandfather, his mother, his brother and sister, his friends... Each of them were presenting in the smoke like wanted to ask for forgiveness; they were resisting the fire to disappear, but those memories ended consume by the power of the flames and vanish in the fire to elevate their figures and become in dense smoke that vanish disappear like images that go up to the sky until losing them in the middle of lonely camp.

All this was happening in a land that was not his... And like that came out the tears from his eyes and his respiration was cutting to become in a disconsolate cry of a soul that was dying of pain and grief, of repentance and desperation, full of fear. His mind reviewing his life, one by one the memories, at the time the tears come out of his eyes and the memories from his mind, leaving it each time emptier...

Hilda, his love; Raquel; Julia, his wife, his children, which were leaving then in total abandonment and without a good example he could never give them. It was clearly pain and repent and in those sobbing moments, appear also all his friends, who one by one were disappearing in the smoke of the same way that his memories. When he was about to finish burning the last documents, Otto was not in existence.

Following the last moment, the instructions of Phase 4, was looking for a total cleaning the trace and not leaving loose end; he knew about Erick, and he also knew that he was not far of having a similar end since Vladimir required to complete the information that he achieves to take from Erick and knew he will come for him.

But it was too late, he closes before the chapter of Phase 4 perfectly, there were no evidence, there was nothing related him and neither the other 12 members of the team not located. Otto destroys all trace, to avoid getting on the hands of the leaders in Berlin, Latin America, Mexico, and United States, as well the high command of Abwher in Germany, that were subdue by the new power and for that moment, Otto did not have an identity, all his memories have been destroy.

Now, he burns the last document, Otto was there watching the consume fire; with a hinge look, he put his campaign uniform and put on the German flag from the Keiser, put the insignia of war from his air battalion and with his pistol like render honor in a total loneliness his funeral image presaging the end. Like that he kept firm and in front of the bonfire until being empty, in a total autism, without watching and hearing, without talking during the whole day and night, sitting in front of that barrel where everything has been eliminated...

Being the early hours of the morning, you can hear noises and steps that were getting closer to the place, Otto like wanted to react, simply turn his face to the place where the noise of the steps was coming over the dirt and saw how in the shadows and poor lighting, the darkness that shadow the faces and the souls of the gather in there, a figure between snapping of fingers that look like counting the steps, Vladimir finally was getting to his appointment with Otto...

"Finally, we meet, little German piece of shit."

Otto reacting, he put his hand on the pistol and took the luck off, but Vladimir interrupted, "Don't gain courage, you know what the rules are. You are well informed and know the protocol (referring to the training that he receives when enter his squadron during the first world war and gave him the Lugger). I see that I'm late, just look at this! how was that possible?! You did not tell me anything..."

Otto was immobile and when Vladimir arrive in front of him, Otto quick took out his pistol and aimed at him; Vladimir put his arms up and said, "Otto don't stress on giving me a shot, because in ten seconds you will get eliminated: there are five marksman pointing to your head... And you won't gain anything killing me... Or would you have the capacity to eliminate the five of them?"

Otto did not let go pointing to Vladimir and being head to head, they look at each other in their eyes and Vladimir said, "Let's do this easier if you pretend to kill someone, point to yourself, to your empty head and that's it! everything is over."

Otto put down the weapon and Vladimir, in that moment got closer and took Otto's weapon while he said, "Otto, this is a marvelous moment for me, but I won't give me that luxury; you have to pull the trigger."

But Otto emits some words, "I knew this will happen, but I'm ensure Vladimir, that at least you will never find the way neither the form to defeat Phase 4."

When Vladimir interrupted, "Phase 4 Germany, EVERYTHING is lost. I'm not interesting anything of that, the only thing I want is power and for your information, I'm more powerful and richer each day."

Otto reproves him, "You will be as powerful and richest as you want, but you will be alone the same as us and you will pay the crimes; I'm sure of that, I'm paying it and I prefer thousand times more being dead that continue with this pain that burns inside me, is a life inferno and that is what you will have..."

"Enough of absurd discussions!

He put the weapon on his hand, several times and subdue him; Otto knew his end, "I won't give you the joy to make me suffer and torture!"

Vladimir got furious when after some minutes searching the information, his partners who capture him discover there was anything to see or to find.

"General Vladimir, there is nothing here!"

Vladimir took Otto's hand with the grasp pistol, cut cartridge with his hand, and put the weapon in Otto's mouth... And shot.

Otto fell on the floor and all his skull vault took all his brain out of place literary Otto was empty. Vladimir threw the body and left him there. Furiously Vladimir left with her empty hands, with no trace to finish his mission.

Next day some woodmen were walking by and saw a body lying on the floor, in front of a barrel full of smoke ashes still; it was Otto's body with a shot in his head and his disfigure face in the middle of a pool of blood.

In that moment, they went to let know the Cumato town, gave notice to the commander who quick went to place and notice that was Don Otto. This news went through the ranch very fast... They took the body to La Barca where was register in the municipal president office a foreign, that was casual there and he was astonished of the fact... It was Vladimir himself, that with an impudence in all his expression and a gibing smile, contemplate how they bring the body of Don Otto in a wooden box that once was the bundle of some pumps.

"What a tragic end!"

In the box emphasize the legend "made in Germany, high quality equipment."

Laughing, left a manila color envelop on the desk of the municipal president to do what he was commanded.

"You know what do you need to do."

He gets up and after of spitting on the body and cursing left smiling from the place. The authorities wrote a dead certificate where declare the death of a German with a fire arm, like a suicide, closing the case. They have the instruction well remunerable by Vladimir, that the public ministry shouldn't realize previous inquire neither give notice to the consulate authorities and have the instructions that if someone wanted or ask information of the dead, to be detain immediately to be investigated; this obligate to no one be present even for to ask for the body of Don Otto. After this he was buried in a common grave, but for his escorting funeral a lot of people were present, since when he was alive helped a lot of people of the towns of La Barca and Brisenas, all of them were present, only were workers, day labored and humble people, no civil authorities or military and none less his family were in his funeral, mainly for the fear to be interrogate or ask about the matter.

They took all his belongings from his body and wrapped in sheets, Don Modesto like unknowing the character and delimitate of the facts, for the fear of risking the life of his family, he kept some belongings that were giving personally by Vladimir after checking and searching the body. Afterwards he discovers some boxes with Otto's private items and gave the contained to a family from Guadalajara that Don Otto sees frequently, and by chance was the one who has little Hilda. So, the family receive a box that was with the name of Gabriel Lopez and it was send by Otto in person a week before dying and contain some belongings, but mainly the money he received as a payment for his services in Mexico. It was the last payment for his activities in Phase 4 in Mexico.

Like that was the ending of the story of Phase 4 in Mexico, with the sacrifice of this heroes, that in many means gave their lives to protect everybody and at the end left the codes open for to be decoded for the German resistant against the Nazi regime. And that happen, such codes allowed decode the attacks that Germany had plan against England and their alliances, dismantle the Nazi army and allowing Germany to lose the second world war.

Regarding Vladimir, he intent to locate Raquel, since he knew about the existence a son with Otto, but Otto was ahead of him since on the last trip to Germany, he stops in Cuba to interview with Raquel and recognize his son as it was. Raquel and her son kept hiding from Vladimir in the interior of the island, and Vladimir never found them. Furthermore, Otto arranges for them that after five years the war ended to send them to Germany since he arrange everything for them to stay with a friend in Berlin, who maintain their whereabouts and inclusive their existence in the anonymous until some years pass, his son named Otto, came back to the island and by chance he join the battle of Fidel Castro to combat the political regime... He was recognizing as a national hero of Cuba, that would make his father proud.

Thanks to these forgotten characters it was a passage inside the story that impact the humanity course, since thanks to them it discovers the intentions of the wicked regime that cloud the brighten of the German city, following this it was protected the most important: the members of the group of Phase 4, a team that continue working for a few yeas more in the nominates until become in a powerful organization and multinational that continue rule and illuminating the destiny of the occidental countries, now under the new mandate, since when fell in the hands of the winners, they made them theirs.

Respecting the descendance of Otto in Mexico; Don Modesto before he dies, send his daughter and grandchildren to the border of United States in a total anonymous and change their last name... Letting in a total forgetfulness the work and life of Don Otto in this land.

While Hilda kept hidden several years until adult age, his secret was well reserved, the little girl became a beautiful woman that went unnoticed before the Vladimir revenge, since her father left her well protected economically since he left her a great amount of his incomes produced in Mexico that he couldn't send to Switzerland, leaving that legacy in the hands of the family that took her, receiving their part, but leaving in favor to the little Hilda a significative amount. She stays forever like the step daughter of that family, without trace of the story of her parents, with a pure German lineage and rich, that ends in the forgetfulness. Years after she got married.

Hilda's mother was murder by Vladimir, but never knew of the existences of Hilda's daughter. She achieves to protect Phase 4 in South America and hides lots of members of Phase 4 that were refugees pursue by the Nazi regime, that later in conceal act to cast that regime of hate and dead and survive the holocaust and Vladimir.

The mother and sister of Otto never return to Germany since the intent of robbing in behalf Johan, the ex-employee, that have in possession their properties, they were investigated and located by the Gestapo since for a long time sustain strong connections with the Jews; Otto advise them of such situation and thanks for them to be in Switzerland territory they never could be detain. After the defeat of the Nazi regime, Johan was murder and all his group of fanatics were judge by the alliance, since the German government never have the power to do justice, resulting responsible of several robbery and murders. Was ten years later that Heidi Marie and her daughter, now a married woman, could come back to claim the little left of his properties, being mainly her husband who will intent to build some of the little his father was build and finally achieving to initiate a new life, with no trace of his brother Otto, that at the end of all, he saves their lives.

Germany lost for the second time in a humiliating way, all the world knew the massacre and genocide charge for this country, who beside of destroying all the legacy of the country fathers; were in ruins; it was lost the 80% of the population, in between them families, friends, and love ones of someone; those who brag about their German nationality were repudiate in the whole world, there were attributing cruel deeds and when the discovery of the concentrations centers, increase even more the German xenophobia; Hollywood did their own, there were no place in the world where all the German were call Nazi without distinction. The silence full his minds; now was the worst: carry with the weight of the defeat and know that the enemies were empower forever of their land, their lives and even their culture.

The Russians claim their part and the unimaginable, as well as the deeply fear for the Germans: the communist arrived at their homes destroying everything on his path and the violation to their women, girls and boys was the price that they must pay for being the greatest losers, thousands of civil innocents that for fear, omission and cowards did not oppose the Nazi regime, they took their dignity and freedom. The story was written for every winner, leaving a pain in a neighbor country which extend for more than 200 years since the communication media, the movies and the same groups that were assaulted in the war oversaw perpetuate the images.

Since the beginning Otto see vaguely the consequences, act with total responsibility, comprehend the fact and the consequences of their actions; forever his trace, he did not leave signs but the legend of a lost little ranch in Mexico, where the people of the place said that some where there is Don Otto working in his garage, some people sees him pass like a shadow by the field, lots of people also said that his soul still wondering around; others said that he is spreading his guiltiness; some others says there because the shame to come back to his country, however the only thing for sure is that he disappear from the world and he is in some other world while his people, his country, erase completely his existence, since there are not documents or evidence of that, the government erase everything about all trace of him, they disclaim to such a degree that Otto never was born, never was a German, and he never existed.

Phase 4 change the name, the best work team and the most professional oversaw cleaning, correct, and continue with their plans, no matter the consequences, the lives, and the people. Millions of persons that still being used to achieve their objective, crating, forming, and erasing at their convenience for the power and business until execute the interest of the new leader in turn, since always will exist a leader, a government, a group that continue managing the interest of this dangerous world organization, that until modern times continue manipulating the lives of the humanity.

Do not doubt, maybe, now you may be seating next to some of them... Since this did not end there...

You should be prepared...

RECAPITULATION

This reflects the life, where we emphasize that truly important is to spread with acts and at the end not being worthwhile all the love for material things or vain world, is another story that give testimonies that nothing happen by chance, that the actions have reactions and everything is a result of the place, the time, the moments, and the interactions of the persons: what we call the social ambient.

The social moment and the influence of a person to other, make the persons conform an intricate web of affective relations and sentimental of all kinds, that conform the ideas, the form of thinking and mold the day to day of everyone. Not for anything, the population knowledge said, "you are who your friend is."

This novel confirms one more time, that we all are part of a mechanism and strategy that the ambient where we develop is forming and never let us surprise the effects of each person in this world; right now, when you had read this novel, you have received a dose of influence, a proof that nothing is forever, everything is present, the pass don not exist and the future is a consequence of the active present.

Contenido

Whitout Trace

Hector Münster
contacto@hectormunster.com

Finished printing in May 2023

Impresos Copitek S.A. de C.V.
Calle 1 #1375 Interior 11
Col. Zona Industrial
Guadalajara, Jalisco, México. C.P. 44940

Editorial design
Rosario Ivonne Lara Alba (Santi Ediciones)
Nance 1370, Col. Del Fresno,
Guadalajara, Jalisco, México. CP. 44900.

Editing by the author,
under the editorial advice of Santi Ediciones.
In self-publishing, the rights are retained by the author.
www.santiediciones.com